I0524051

Fourth Edition

In Search of
Brandon Springs

Second novel of the Brandon Springs series

**In dedication to my soul mate and wife,
Gwyn,
and to my four children**

Rob Williams
2023

In Search of Brandon Springs
Fourth Edition Published by Rob Williams through Winged Publications 2023

Printed in the United States of America
First Printing: 2009

ISBN: 978-1-0881-5654-4

Chapter 1

RAYS OF SUNLIGHT spilled through windows of the house, as its owner quietly began the day's work. It was an unusually lazy morning for Ryan Walker, so the effort began at a slow and relaxed pace. A knock at the front door interrupted his meticulous effort to repaint the kitchen of his recently inherited home in Brandon Springs.

The sound of the knocking seems much too light to be made by the thick hands of Pete Johnston, but I can't imagine why anyone else would be standing on the front porch.

As he briefly examined his handiwork, Ryan's eyes captured a spot missed by his brush. A year earlier, it would have driven him crazy to not correct this imperfection before answering the front door. However, recent events in his life caused him to become a little more laid back.

Ryan made his way down the hallway to the main living area. His curiosity heightened, he took hold of the knob and opened the door. Instantly, the young woman at the door threw her arms around his neck and sobbed uncontrollably. Between sobs he heard her whisper repeatedly, "Thank you."

He recognized her, but he could remember only one occasion on which he had previously encountered Layla. After several seconds, he managed to loosen her hold on

1

him. Nervously, she stepped back a few inches. Wiping tears from her face, she stammered, "I'm sorry… I just can't thank you enough."

"What are you talking about?" he asked, somewhat shocked.

Reaching into her ample purse, she handed him a large envelope. The only words written on it read, "For Layla Quick." The envelope had already been opened. Without thinking, Ryan reached inside and brought out a stack of wrapped one-hundred-dollar bills. Quickly, he returned the money to the envelope and shoved it back into her hands.

"I didn't give this to you!" he gasped. "Where did you get it?"

A smile spread beneath her reddened eyes.

"It was right where you left it, silly," she stated in a half mocking tone. "It was in the passenger seat of my car. I just don't know how you knew which car was mine."

Layla explained how unusual it was to find her car door to be locked, for she never locked it. Her aged vehicle was not exactly the envy of passersby, and it rarely contained anything of value. Looking through the driver's side window she spotted the envelope lying on the front car seat. Layla opened the door, picked up the envelope, and slid into the seat behind the steering wheel. Puzzled, she examined the handwriting to determine who might have placed it in her car. Closing the car door and placing the envelope in her lap, she searched to see if she could spot someone near the car. She expected this to be a prank played by another waitress or a friend.

"What if a spring-loaded rubber snake pops out when I open the envelope?" she thought. *"I bet someone is hiding nearby, waiting to enjoy my reaction to this joke."*

She saw no one, so she opened it and pulled out a healthy stack of money. Frightened, she quickly placed the cash back into the package and locked the doors of the car.

Her hands began to shake as she spread the envelope open and peered into it. Inside was a note stating that this was a ten-thousand-dollar gift to her from an anonymous donor. Pulling the stacks of money back out, she quickly confirmed the amount. As tears began to roll down both cheeks, she scanned her memory for the possible source of this gift. Almost immediately, she thought of Ryan. Recalling her conversation with him on previous occasion, she remembered that he had inherited a home and property just outside of town.

"He must have inherited money, as well," thought Layla.

"What made you think the money came from me?" Ryan asked.

"OK, you can pretend it didn't come from you," she said, smiling. "I just want you to know how grateful I am."

Please believe me when I say that I did not give you that money!" Ryan exclaimed.

"OK, OK, I'll take you at your word," she said, still not believing him. "So, who did it then?"

"Well, apparently, whoever it was wanted to remain anonymous," Ryan replied. "I would put that money in a bank account, if I were you."

"I don't know," she answered. "I'm afraid the bank would ask questions, and I'm not sure what the IRS would do if they knew about it."

"I believe you can accept ten thousand dollars per year in gifts without the government taking a chunk of it," Ryan said. "Whoever gave it to you probably took that into account."

"Ryan has to be the donor," she thought. *"Why else would he know how much money could be received as a gift?"*

They talked for a few more minutes, and Layla agreed to place the money in a bank account. As she left him, Ryan attempted to read her face and body language as to determine whether she still believed him to be the donor. He wasn't sure.

RYAN THOUGHT BACK to the one previous meeting between himself and Layla. On that day he was about to return to Boston from a previous visit to Brandon Springs, when he stopped at a familiar café that served a hearty breakfast. As he pulled into the crowded parking lot of the small diner, Ryan noticed the interesting mix of beat-up farm trucks and well kept large moderately luxurious cars. All were American made. It was obvious to him the locals considered this to be a place to frequent on a Saturday morning. The trucks belonged to farmers, who were in the process of leaving the café to begin another workday. The large cars belonged to the retired elderly, who were in no rush to leave the company of old friends.

As he entered Elva's Café, he realized that the tables and booths were all taken. There were only a couple of available stools at a bar that stretched from the register on the left to a swinging half door mounted on the right wall. Ryan was an outsider of sorts, but most of the patrons knew who he was. They had seen him and his aunt in town during a previous visit. His Aunt Sally had known almost everyone in town, and a number of them had seen Ryan at her funeral. He even recognized a few faces in the crowded restaurant. As he made eye contact with some, they nodded to acknowledge his presence. Ryan found his place on a stool at the bar and was soon approached by a small waitress with large brown eyes. Her dark brown hair was pulled back neatly under a hair net, and a cautious smile greeted him as she asked for his order. The slight nimble fingers of the waitress jotted down his order. She turned away to call it out to the cook and moved on to other customers. Just as she returned to bring his coffee, he felt a heavy hand on his shoulder. Turning, he glanced upwards into the familiar face of the farmer who rented the front acreage of Ryan's recently inherited land. Standing beneath his huge frame was his short, and slightly plump, wife.

"We are so sorry for your loss; you were blessed with such a fine aunt," the man began. "It's really good to see you again. Will you be in Brandon Springs very long?"

"I'm just here for a quick visit," Ryan replied.

Still mindful of the loss of Ryan's aunt, the wife tenderly asked, "Would you consider eating supper with us tonight?"

Before he could answer and saving him from any embarrassment for not remembering her first name, she continued.

"Here, I'll write down the address and draw you a map on this paper napkin."

At the top of the napkin, she wrote the names, "Pete & Eunice Johnston," and scribbled a phone number. She then began to draw a small map to their home.

As she prepared the map, Ryan told them that he would not be in town that evening. He explained that he was on his way back to Boston, but that he would be glad to have a rain check on the meal.

"Thank you so much for the invitation," Ryan said. "I'll give you a call next time I'm in Brandon Springs."

With that, the couple left the café in a large late model white pickup truck. Soon afterwards the waitress placed before him a generous ham and cheese omelet, a side of bacon, and a tall thin glass of orange juice. She announced that she would be back shortly to see if his coffee needed a warmup. She then turned quickly to serve her other customers. He salted and peppered the omelet to his liking, and he began to consume the meal at a deliberately relaxed pace. Ryan enjoyed each bite. Sure enough, each time his coffee cup reached the half empty state, the waitress refilled it. He watched to see if she was giving him special treatment, and he found that she gave everyone in the café the same care. It was his opinion that she must have been doing this job from a fairly young age, because she was quite good. Ryan watched in amazement, noticing how easily she accomplished the feat of carrying two plates of food on each slender arm. His waitress was small, but she apparently was much stronger than her frame initially implied. The last time she approached with the coffee pot, he told her that he was ready for his check. She sat the pot on the table and thumbed through her pad until she came across his order. Tearing it from the pad, she gave him a smile and placed the ticket beside his now empty plate.

"Was it good?' she asked in a deep southern dialect.

"Oh, it was great, and so were you," he replied. "You did a great job, Layla."

He had noticed the name tag on her uniform.

"Actually, I don't think I've ever met anyone with the name," Ryan continued in a courteous manner. "It's unique, and really very pretty."

"Thanks, but you didn't grow up with the name," she explained. "No matter where I go, it seems some guy has something crude to say. I attend church regularly, and even there I've been ribbed about it."

"What about your middle name?" he asked. "Have you considered using that name instead?"

"My name is a mix of Rock-&-Roll and country," she replied. "Layla Jo Quick. If I go by Jo Quick, then it sounds like a guy's name."

"Your name is Layla Quick?' he asked, with a slight glimmer in his eye.

"See what I mean? You just met me, and you're thinking things," she said, with a look of slight disappointment.

"Hold on, I'm not doing anything," he said. "I don't even know you. I was just trying to help, but I guess you're pretty sensitive about it."

"Sorry," Layla apologized.

It was at that moment that he noticed something on deeper level. Though she openly spoke with him, he sensed no flirtation in her voice. There was a heaviness of heart spilling through her eyes, even when her mouth gave way to a sincere smile.

"Are you OK?" Ryan asked. "You seem to have a lot on your mind, that's all".

"Oh, I probably have plenty on my mind, but that's not your problem," she replied. "Everyone has to live with their own mistakes."

She left him to care for other customers. In recent months, Ryan had begun to observe others more closely and consider the lives of those he met. He watched as she made her rounds, and he estimated her to be in her mid-twenties. Soon a woman, he guessed to be in her fifties, entered the café with a young girl in her arms. Immediately the child was passed to Layla, and the little girl gave her a deep hug. The two women talked for a few minutes. Eventually, the little girl was given back to the older woman, and the two left the restaurant.

Layla approached Ryan with a full pot of coffee.

"Are you sure you wouldn't like a warmup?" she asked.

"Sure," he replied. "Was that your daughter?"

"Yeah, she is such a wonderful blessing," she answered. "She is not one of my mistakes, but the way she came about was. Her father and I weren't married, and he really isn't a part of her life now. My mother keeps her while I work."

"I guess that would be difficult," Ryan responded.

"It's OK," she explained. "All three of us live in a trailer, and we take care of each other. My father was able to pay the trailer off before he died last year, so we're fortunate".

Before thinking, Ryan told her about losing his own parents during a home invasion. Her openness, regarding her own personal life, invited openness from others. She never complained to Ryan or to anyone about her difficulties, but she felt no need for secrets.

"When I found out that I was pregnant, the reaction of my boyfriend was not what I expected," she revealed. "He wanted me to have an abortion. When I told him that I just couldn't do that, he left. Someone told me that he might have moved to Atlanta, but I don't have much use for him anymore. I don't care where he is. Except for my mother, my church has given the greatest support. I don't know what I would do without either of them."

"Are you doing OK?" Ryan asked.

"We get by," she responded, with a slight smile. "God has really blessed me. Like I told you, my mother takes care of my daughter while I'm at work - and the trailer is paid off. I don't have a house payment."

"Do you like your job, here?" Ryan continued. "I couldn't do it. I would have food all over myself and everyone around me."

"You probably would get the hang of it; the folks here are nice and it's all I know," she replied, as a smile began to take hold. As she spoke, a mental picture of food covering both Ryan and customers flashed through her mind. The smile broadened as she continued.

"It beats the first job I tried. I tried working in a chicken house, but I really didn't like it. As a waitress here, they even provide me with a uniform. I don't even have to buy work clothes."

He found himself at ease with her. Conversation seemed to flow between them naturally, with little thought being given.

"What did you want to be when you were a little girl?" Ryan pressed.

"You mean besides being a princess?" she said, as the smile gave way to a chuckle. She scanned the café for customers in need of her care, but found none. "I thought about being a nurse when I was in high school. I would have to go to nursing school or college to do that."

"Nurses have uniforms, also," he replied. "I can see you as a nurse and I bet you would be good at the job. As a waitress, you seem to genuinely care about the service you provide to customers."

"I don't have the money to go to school," she explained. "Even if I did, it would mean leaving my daughter Kaylee with my mother even more than I do now."

"You seem like a good person, and I think good things will eventually come your way," Ryan stated.

In his heart, he genuinely wished good things for her. Picking up the check, he followed her to the cash register, where the waitress totaled it up.

"I hope things go well for you," he said, as he handed her a 30% tip.

As he walked toward the door, he heard a sheepish reply from Layla. "Thank you, so much. I'm sorry. I didn't mean to talk your ear off."

Opening the door of the cafe, he turned to face the waitress.

"You're welcome," he replied, with a smile.

As he made his way from the small restaurant, he wondered what caused some parents to give children particular names. In school he knew a boy named Fredrick Alexander Turner. The full name sounded somewhat dignified, and Ryan felt sure that part of the name came from an ancestor of some significance. However, the young man could never have anything monogrammed with his initials. To Ryan it seemed the parents should have been smart enough to realize what they were doing. Nevertheless, he felt he couldn't change the world. This morning, he had things to do. He had to drive all the way to Knoxville, turn in the rental car, and make his flight for Boston.

That encounter with Layla had been a couple of months prior to her visit to his home this day, and that occasion produced the only conversation he remembered having with her. Ryan recalled the fact that she had left an impression on him after meeting her at the café. There was no romantic attraction, or even an endearing mannerism which captivated him. It was almost as if there was something spiritual about the young woman, for he remembered no striking qualities regarding her beauty, wit, or intelligence. In fact, her speech seemed to be that of someone poorly educated. This waitress had given up on personal ambitions beyond her current state. She seemed to accept her lot in life. She had frequently been in his thoughts for a few days after that encounter in the cafe. He remembered asking prayer for her in the Sunday school class of a church he visited in the Boston area. Ryan had decided to visit that church after finding a church bulletin on the corner of his desk at work. He didn't know if someone had inadvertently left it there, or if a fellow employee was giving him a subtle invitation. However, he had not thought of her since asking for prayer on that occasion. Now, he doubted that he would ever forget Layla.

RYAN WAS BEGINNING to understand that it is in our handling of what comes our way and in our attitude regarding how blessed or cursed we think ourselves that determines how full life is perceived by the particular soul living it.

There are those whose lives are considered ancient by others, who see their own journey as only beginning. For some, the experience of living a comparatively short life may seem to last an eternity. Compared to eternity, or even the history of man, each life occupies only a whisper of breath in the story of mankind. However, each existence has purpose and reason. Some begin to understand that purpose during their lifetime, and others do not. There are a few individuals who view themselves as having been granted two lives.

Such was the case with Ryan Walker. He was a changed

man, and it seemed to him that he had been granted a second life. During his first thirty years, he had formed a certain line of reasoning regarding his existence on earth. Ryan had established personal methods for handling things that came his way. For a time, they appeared to work relatively well. He had begun to master those procedures and processes he had defined for his own life. Ryan thought he had attained a certain level of comfort in his perception of where he wanted to go in life, and of his progress. All of this changed during an earlier brief visit to a very small town. He wasn't sure how, but those days and events with the people of Brandon Springs had caused this former perception of life to fall away as leaves from a maple tree on a windy fall day. He was like a man learning to walk again. He was unsure and a bit clumsy with each attempted step in this new life.

In the classroom of life, his newfound awareness and appreciation of those with whom he came in contact seemed to erase the board of previously held life lessons. He now found himself thrown into an entirely new study of the subject. Ryan began noticing people. No longer were they simply objects passing by him on a sidewalk or sitting at other tables in restaurants. Each form contained a living soul, housed within particular genetic traits, and shaped by personal experiences, desires, and purpose. He wasn't sure whether the source of this understanding was from God, or people, or experienced situations. Ryan felt he had come to a point in his life where the light seemed to come on. Regardless, he wasn't the same. In his embrace of this change, his focus deepened.

I'm essentially the same soul traveling around in the same body. It's just that my perception of myself and others has changed dramatically, and the significance of so many things in life have also changed. My personality is my own, but it's like an inner river carrying my thoughts and feelings about a host of subjects have completely changed course.

For three months, since being released for the second

time from the hospital and his return to Boston, Ryan maintained regular correspondence with two children who tragically lost their mother in the same accident that had almost taken his own life. There was a bond between them. It wasn't only the fact that he shared a similar loss, that of his own parents' death at the hands of a burglar. There was a true connection of love and caring.

What are the chances of someone to be involved in two separate automobile accidents within a period of a week, in which each accident took a life?

Ryan was only slightly comforted in the fact that neither case was found to be his fault. A mother of two, a schoolteacher and wife of an attorney, died because she tailgated Ryan in a heavy downpour. As a result of this accident, Ryan suffered a serious concussion. While hospitalized for several days, he dreamed vividly of life changing events. To some degree, those dreams became part of his reality.

A few days later, while Ryan was a passenger in his beloved Aunt Sally's car, the elderly woman lost control and died when the vehicle slammed into a large tree. He was badly shaken up during the second wreck, and lost consciousness for a while. Because of the concussion sustained from the earlier accident, the doctors decided to keep him in the hospital for a couple of days for observation. During his second stay in the hospital, he met and came to know John Oliver, the fiancé of his nurse Patsy Smith. Patsy had caught Ryan's eye during his first hospitalization, because he was physically attracted to her and because he truly enjoyed her company. However, he found John to be a truly likable person and his friendship with them both became strong.

His Aunt Sally was buried between her recently departed brother Andrew and her earlier deceased husband. To Ryan, she seemed to be laid to rest exactly where she should have been. He inherited the land and the small old country home, where both Sally and Andrew lived their last days. After her funeral, he stayed in the old house for a week before returning to Boston. Each evening during that week, he visited with Patsy and John. The friendship grew quickly and deeply, and they continued to call each other often after he returned to Boston.

While unconscious in the hospital, Ryan had often been visited by a stranger in his dreams. He fully recovered from the physical injuries suffered during in the auto accidents. However, both dreamed and real experiences had permanently affected him. Sometimes situations and events fall in such a way as to shove us in the direction of genuine positive change.

He found his relationship with his aunt to be inspirational, but he had no idea of the extent to which his life would be further impacted by a simple encounter with a waitress. On rare occasions, life changing events are injected into a seemingly insignificant day. Such was the case for Ryan Walker on that Saturday morning of finding Layla at his front door.

Chapter 2

WORK IN BOSTON was not the same for Ryan. His job was the same as before, and his fellow employees were the same people. Ryan was not the same. He missed the uncomplicated lives of those lived in the Brandon Springs area, and he missed his last relative, Sally. He hungered for true relationships with people who cared deeply for him, and he craved the simple honest life of those in that small town. No longer was he totally absorbed in efforts to make career enhancing impressions on those who had the power to pull him into the upper levels of his profession. No longer was he interested in individuals only for lessons learned which would empower his own life and ambitions. He wanted true friends, and he had none in Boston. Ryan had none because he had never been a true friend to anyone. He had never truly taken an honest, personal, and caring interest in anyone else. The people with whom he worked had come to know his shallow intents regarding his relationships with them, and each determined that Ryan was one to be kept at arm's length.

He no longer visited the fine restaurants in the North End, when he went out after work. The food was wonderful, but there was something lacking. Ryan longed for what he had experienced in Brandon Springs. He decided to seek out the establishments of more common people, in hopes of finding it. He went to the restaurants near the docks, and frequented diners in somewhat seedy areas of town. On one occasion, he was robbed at gunpoint. He became a little less venturesome after that experience, and Ryan eventually settled on a couple of diners near the docks.

One night, just as he was about to begin his supper, the cafe he visited was emptied because someone called in a bomb threat. While standing outside, waiting for the police and restaurant staff to give the "all clear," he decided that he could no longer wait to use the rest room in the cafe. He walked briskly for a couple of blocks to a less populated area. Just as he entered a nearby alley to relieve himself, he came face to face with a wild-eyed young man. Those eyes, picking up fragments of light from the street, seemed to take on an inhuman glow. Ryan felt a chill, as if an icy stream of water ran down his back. His body tensed. For a moment he stared motionless into the glaring eyes before him. Then slowly he held up both hands, and cautiously backed out of the alley. Still silent, the young man's eyes grew even wilder as he followed Ryan out into the street.

"You snotty jerk," the man stated, in a defiant southern dialect. "Did you think I was going to rob you? Just because I'm not dressed like you, you think I'm a thief. You jerk! I hate this place. I just hate this town!"

With that, the tall young stranger shoved both hands into the pockets of his jacket, walked past Ryan, and headed in the direction of the diner. His timing was perfect, as the police had just given the "all clear" and café staff announced to the waiting patrons that they were allowed to return to their meals. Still shocked by the reaction of the young man, Ryan stood for a moment watching the people file back into the café. Apparently, a local high school kid had played a prank with the call. Years had passed since the terrorist bombing in New York, and younger people had no clear memory of it. To them, they saw relative harmless opportunities to frighten adults. However, most adults found no humor in pranks of this nature. For the police, and for those whose memory was still fresh with the deaths of thousands, these prank calls were no laughing matter. As Ryan again entered the cafe, the waitress signaled for him to be seated again at his table. Waiting to be seated, the young man he met in the alley was still gazing at him with those wild eyes. Ryan told the waitress that he would return to the table on his own, and he then headed directly for the man. As he approached, he could see that the young man's facial muscles harden. Standing with eyes scanning one another, Ryan attempted to explain.

"I'm sorry. I was robbed by a guy last month, and I'm a bit … cautious…, maybe somewhat a little scared. I already have a table. Would you care to join me?"

Ryan would have never done something like that six months prior. He would not have even been in that café or even spoken to this fellow. The young man's face softened, and his eyes became more inquisitive. For a moment, he scanned Ryan's face for answers to his own questions about the conversation. He quickly sensed that the offer was genuine and the apology sincere. Though still piercing, the young man's eyes relaxed.

"Alright, that sounds OK," he responded.

He accepted the invitation, but he was still not comfortable with his host. As a child following an unfamiliar babysitter, he followed Ryan to the table. He cautiously studied the man walking before him, while scanning the tables for dangerous individuals. Stopping, Ryan turned and politely offered him the seat across from his at the table. The young man removed his jacket and placed it on the back of his assigned chair. Both men took their seats simultaneously. After taking a sip from his drink, Ryan motioned for the waitress to come over.

"My name is Ryan Walker," he stated, as he extended his hand to the stranger.

Still with the intense questioning stare, the man clasped his hand firmly.

"Larry Chatterson," he announced, in a distinct southern drawl.

Larry's hand was large, lean, and rough. It was apparent that hard physical work was no stranger to the fellow.

"I am sorry for the reaction outside," Ryan began. "I'm still a little shaky from the robbery, and I didn't expect to see anyone in that alley. Honestly, I stepped in there to take a pee, and … I still really need to go. So, if you will excuse me for a minute… I'll be right back."

Chatterson quietly nodded, and Ryan was quickly off in the direction of the men's room. Larry scanned the menu, as the waitress approached to take his order. He didn't notice her arrival at first. As she stood silently near the table, the waitress took the opportunity to look her customer over. Though his dress was not impressive, she couldn't help but take note of the large muscular hands which held the menu. Her study of his wide shoulders was interrupted, as his eyes met hers. Larry Chatterson was a striking figure, and she felt a little self-conscious as she inquired as to what he would like to eat. Larry placed his order, and then began to study Ryan's temporarily abandoned meal. As a detective on a crime scene, he thoroughly examined the manner in which the meal had been left. He quickly concluded that Ryan was a thoughtful, neat, and organized individual.

"The napkin is neatly folded beside the right side of the plate, and the eating utensils were placed on top of the napkin in an orderly fashion," thought Larry." Apparently, the announcement of the possible bomb had not caused him to panic, and he had taken time to think about how he wanted to return to his meal. The content tells me that Ryan has an expensive taste, and that he is accustomed to eating well. Only a few bites are missing from the prime rib, and to the left of the main course the salad is mostly eaten. Prime rib on a payday might not be that unusual, but this is a Thursday

night."

Chatterson ordered the largest hamburger on the menu, an order of fries and a soft drink. A moment after Ryan returned to his meal, Larry questioned him.

"OK, who are you? You said that your name is Ryan, but who are you?"

There was something about the directness of the question that Ryan liked. This fellow was right up front and believed in wasting no time getting to the point. Ryan had grown tired of games and found the question refreshing.

"Nobody special," Ryan replied.

"OK, what do you do?" Larry asked. "I mean, besides taking a leak in a dark alley. I'm sure you must have a job."

"I work downtown at Freemont Corporation," he stated. "Anything else?"

"OK – what do you do there?" Larry asked. "I bet you're a paper pusher."

"I'm a systems analyst," Ryan answered. "In college I double majored in computer science and in business. Is that OK with you?"

"What are you doing down here?" Larry pressed. "Why aren't you in the North End, or entertaining guests in your condo or something? You're probably out looking to buy drugs or something."

"My turn," quipped Ryan. "What do you do for a living, and why are you here?"

"Fair enough," replied Larry, in a backwoods southern drawl.

He paused for a moment before giving his answer.

"I'm here because I live in this neighborhood. I moved here because I wanted to work on the docks, but it didn't work out. It's not the best job in the world, but I wash dishes at another restaurant. I don't eat where I work, because I want to be off work when I am off work."

"Fair enough," Ryan replied in turn. "I used to eat at the North End, but I guess I got tired of it. The food is very good, but I found that I just can't relax while I'm there. Besides that, the food here is pretty good."

"I guess that makes sense," answered Larry. "I doubt that I would be able to relax there either."

With a bit of caution, Ryan asked, "So why didn't the job on the docks work out? If you don't mind my asking..."

"I worked on the docks in Mobile, Alabama," Larry explained. "When I heard of the wages paid to dock workers up here, I left and decided to give Boston a try. Not only do you have to belong to a union, but it is really a tight knit group here. You have to either know someone or have a family member working to get on. I don't know anybody, and my family is hundreds of miles away. I have a only high school education, so my alternatives were pretty limited. I took the job washing dishes."

"Do you plan to go back to Alabama?" Ryan asked.

The waitress arrived with Larry's meal. He politely thanked her for it, and then turned back to his host.

"No, not yet anyway," he quietly replied. "I haven't decided what I will do. I don't plan to wash dishes forever, and I'll probably find something else. I'm not married, so I am the only one this job is affecting."

"Have you ever thought about going to school at night?" Ryan asked. "It would probably help you find other options."

"I can't afford school on what I make," he explained. "I do read at night, and the library is a fairly cheap alternative to school."

Ryan was intrigued. He never expected the man who had startled him in the alley moments earlier to be the type who regularly spent time in a library. The wild eyes that had been so frightening outside were now softened, but their clear blue color was still striking against the tanned and somewhat weathered skin of this young man.

"How long have you been going to the library to read?" Ryan asked.

"Oh, I've done that for years," he stated. You know, it's really sort of foolish to buy books, when there are so many available for free. They even have newspapers from all over the country there. It would cost me a load to buy so many papers. It's pretty cool. I can find out what is going on all over the country, by visiting one place. They even have the Wall Street Journal."

"You read the Wall Street Journal in the library?" gasped Ryan.

"Well, I read it the first time when a guy left his copy on a bus I was riding," Larry replied. "The whole thing was about MONEY, and businesses that make MONEY. I decided that it might be a good idea to read it, since I didn't have much MONEY. I thought I might figure out how rich people make MONEY. Couldn't hurt. Actually, it was interesting. The problem is that you have to have money to invest, in order to earn that kind of money I don't have any extra money right now. But I still think it's interesting."

Emphasizing the word "money", Larry made his point. He felt trapped by his lack of money. As the meals were consumed, Larry talked about rates of return and different types of dividends. Ryan became more and more amazed at this fellow. Larry had detailed understanding of a variety of money markets and could quote the highs and lows of various stocks over a period of time. What Ryan found most incredible was that Larry thought all educated people read the Wall Street Journal and understood the details of finance. He talked about some aspects and trends that Ryan never considered or even cared about.

Eventually, Ryan noticed a disgusted stare from the waitress. It was almost time for the café to close, as they had occupied the table for hours. She wanted a steady turnover of customers on that table in order to make the tips she needed. Ryan immediately understood the situation, placed an exceptionally large tip on the table, and offered Larry a ride home. As they were leaving the diner, he never saw the grimace on the face of the waitress evolve into a relieved smile.

During the month of July, they met regularly at the café. The waitress remembered Ryan and always greeted the two with a smile. Ryan never had a real friend, and he was amazed at how well they hit it off. Larry wasn't a well educated professional, but he seemed to be very knowledgeable about a variety of subjects. After Ryan was able to ignore the backwoods southern accent and slightly poor grammar skills of his new friend, he realized that Larry was unusually intelligent, and self-taught through his reading at the library.

Their backgrounds were very different, in that Ryan had lost both of his loving parents and Larry's father was abusive to everyone in the family. His old man was an alcoholic and had terrorized his wife and children on a regular basis. Larry had no interest in church, but he was a very honest and open individual with strong work ethics and strict morals. He never drank. Larry had seen enough abuse as a child and was deathly afraid of becoming like his father. He had no use for alcohol.

Larry's mother was a soft spoken and kind woman, who had made the mistake of allowing herself to fall in love with an unstable man. Academically, she was very bright. However, she had exercised poor judgment in becoming involved romantically with the high school football star without really coming to understand who he really was on the inside. They were married immediately after graduating from high school, and it wasn't long before the glory of an athlete was replaced by the mundane reality of being a low wage earner who felt trapped in the responsibilities of being a young husband. The drinking started within the first year, and so did the abuse. During their high school years, Larry's father had reserved his brutality for players on the other teams. His poor ability to handle the responsibility of caring for a family, combined with realization that he had moved from the place of being a local celebrity to being viewed as just a lower class citizen, caused the mean streak in his personality to spill over into the household. He could not afford to lose his job, so he maintained control in the workplace. Once he arrived home, the heavy drinking and violence began. Larry had inherited his athletic frame from his father and his intelligence from his mother. The majority of his personality was very similar to hers.

WITHIN A SHORT PERIOD OF TIME, Ryan began to realize that the wild look he had seen in Larry's eyes that first night in the alley had actually been an expression of fear. Larry was as startled as Ryan, at their meeting. Different people react differently to fear. Some people cower away, and others become wide eyed and alert, as to be ready for what ever threat comes their way. Larry was dealing with more fear than Ryan could have imagined. He had come to a strange city, knowing no one. His quest for a high paying wage failed, and he was left living in one of the roughest sections of Boston. He saw much of the same brutality of his father in the eyes of some of the men in his neighborhood. Although he was physically strong, like his father, he had no stomach for violence.

Ryan enjoyed his newfound friendship with Larry, but his satisfaction of living in Boston was growing thin. The excitement of big city life and the prestige of his professional career were no longer as glamorous as they once were. He thought about Brandon Springs a lot and made a decision to fly down there once a month to make sure the old home was alright. Ryan determined he would fly to Knoxville, Tennessee and rent a car for the remainder of the trip. The flight would only take a little over four hours, and the drive about an hour and a half. He checked several airlines leaving from Boston and found several leaving between 3:30 PM and 5:00 PM.

If I make arrangements to leave early on a Friday, I would be able to catch an early flight and be at Andrew's old home as early as 9:30 PM. I would have Saturday to relax and enjoy the old place and could leave to come back Sunday afternoon.

Just the thoughts of returning to Brandon Springs caused a warm peace to spread across his lonely soul. Ryan missed his Aunt Sally, and the times they had shared together in that small Appalachian hamlet. Since she passed away, he no longer had any remaining family members. Larry now seemed to be the closest thing to family.

Sally had left him the old home and the land that she had inherited from her brother Andrew. Summer was passing, and he was sure that the grass needed to be mowed and weeds pulled from around the old home. He needed to return, for he realized the place shouldn't be left in that shape.

It's settled. I'll spend the following weekend in Brandon Springs. I had dream about a shed containing a mower and tools standing behind Andrew's house. I'll purchase a shed building for a lawn mower and place it in that very spot behind the old home.

The next day, Ryan called a local lawn and garden store in the vicinity of Brandon Springs and ordered a metal shed to be delivered and set up. His excitement about this project grew, just as had when he had the home painted months before. Ryan couldn't contain himself. He placed another call to the store and ordered both a riding and push mower to be delivered to the place. He was like a child the night before Christmas, and he was giving his credit card a workout. All of the goods were to be delivered and set up Thursday of the following week. Adrenalin ran so strongly that he could not rest until he had used his laptop computer to book the flights and rental car.

For the next few days, he found it difficult to concentrate on his work. He found himself daydreaming continually. Ryan envisioned what the shed looked like, wondering if it really looked the same as what he had dreamed. He saw himself cutting the grass and resting afterwards sipping a cold soft drink on the front porch, as he inspected the freshly cut yard. He was definitely not the same person he been several months earlier, when he had felt so irritated at the thoughts of returning to Brandon Springs. No longer did his view of the town consist only of memories of his boring and dull visits as a child. Even those reflections were remembered differently, as he had learned to treasure his relationship with his Aunt Sally. The memories of visits there with his now deceased parents were now looked on with warmth and fondness. The effects of time and events, shaped by the hand of God, had changed him and his outlook on life. Facts had remained the same, but his perception of events caused them to take on new meaning.

He obtained permission to leave work at 3:00 PM on Friday. Ryan had worked overtime during the week to make sure his work was done. He planned to only be gone during the weekend, so he was able to easily place the clothes he needed in his backpack. He only needed this one carry-on, as he boarded the plane for Knoxville. It fit perfectly in the overhead, and he eagerly dropped into his window seat in coach class. When traveling for work in the past, he always enjoyed his flights in first class. Now, he looked forward to meeting the regular people in coach, for they seemed to be more talkative and interesting. The plane accelerated down the runway and lifted off. He watched the skyline of Boston fade away, and thoughts of the drive from Knoxville to Brandon Springs filled his mind.

At last, I'm returning.

Chapter 3

AS RYAN DROVE AWAY in the rental car from the airport at Knoxville, he was filled with anticipation. He estimated that he would arrive in Brandon Springs no later than 8:00 PM, if he didn't stop to eat. However, in time, his stomach began to speak louder than his desire to arrive at Andrew's old home.

After all, there will be no dinner prepared at the house and no one waiting up for me.

The lights of a fast-food restaurant beckoned to him, and he succumbed to its enticement. He pulled off the interstate highway, and onto a service road lined with a handful of restaurants and a motel. Ryan didn't even remember opening the door of the restaurant. Standing in front of the cashier he attempted to scan the menu but found he couldn't concentrate. He was hungry, but thoughts of the land and the house filled his mind to the point that the menu seemed to be just a meaningless collection of words and numbers. After a moment of silence, he announced that he would take a number five. It wasn't until after he placed the order that he realized that it consisted of a chicken sandwich, a medium soft drink, and fries. It didn't really matter, for he desired only to quickly eliminate the growling in his stomach before moving down the road. At last, his order was up. Ryan gathered the tray of food, and he took it to a booth near a front window. Although the food was not exceptionally tasty, it was quickly devoured.

It was particularly dark that night when he left the main highway for the rough pavement of the old county road leading to the small village. Vibrations rising from car tires grinding against the road seemed to sooth him. He felt at home. There are some who place a crying baby in a carrier on top of an electric clothes dryer, allowing the warmth and vibrations sooth the child to sleep. Ryan felt remarkably at peace as he drove. He made a last stop before reaching the house. At a corner convenience store, Ryan purchased a soft drink and a bag of peanuts.

Standing before the front door of the old home, Ryan found that everything was dark. He had left no lights burning when he was last there. He lowered his backpack to the front porch. Holding the soft drink and bag of peanuts in his left hand, Ryan retrieved the keys from his pocket with his free hand and purposefully slid the house key into the lock. Before turning the key, he paused for a moment. He listened to the distant sounds of barking dogs, carried across still country air. Almost a mile away, dogs were still announcing his presence to the owners of houses he had passed along the way. He was surprised how distinctly he could hear them. The dogs quieted, and Ryan heard the lock loosen its grip on the door. Hinges sung a song of welcome as the door gently swung open. He blindly reached inside for light switches and flipped them on. Both the main living area and front porch were flooded with a warm glow of light. Ryan grabbed his gear and went inside.

He was alone in the house, but it didn't seem so. As he stood motionless and silent, he could still hear the echo of his beloved aunt's voice calling him to breakfast during those precious days they shared before her death. Ryan had never felt so much at home as he did in this old house. As a child, he was bored to tears during his visits there. Without the presence of a TV, or even air conditioning, he would count the days and hours before he would leave. The home was now different because he was now different.

Ryan placed his backpack in the bedroom, which he had prepared for himself on an earlier visit. He pulled back the comforter and sheets of the bed. Ryan carried the soft drink and bag of peanuts into the living area and dropped into a chair. He sat in quiet peace for a moment, and then listened to the hiss of the drink as he opened the bottle. It was as if he was absorbing everything around him. He lazily ate the peanuts and drank the soft drink. Ryan sat almost as still as the empty furniture in the room, listening to the muffled outdoor sounds penetrating the quiet night air.

Another car must have driven the road to Brandon Springs. Dogs are barking again.

The blinking of his eye lids slowed, and his breathing became almost silent. Just before he drifted into the land of dreams, he forced himself out of the chair and made his way to the bedroom. He dropped his clothes on the end of the bed and slid between the sheets. Ryan had not even turned off the lights in the living area, but it didn't matter.

This room has suffered darkness for too long.

Ryan allowed the burning lights to smile brightly throughout the night. The bedroom light was off, but the gentle glow of the lights from the living area spilled faintly across his face as he fell into a peaceful sleep.

RYAN AWOKE TO THE RAYS of the morning sun blazing a silent form of reveille across the bedroom wall. With narrowed eyes, he arose and clumsily opened his backpack and found his toiletry kit. Once in hand, he shuffled his way to the bathroom across the hall. Ryan relieved himself of the remnants of the soft drink he had consumed the night before, brushed his neglected teeth, and shaved. It was enough to bring him to a state of being fully alert.

He went back into the bedroom and fished out clothes for the day. Ryan placed his fresh pair of underwear on the closed toilet seat and hung his other clothes on the hook which was mounted on the back of the bathroom door. He gathered soap, shampoo and conditioner from his toiletry kit and placed them in their proper positions in the shower/tub. Dropping his worn underwear to the floor, he then proceeded to start the water. Once satisfied of the temperature, he vigorously showered. He really enjoyed the powerful spray coming from the old showerhead. It had been made during days when no thoughts of water conservation were incorporated into its design. The powerful volume of water readily blasted the soap from his skin, and the stream pounded his body almost as a miniature massage. It felt great; it was invigorating.

Upon turning off the water and pulling back the shower curtain, he realized his situation. He had neglected to bring a towel from the hall closet. He shook some of the water droplets from his hands and feet into the tub, before making his streak to the closet. Although the house was a fair distance from the road, he had left the bedroom blinds up and the bedroom door open. Sunlight bathed his body as he exited the bathroom and into the hall. Hidden from the revealing window, he dried himself in the hallway. Ryan then used the towel as a makeshift kilt while making his way back to the bathroom.

Once dressed, he dried the hall floor with the towel, and hung it on the hook on the back of the door. He felt the empty churning of his stomach and remembered that he had emptied the refrigerator before leaving the house the previous time. Ryan emptied his backpack and placed the remaining clothes across the top of the bedroom dresser.

He was ready for the day. The first order of the day was to place a call to Pete Johnston, as he had promised to have dinner with them on this visit back to Brandon Springs.

"Hello, Mr. Johnston," he began. "This is Ryan Walker. I promised I would call the next time I arrived in Brandon Springs."

Pete Johnston was delighted to hear from him, and immediately extended the invitation to Ryan for dinner. Ryan could hear Mrs. Johnston in the background giving her husband instructions regarding his visit.

"What time should I arrive?" he asked.

Pete responded, "How about 5:00, if it's not too early?"

"Sure," Ryan replied.

"Good! I have something that I want to show you," Pete said.

Taking the phone away from her husband, Eunice Johnston added to the conversation.

"Make sure you bring an appetite, because we'll have plenty," the little wife chirped, in a southern backwoods accent.

With the end of the call, he was ready to begin his plans for the day. The morning sunshine warmed the right side of his face as he stepped off the front porch and made his way to his car.

Stopping at a local hardware store, he bought a large gas container for use with the newly purchased lawn mowers. He went to the nearby convenience store for a couple of cans of oil, and to fill the container with gas. Ryan placed the container of gas in the trunk of the rental car. He drove several minutes before finding a home decoration store, and he began to smell gas fumes from the trunk. As he parked, he decided to leave his car windows slightly open while he visited the store. He asked an employee of the store to select and arrange artificial flowers suitable for the outdoors. Informing the woman that one arrangement was for a man and the other for a woman, he explained that he wanted them to be mounted in durable vases. He intended to place them place on the graves of Sally and Andrew.

Upon returning to the car, he found the gasoline fumes to be almost unbearable. Alarmed at how strong they had become; Ryan fully lowered all the car windows. After placing the vases of arrangements in the front floorboard, he slowly made his way to the cemetery behind the church. He was careful not to tip over the arrangements as he drove. Gingerly carrying the arrangements to the gravesites, he knelt in front of Sally's marker. The graves of Andrew, Sally, and Sally's husband were equally empty of signs of respect and affection. Although the funeral sprays had been removed from Sally's grave a few months before, hers was the most obvious. Ryan had selected her tombstone. Though it wasn't large, it was much more prominent than the small flat ground level markers of Andrew and Sally's husband. Ryan had considered giving her a larger stone that would equally mark the space of both Sally and her husband, but he really didn't know the man that well. He placed the masculine vase and arrangement in front of Andrew's flat marker and set the more feminine arrangement squarely between Sally's and her husband's markers. The flower arrangement was truly for her, but he believed she wouldn't mind sharing it. During her life she had been such a giving soul.

Weeds sprouted from around the markers of each grave, and he finished the visit by pulling them out of the ground and tossing them into a nearby trash bin. Satisfied, he left to inspect the ordered shed at the house. Ryan had to drive the entire way with the windows down, for the interior of the rental car was now permeated with gas fumes. Early fall had begun to replace summer, but the winds from the south caused the air to be much hotter than normal. It felt more like mid-summer, and the forecast for the weekend was for the temperature to reach near 85 degrees Fahrenheit. The heat was quickly rising, so he elected to run the air conditioner on high in an attempt to cool himself and push away the fumes. His mind was fixed on cutting the dying tall shoots of grass that surrounded the old home. The grass had stopped growing by this time of the year, but he realized his neglect to cut it during the summer had probably left an unintentional advertisement that home was abandoned. He would not make this mistake again.

After arriving at the house, he left all four car windows down and quickly removed the gas container and oil from the trunk. As Ryan rounded the corner of the home, the shed came in full view. The metal building stood almost exactly where he had envisioned and requested it to be placed. He slid the metal doors apart with ease. Inside, both the riding and push mowers sat on the layer of gravel he had requested to be spread inside the shed. He had to slightly bend his head down to enter the small building, and he was pleased to find the owner manuals for both resting on the riding mower seat. Six months ago, he would have found it ridiculous for a man to be seriously interested in a riding mower, but today the rush of adrenaline flooded his body as he began to push his man toy out of the shed and into the sunlight. Ryan could hardly force himself to browse the manual before grabbing the container of gas to fill the tank. Checking the oil level, he found that none needed to be added. He had managed to skim through the document before pouring gas into the riding mower, but now he could wait no longer.

He placed both manuals on top of the push mower engine, still within the shed. Ryan then straddled the riding mower as a cowboy about to ride his steed to corral a herd of stampeding cattle. Ryan reached near the engine of the mower and squeezed the plastic bulb to push the right amount of gas into the chamber for starting. He placed the throttle in the starting position and made sure the blade was disengaged. Turning the key, the engine began to clear its throat in preparation for a warmup melody. It then burst into full song as the internal explosions fired one after another. He moved the throttle into the running position and felt the power of the mower beneath him vibrate with promise of things to come. Without engaging the blade, he pushed in the clutch/braking mechanism and dropped the beast into the second of seven forward gears. Slowly releasing the clutch, he felt the mower began to move forward.

I want more speed.

He experimented with the gears until he decided that fourth gear gave him the desired acceleration. He sent the mower galloping off to the front yard. He then brought it to a halt, in order to engage the blade. Once the blade was engaged, grass immediately shot from the spout on the side of the machine. He gingerly released the clutch until the mower slowly began to creep. Within the first seconds of forward movement, the engine began to cough and chug. He realized the grass was too deep for this blade setting. Pushing the clutch back in, he raised the blade a couple of notches. Trying again, the mower purred consistently as it trimmed the tops of grass shoots. All was well until he heard a loud noise, felt a bump, and caught a glimpse of something metallic shooting from the spout and across the lawn. Fearful that a part had broken loose from the machine, he stopped the mower immediately. Upon inspection of the metallic object, he found it to be a mutilated beer can. Ryan had failed to inspect the overgrown yard for trash and debris. Many cans were left by trespassers who had used his property as a place to consume mass quantities of brew. He suddenly felt a mixture of gratitude, anger and humiliation. Gratitude, in that, he had not damaged the mower. Anger, because someone had placed trash in his yard and abused the sanctity of his property. He felt humility for being so caught up in the moment that he had neglected to inspect the yard before mowing. For a time, the emotions of each cycled through him until it settled in to being simply grateful, he had not damaged his newly acquired steed.

He found a box of kitchen sized trash bags in the house. After a diligent inspection of the yard, four of the bags were filled with the debris he collected. Straddling his trusty mount, he began the job again. After Ryan completed one pass on a high setting, he then lowered the blade for another pass. It was 11:00 AM, when the mower was parked inside the shed. The serious heat of the day was beginning to set in, and he decided to retreat into the house for something to drink. Only after opening the refrigerator, did he remember it had earlier been emptied of soft drinks during a prior visit to the home. He quickly filled a glass with tap water. Over half the glass of water was gone when he brought it down from his lips. He quickly refilled it and made his way for the front porch. Ryan sat on the front steps and admired his handiwork. Suffering under the rising heat, he removed his shirt and continued to sip the water.

After a brief rest, he decided to begin trimming with the push mower. Returning to the shed, he picked up the mower owner's manual and returned to the kitchen. He glanced through the pages until he was satisfied that he had mentally digested enough of the material. Ryan placed them in a kitchen drawer for future reference. He refilled the glass with water twice before it left his hand for a temporary resting place beside the kitchen sink.

He filled the push mower with gas and began the process of trimming. By the time he returned the push mower to the shed, rivers of sweat poured down his forehead, chest, and back. The sun beat down upon him. Each slight breeze brought welcome and cooling refreshment, as it caused his sweat to evaporate into the heated air.

He revisited the shower, reused the towel, and dressed himself for a second time that day. Ryan called Patsy on his cell phone to let her know he was in town. He agreed to have a late Sunday lunch with her and John the following day before flying back to Boston. The discussion about food made him realize that he had not eaten lunch, and it was now approaching 1:00 PM. His visit to the Johnston's was only four hours away. He drove back to the convenience store and purchased a six pack of cold soft drinks and several bags of peanuts. Returning to the house, he drove slowly up the gravel drive and admired the yard he had earlier prepared. Although the heat of the day had established itself, he lowered the window in his car to take in the bitter-sweet smell of the freshly cut grass.

There is something unusually gratifying about the results of manual labor. Once done, one can observe the outcome and instantly realize the improvement one has made.

As he rolled to a stop and exited the car, he felt like a king looking out over his kingdom. His royal highness trod up the front steps with a six pack of cold soft drinks as his sword, and several bags of peanuts as his scepter. He placed all but one can of soft drinks in the refrigerator, beside a lonely bottle of ketchup. He then placed all but two bags of peanuts in the kitchen drawer containing the mower manuals. Returning to the front steps, the king seated himself on his throne and consumed the drink and peanuts. There, sitting on a step and leaning his back against a porch post, he slowly dined for half an hour and considered the extent of his blessings.

Later, as he drove to Pete Johnston's place, he battled within himself as to whether he should attend Sally's church or climb to the top of the mountain on the following day. He was torn. Ryan loved the land, especially the mountain top. However, he had great respect for Sally's pastor. In his view, this man was vastly overqualified for this small rural church. Besides respect for his education, intellect, and wide experiences, Ryan found the pastor to be very personable. He genuinely liked the man. The decision still hung in his mind as he rang the doorbell of the Johnston home. As soon as Pete opened the door, all thoughts were focused on his host as he was welcomed inside. Eunice explained that they planned to begin eating around 6:00 PM, giving the men a chance to visit beforehand. Ryan had given little consideration as to what Pete had promised to show him. Almost immediately the large farmer invited Ryan to "hop in the truck and go for a little ride." He didn't really know Mr. Johnston very well, but Sally had thought highly of him. Besides that, Ryan received enough payment from the farmer for rental of the front acreage to more than pay all the yearly taxes on his recently inherited property. He quickly agreed.

They drove down a thinly graveled road until they

neared a large pond. Upon exiting the truck, Pete hoisted a feed sack from the bed of the trunk and invited Ryan to come with him to the pond. Once there, he dropped the sack to the ground and asked Ryan to toss some of the contents into the pond. With a questioning glance, Ryan obeyed. Reaching in, he brought out a handful of dried corn pellets and tossed them into the pond. As soon as they hit the water, the pond began to explode into a state of frenzy.

"What in the world was that?" Ryan snapped.

"Catfish!" exclaimed Pete, wearing a broad grin. "I love catfish, and these are a cash cow for me."

"Cash cow?" questioned Ryan.

"I sell most of these fish to local restaurants," he explained. "These are grain fed, to give them the best taste."

Reaching his large hand into the bag, then with one motion, Pete let fly a consistent spread of corn pellets across the surface of the pond. Again, the surface of the water erupted.

"Go ahead," Pete encouraged. "Toss in a few more handfuls. I'll tell you when I think they've had enough."

Ryan obeyed and was amazed the fish so easily went after the feed. He wondered if fish actually had more brains than he had previously imagined. As he tossed in another handful of pellets, he considered the possibility that fish could be trained. Ryan remembered a girl he knew in high school, who for many years had a large fish in an aquarium. The fish would come to the surface to be petted whenever she placed her hand across the surface of the water. He said nothing of this matter to his host, and he continued to toss the pellets until Pete signaled that the fish had eaten enough. After they were seated in the truck for the return ride back for supper, Pete began to share an idea.

"I like the taste of catfish, but nothing compares to freshwater largemouth bass," Pete explained as he started the engine of the truck.

"I can't say that I have ever had freshwater bass," Ryan

answered.

"You will tonight," Pete revealed.

"If you enjoy the taste of bass so well, why don't you have some in your pond?" Ryan asked. "Maybe you do, and I just didn't realize it."

"No, I don't," he replied. "And I will tell you why. Bass require running water to do well. They are alright if you have a larger lake, but they really do well in moving water."

"You mean like a river, or stream?" Ryan asked.

"Well, yeah," said Pete. "The problem is that most people don't have a river; and even if they do, they would not be able to stop the bass from moving downstream to be fished by someone else."

"That makes sense," said Ryan. "I guess the same problem would occur with a stream."

"Not entirely," explained Pete. "We can continue this discussion later. We are almost back at the house now, and supper should be ready. I'll explain how a stream can be used after supper."

Ryan found it interesting that Pete didn't want to talk about it during the meal, but he didn't ask questions. They exited the truck and went inside to the combined smells of fried fish, hush puppies, fried okra, and corn on the cob. Eunice was placing the last plate on the table.

"What will you have to drink?" she asked. "We have iced tea, (sweet or unsweet), soft drinks, milk, or water. What will you take?"

"Sweet tea will be fine," Ryan responded. He knew that many people in the south prided themselves on the making of iced tea, and he considered the possibility that the Johnston couple would be drinking the same. He was correct in this assessment, as sweet, iced tea was poured in each glass.

"We aren't very formal around here," she continued. "Have a seat right here."

They took their places. Then she glanced over at her husband and said, "Pete, would you turn thanks?"

Pete had already taken off his hat before sitting, and he responded to her request. "May we bow our heads, and give God thanks for all He has provided?"

Ryan closed his eyes and bowed in agreement. Pete thanked God for the presence of his guest and asked God to bless the hands of the person who had prepared the food. He then thanked the Creator for health and other blessings. He ended the prayer by asking God to use the food to nourish the body of each person at the table.

The platters of food were passed first to Ryan, and then the hosts loaded their plates.

"Some like to eat fish and hush puppies with ketchup," Pete explained. "I eat them with and without. Try it, and see which way is best for you."

"I've eaten hush puppies and catfish with my aunt, before," Ryan responded. "I like ketchup with them both."

"OK, but you ought to try a bite of the bass without ketchup, so you can taste the difference between it and catfish," Pete encouraged.

Ryan did, and he was amazed that the freshwater bass had very little of the 'fishy' taste that was more common with catfish. "This is really good!" he replied.

His plate was soon empty, and he was offered more.

"I've cooked plenty, so eat all you want," Eunice offered. "But make sure you leave room for hot apple cobbler with ice cream. That's what we have for dessert. If you don't like apple cobbler, we have some store-bought cookies."

"No, I love apple cobbler," Ryan confessed. "I'll make sure to leave room. This fish is really good, and I am surprised that Aunt Sally never cooked any during a visit."

"Well, she didn't have a boat and she didn't really have a pond with fresh water running into it," Pete said, looking over at his wife with a little sheepish grin.

"That's enough of that at this table Mr. Johnston", she warned. Turning her attention to her guest, she stated, "No, Ryan, you're just fine. Pete needs to mind his manners, that's all."

With her head slightly tilted down, she gave Pete the same serious "you had better behave yourself" glance that is so often given by mothers to children. It was a bit comical for this small woman to treat this huge middle-aged man as if he were a child.

"Yes, Mama," he replied with a sly grin. "I'd hate to get a whupin', right here in front of Ryan."

By this time, she had approached the table with the cobbler and a large knife. Just as his Aunt Sally had done, while handing out a verbal rebuke while holding a knife, Eunice pointed the knife at Pete and warned, "You best behave, if you know what's good for you."

The sly grin on Pete's face, broadened into fullness. His eyes danced, as he glanced over to Ryan.

"She means it, too," he explained. "You don't cross that woman," he warned, still wearing the broad grin.

"Are you ready for that apple cobbler?" she asked her guest. "Pete might not get none, if he don't shape up."

"Absolutely," Ryan replied. "Thank you."

She carved out a healthy square piece from the cobbler and placed it on a small dish. She then asked "Would you care for ice cream on top? The cobbler is still hot, and I have the ice cream right here."

"Sure," he answered.

She dipped a large scoop of vanilla ice cream and placed atop the hot apple cobbler. She set the dessert in front of Ryan and placed a clean fork beside the plate. Turning to her husband, she asked "Mr. Johnston, are you going to act right?"

"Yes, I'll be good; and I want two scoops, please Ma'am," he responded.

She prepared his with a grin and set it before him. She

cut herself a smaller piece, but didn't include the ice cream.

Changing the subject, Ryan asked "Why does the bass taste so different from the catfish?"

Pete explained, "A catfish is a scavenger, eating mostly from the bottom, while bass are game fish. A bass eats mostly living things, like smaller fish and frogs. I'm sure the difference in diet, is the main reason. That is why people prefer grain fed catfish, instead of the catfish that scavenges the bottom. There is a difference in taste."

"Mrs. Johnston, this cobbler is delicious," Ryan complimented.

"Please have some more," she offered, standing up over the cobbler.

"OK, just a small piece without the ice cream," Ryan said.

She quickly cut it and placed it on his dish. "Anyone care for coffee?" she asked as she moved into the kitchen.

"Sure, I'll take a cup," Ryan responded.

Eunice asked him how he liked his coffee, and Ryan requested only sweetener to be added. She brought a cup to each and announced that they could stay where they were while she cleared the table and washed the dishes. Ryan considered asking her if she needed any help, but decided that she was leaving the two of them there for a reason. As soon as the table was cleared, Pete confirmed it.

"She doesn't like for me to talk business at the table, while everyone is eating," Pete explained. "She considers it to be rude. I have a proposition for you to consider, and I want to assure you that I have no intention of putting pressure on you in any way. In fact, after tonight I will not bring the subject back up unless you want to talk about it at some future date. Fair enough?"

"OK," Ryan replied.

Pete began, "I currently pay you rent in order to farm the front acreage of your property, and I began that as a deal made with your Aunt Sally before she died. If you should ever decide to call off the deal, just tell me. I am making a profit, but I really don't need it. Should you ever decide that you would like to end the deal, I want you to know that I would not hold you to the agreement."

"No, I 'm glad to have you farm it," Ryan stated. "It helps me probably more than it does you. It really helps with the property taxes. I'm not here often, and it is also to my benefit to have someone coming over to the place in my absence. I think it might contribute to keeping strangers off the place. Thank you."

"I have a proposal," Pete offered. "Besides the rental of your front property, I would like for you and me to participate in something together. What I propose is that you and I put a pond behind the house."

Pete believed in laying his cards squarely and openly on the table. He continued.

"Let me finish explaining, and then I'll answer any question you might have. Earlier, I told you that bass need running water in order to do well. In a few years, I will not want to have to transport and launch a boat every time I want to fish for bass. I plan to sell my boat, eventually. In fact, I am already a little tired of maintaining a boat. When the time comes, I would like to still be able to fish for bass from the bank. I have a couple of friends, who have a place on the lake. However, I don't always have access to their property. To get to the point, bass need running water; and you have a small stream. I would like to dig out a pond at one corner of the stream, just enough to allow fresh water to come in and then spill back out. I wouldn't disturb the majority of the stream. The pond would need to be no smaller than a quarter acre, and it would have to have spillovers where the water enters and exits. I don't want to sell the bass; this would only be for our personal fishing. I would like to be able to come over and fish it anytime when you are not at home, and I would like to be able to fish it only if I gained permission from you during the time while you are staying there. It will take several months to stock a pond and would take two to three yeas for the fish to grow to a reasonable size. It would only be for our two families to enjoy; and for only as long as I live or have the ability to fish. In this joint effort, you would provide the land and access to the pond. I would provide the equipment to dig the pond, construct the spillovers, and provide maintenance in stocking the fish. We would equally share in the bass, only on the basis of our personal private fishing."

Ryan was a little shocked at the idea. Scenarios began to run through his head, and he quickly pondered several pluses and minuses of the proposition. Before he could answer, Pete continued.

"I would like for you to think it over for a while. I will try to answer any question you might have."

"What about legal matters?" Ryan asked. "I know that there is a legal agreement regarding the farming of the property. Would we draw up something along those lines if I should agree to this?"

"Whatever agreement that pleases you, would be fine with me," Pete replied.

"How deep would it need to be?" Ryan asked. "I'm a little concerned that a child might sneak onto the property to fish the pond, and possibly drown while I'm not present." He was mindful of the boy, Tommy, who drowned in the presence of his Uncle Andrew. He would never forget the impact of that event on his uncle's life.

"The deepest area would be in the center, at about fifteen feet deep," Pete answered. "They need to move to cooler water in the heat of the day. There is never a guarantee that some kid won't decide to try his luck at fishing. I have several rolls of eight-foot chain link fencing, but it would take more than that to fence in a quarter acre. It also wouldn't stop a determined kid, so I think it would probably be a wasted effort. The pond would sit a good way from the road, and it might not be seen unless someone came up to the house."

"I've found evidence that someone has been drinking on the property," Ryan explained. "I wasn't very happy when I found it. What about a privacy fence to block the view?"

"It might work if you put a *'Beware of the Dog'* sign on it," Pete said with a chuckle. "It wouldn't do much good if they never heard the barking of a dog from behind the fence. A fence like that has a downside. It would prevent me from seeing anyone back there, while I farmed the front acreage; and you couldn't see them from the house. My best advice, would be to place a 'No Trespassing – Private Property' sign at the road."

"I think that would be a good idea, regardless of the pond," replied Ryan. "Thanks. I'll make a point to do that before I leave. I will have to think about the liability of having a pond, but the sign might release me of legal problems. I would still hate for a child to fall in."

"Well, give it some thought," Pete continued. "If I dug the pond, I would move the dirt to the mountain side of the stream. An earthen berm would be an advertisement that a pond was behind it, and the best way to keep a stranger away is to make the area very visible from the house. I have known people to place a pond in the woods, or plant trees around a pond, in order to block the view of the water from the road. To me, this only served to keep the strangers hidden from view of the property owners."

"You have a point; I had not thought about the fact that hiding the pond would result in allowing trespassers to feel more secure," Ryan responded.

He was silent for a moment. The younger man's eyes danced about, indicating that he was deep in thought. Then, in an instant, Ryan became calm and assured. In his mind and heart, it all came together. Fixing his attention back on the farmer, he replied.

"No, I trust your judgment regarding the matter. You've

been a good partner in the rental of the front acreage, and you've been a good neighbor."

In a sudden act of decision, and even as a surprise to himself, Ryan stood and held out his hand to Pete. Pete slowly stood.

"Are you sure you don't want more time?" Pete questioned.

"No, Pete," Ryan answered. "I have a tendency to be overly concerned, at times. Sally thought highly of you, and you could not have obtained a stronger reference."

Pete smiled. His powerful hand reached out for the hand still extended by Ryan.

"Thank you, son," the farmer quietly responded.

Ryan sensed, in that hand clasp, the sincerity of the moment. He realized for the first time the man to man respect that men of old extended to each other, when they joined hands and quietly looked each other honestly in the eye. If this situation had come about with another individual, or even at another time, the younger man might not have made a decision of this type so quickly. A year prior, he certainly would not have taken this risk without having a legal agreement on hand. On this day, and in this hour, Ryan experienced something entirely new to him. This was a vow between men; and the honor and respect exchanged between the two made him feel a sense of strength he had never known before. For the first time, he knew he was no longer an outsider in the small community.

Chapter 4

THE NEXT MORNING Ryan awoke as the fall sun began to spill a familiar red glow across his bedroom wall. After returning home from Pete's the night before, he determined that he would spend the morning climbing the mountain. Without a shower, he quickly dressed and placed two cold soft drinks and three packs of peanuts in his now empty backpack. Before stepping off the small rear porch, he dropped his head in reverence for God and the beauty of the day. He asked God to be with him during the day and asked for a Divine touch regarding his relationship with Pete.

It's Sunday, but I'll excuse myself from Sally's church today. I'll worship God in the natural surroundings this property offers, in God's creation.

Within minutes he was quickly making his way up the mountain rising behind the house. He moved very quickly, and within a couple of hours he passed the familiar flattened area on the side of the mountain. Ryan pressed on, for his goal was to not stop or eat until he reached the top. It was early fall, and the dense foliage that covered the mountain during he summer months was beginning to thin. With many of the leaves fallen on the ground, he found it more difficult to follow the path which led up the slope. Since returning to Boston after the accident, he had begun to exercise. Ryan was now running two miles, three times a week, and his times were improving. Since the last time he made the hike, he could tell a dramatic difference in his stamina. During most of the ascent up the mountain, his thoughts were filled with visions of the pond he and Pete would share.

By the time he reached the top, the time approached 10:00 AM. It had taken him almost three hours to ascend the slope, and he was to join Patsy and John for a late lunch at 1:30 PM. He wasn't concerned, because he knew that the hike down the mountain would be much faster than hiking up. Ryan would need to arrive at the house by 12:30, in order to shower and drive to the neighboring town where Patsy lived. He rested, while standing bent forward with a hand placed on each knee. After a moment, he dropped his backpack to the ground and removed a soft drink and a pack of peanuts. As he consumed both, he walked over the crest and found the view of the other side to be much more revealing than before. During the summer, the leaves of the trees hid what he now witnessed. Below him, at the base of the next hill, was a small rural wood frame church. As the morning sunlight reflected off its white painted facade, the small structure stood out against the brightly colored autumn leaves. A thin lightly traveled road ended in front of the building. A small cemetery lay beside the church, and about a half mile down the road was a small white house with a tin roof. He scanned the countryside before him for other larger roads that might tie to this area and could find none. It seemed really isolated, and he wondered what type of church it might be.

Ryan had no time to examine the church more closely, as the time had arrived for him to make a speedy descent down the mountain. He stood for a couple of minutes with his eyes closed. Ryan felt the gentle mid-day sunshine warm his face, as he breathed in the clean fresh fall air. He regretted not having more time, but was glad that he was able to experience the mountain again.

As Ryan made his way down the slope, he could not

stop thinking about that small rural church. It's peaceful setting and simple frame was as enticing as an elegant painting of a country setting that existed only in the mind of an artist. Each time he had attended church in Brandon Springs, it had been to Sally's former church Because of her, the people there showed him favor. He had great respect for the pastor, and usually gleaned a life lesson from the sermon. However, he felt compelled to find and visit this little church. The image of the simple building, set against the rustic pristine landscape, was etched in his mind. Far removed from traffic, it almost seemed to be placed there from a time lost long ago. As he thought about it, an almost overpowering sense of peace came over him.

When he arrived at the house, he had only time to pack, shower, and drive to meet Patsy and John. In fact, it was fifteen minutes beyond the agreed upon time when he parked his vehicle at the restaurant. As Ryan entered the front door of the establishment, he saw the two talking while sitting in the waiting area. He imagined that they were discussing his late arrival, but was relieved to find he was not the subject of conversation. The couple had earlier attended a church service, and the pastor's sermon was the topic of discussion.

"I'm sorry to be late," he apologized.

Patsy broke off the conversation with John to reply, "We had become a little concerned, but decided that the church service in Brandon Springs may have gone beyond the normal time. Is everything alright?"

"I'm fine," he explained. "I can't blame it on a church service, because I decided to hike up the mountain this morning instead."

Noting a slight look of disappointment on Patsy's face, he continued.

"Well, I 'm not a member of Sally's church, and I have only attended there a few times."

"You don't have to explain to us," John answered. "Your attendance in church is between you and God."

"Thank you," Ryan replied, giving Patsy a slightly defiant glance.

He really enjoyed her company, but he had always detested any type of judgmental attitude from others. He was thankful for John's statement, and the momentary instance of quiet internal rebellion left him.

The restaurant hostess announced that their table was ready, and led them to it. Patsy was still working as a nurse in the local hospital, and John managed a local department store. Ryan was unable to determine whether they were really in love with each other, or if they had become engaged because it seemed the next logical step in their relationship. They attended the same church and had dated since John graduated from college. Patsy was twenty-six and John was twenty-seven. The two had been together for about five years, and they seemed to be well suited. Yet, Ryan observed something that bothered him.

Maybe it's actually something I don't see. They seemed to get along, but a certain chemistry seems to be missing. I don't see that spark that see in some couples. It's hard to put my finger on it. It's like there's no mingling of souls. Larry and I seem to have a closer relationship than this couple.

Not that he had any inclination of romance toward Larry, but they were men of kindred spirits. Patsy and John reminded him of two sculptured figures on each side of the entrance to a mansion, or a museum. They were of good taste, attractive, and well made. However, they didn't seem to deeply interact with each other. Their discussions even appeared to reside on the surface; eye contact never seemed to penetrate the core of either person.

There is no mingling of souls.

As they were seated, the couple continued their discussion regarding the pastor's message. Ryan sat silently, until the conversation was pleasantly interrupted by the waitress asking for the order of each. He loved both friends, but he had become weary of the talk. The two men ordered steak dinners and Patsy asked for a salad with chicken strips.

On a personal level, the waitress quickly sized up the party. She noted that Patsy and John were the couple, and that Ryan was the single guy. The waitress gave him a smile as she filled their water glasses. Without thinking, Ryan watched her as she walked away from the table. Her movements were genuinely feminine, and her figure attractive. When his eyes returned to the woman seated across the table, he realized that Patsy had been watching him.

"Well, she sure caught your eye," Patsy said with a teasing tone.

"I don't know her, but she is easy on the eyes," he admitted. "I bet she's trouble."

Changing the topic, John asked, "What do you think about our pastor's sermon? I think we've almost left you out of the conversation. I'm sorry."

"I doubt that I know enough about the Bible or spiritual matters to have a valid opinion," Ryan offered.

"The subject concerns the second coming of Christ, or what some call the *Rapture*," John explained. "The Bible warns about a period of tribulation and suffering brought about near the second coming of Christ. Patsy agreed with the pastor, in that she believes that Christ would come for God's people before that time of tremendous tribulation. She believes that a loving God would certainly rescue Christians from that type of suffering and would call them to Heaven before it began."

"That sounds reasonable," Ryan responded.

"Christians have suffered horrendously during particular times throughout history," John stated.

He noted the suffering of the early Christians at the hands of the Romans, of Christians who suffered behind the Iron Curtain at the hands of the Communists, and of those suffering today in some Muslim countries in the Middle

East. He reminded them of the Biblical scriptures indicating that Jesus would return when the last heavenly trumpet sounded. To him, it seemed that a great deal of the predicted tribulation would occur before that last trumpeting.

Changing the subject, Ryan began to tell them about his friend Larry. They laughed as he told them how they met, and he explained his surprise of learning about Larry's pastime of reading nightly in the public library. Both found it interesting when Ryan gave examples of Larry's incredible self-taught knowledge, and of his unusual intellect.

"He sounds like Abraham Lincoln," Patsy offered.

John was suspicious. He pointed out that some of the more dangerous people observed by the FBI were uneducated and extremely intelligent individuals, having very little self-discipline, being somewhat lazy, and only able to earn a meager living by a low wage job.

"These types of people are prime suspects for major crime, or they fit the profile of several persons in history who were known to bring about serious civil unrest in societies," John warned. "I would be somewhat careful in becoming overly involved with Larry, but I'm curious to know more about this man."

John asked questions regarding his place of origin, family life while growing up, and whether he had ever been married. Although he was concerned, it was apparent that he was also somewhat fascinated. As the conversation continued, Patsy quickly lost interest. She became bored, even to the point of feeling a bit irritated. Several times she tried to bring the discussion back to the topic of the church sermon, but John and Ryan were firmly fixed on this unusual individual.

Careful not to betray his friend's trust and confidence, Ryan told them only the information of which he felt sure Larry would not be sensitive. He explained how his friend worked on the docks in Alabama, but that he had found it almost impossible to obtain a similar job in Boston. When he told them that Larry was currently washing dishes for a café, this fact seemed to captivate John's attention.

"While going to college, I washed dishes for the school cafeteria with three other students," John said. "I clearly remember the day when the police arrested a fellow cafeteria worker, who was charged with heading up a ring of drug dealers on campus."

Ryan offered nothing of Larry's family life or personal history. He disliked John's insinuations and maintained his loyalty to Larry.

The waitress delivered each order, and Ryan's focus of conversation was only interrupted when he felt her graceful hand on his back as she refilled his glass of water. Patsy and John were not able to see this, but her touch was not missed by Ryan. He made a conscious effort not to allow his eyes to follow her away from the table this time, but he found the task difficult. Even after she departed, he could imagine her caressing hands gently giving a massage to his shoulders. He summoned every ounce of mental discipline and returned his attention to the conversation. It had been months since he had gone on a date, and it was becoming very apparent to him that he had really become lonely for the touch of a woman.

The waitress never placed her hand on him again that night, but it was obvious that he was in her sights. She never let his glass become less than half filled, but had almost ignored Patsy and John. Each time Ryan's glass was filled by the waitress, Patsy would give him a teasing glance. Patsy once stuck out her tongue out at the waitress, as the woman walked away after having left her with a mostly empty glass. Though this was a bit juvenile, Ryan welcomed the break from the theological discussion that kept resurfacing during their conversation. Just before he left the restaurant, Ryan placed a healthy tip on the table for the waitress.

WITHIN TWO HOURS OF LEAVING Patsy and John, Ryan was boarding a plane in Knoxville. He hoped that his flight back to Boston would be more enjoyable than the earlier one he had taken to Knoxville. On the way down he had a window seat, but most of the trip offered a view of thick clouds. The inability to have a view only added to the real problem, the lack of comfort. He was wedged snugly beside a large fellow with ample hips, a barrel chest, and broad shoulders. The man's lower half was so large that he barely squeezed into the seat, and his upper half spilled over into the area that should have been reserved for Ryan. Once they were in the air, the man dropped into a heavy sleep; and he snored lightly until they landed. The enormous head of this passenger rested on his chest, cushioned by a large roll of fat that hung from under the chin and acted as a small pillow. The fellow slept like a baby. Ample pouches of fat along the man's ribcage prohibited his arms from hanging directly from the shoulders. Instead, they angled out from the body so that the man's elbow positioned itself completely over Ryan's armrest. Ryan experienced the entire flight leaning against the side wall of the plane, with his own arms fixed tightly against his rib cage. His bodily movements were so constrained, that his neck was stiff for a couple of hours after disembarking.

During that trip, he had another reason for being glad to reach the terminal in Knoxville. Throughout the flight he had resisted waking the man beside him so that he could use the restroom on the plane. The two cups of coffee consumed in the restaurant were screaming to be released from his body. As he hastened to the closest terminal men's room, he tried to focus on loosening his stiff neck to take his mind off the stretched walls of his fully expanded bladder. Standing at the urinal, he found welcome relief. During his time before the ceramic fixture, he considered the story of the lion being so grateful to have a thorn removed from his paw. He felt he could relate. As he allowed the pressure to subside, he studied the etchings in pen and pencil scribed on the wall before him. Ryan wondered how tomorrow's cultures would view the restrooms of today.

Would this room become a revered place of historical significance, and the crude writings upon it viewed as prized archeological etchings of peoples lived long ago?

It is amazing how relief from discomforts can put things into an unusual perspective; and it is mystifying how the mind decides what to hold as significant information to be retained. This moment would be included in the memories retained by Ryan for the remainder of his life. Why would the event of standing at a urinal be as vividly stored in a mind, as the memory of meeting a famous person or visiting a significant place? When fully appreciated against the crisis of the hour, many of the remembered joys of life can sometimes be measured by some of the more mundane and simple events.

On this flight he had an aisle seat. This would have to be better, for the seating assured him that he would not be trapped. Finding his row, he placed his backpack in the overhead and dropped into the aisle seat beside a rather plain looking woman. She was a petite framed person, whom he guessed to be approaching her forties. She politely greeted him with a tired, but genuine, smile. Once they ascended to almost cruising altitude, Ryan introduced himself. Her name was Mary, and she lived in a suburb just outside Knoxville. She was on her way to Boston to be with her father, who was having brain surgery for a rapidly growing tumor. He was under the care of a renowned specialist there who had been recommended by a neurologist in Knoxville. Ryan told her a little about himself, but refrained from telling her about his deceased parents. He wanted to avoid any discussion of death, hoping to help her maintain as positive an attitude as possible concerning her father.

"Do you have children," Ryan asked.

"I have a boy and a girl," Mary replied.

Pausing for a moment, she continued. Mary told him that she had lost a 10-year-old daughter after many years of battling a childhood cancer. From somewhere beneath her kind face, visibly marked from years of pain and concern, her eyes and voice spoke with a remarkable sense of peace and inner strength.

He then told her about losing his parents, and of recently losing his Aunt Sally. As she attempted to console him, he interrupted her.

"I can't imagine the horror and desperation of helplessly watching a child suffer over an extended period of time, and then have it all end in her death," Ryan said.

"It wasn't easy, but I am so blessed to have been given two healthy children," she softly spoke.

Ryan sensed strength in her that he had seen in his Aunt Sally. She had risen from devastation and disaster and focused on the positive aspects of her life.

"I just don't understand why things like this happen," he painfully stated. In his mind he could envision Mary wearily caring for her daughter, who suffered year after year until death released her.

"This place is not Heaven, and good people sometimes find themselves in very difficult situations," she replied.

She had spent so many years caring for someone in pain that she naturally reached out to comfort any suffering soul with whom she came in contact. Ryan wasn't only suffering because of his realization of her past pain and grief; there was more to it. He was carrying around his own struggle. He was not the person he had been six months before, but he still was deeply struggling within himself for life's answers. She didn't really understand the details, but Mary sensed the silent battle raging inside the man seated beside her.

Ryan laid his head back against the seat and closed his eyes. He reflected on the theological discussion that earlier consumed his two friends at the restaurant. In comparison to the agonizing death of a child, it seemed intensely trivial.

What difference did it really make, as to when Christ will return to earth, in the light of a dying child or a real struggle like facing brain surgery?

He almost felt anger toward them.

Before leaving Mary in the airport, everything within him wanted to reach out and hold her in an embrace. Not an embrace of romance, but an embrace of deep concern and care. He wished he could hold her so tight that every sorrowful event in her life could be squeezed from her slight frame and vanquished into Hell itself. Knowing how inappropriate that action would be, the best he could do was to pat her on the shoulder and wish her and her father well.

OVER THE NEXT TWO DAYS, he could not shake himself from his encounter with the woman on the flight. He attempted to tell Larry about her, but his friend was concerned with his own difficulties in finding a better job. During the conversation with Larry, Ryan made the decision to visit a mission for homeless people he had seen in Boston. He invited Larry to come with him, but his friend flatly refused to take part in it. When asked why, Larry simply stated that he was uncomfortable with the idea. Ryan considered the possibility that John had been right in his assessment of Larry.

John's suspicions of Larry could be correct; maybe he really did have something to hide. Was it possible that Larry refrained from going because some criminal element at the mission might recognize him as a fellow accomplice in wrongdoing? Do I really know Larry?

Ryan searched his heart and decided to give his friend the benefit of the doubt. He truly believed Larry to be honest and open. Ryan felt comforted in reminding himself that Larry would certainly confess any wrongdoing, if asked.

Saturday morning, Ryan opened the door to the mission and made his way to the director's office. After a short conversation, the director had someone on staff take him to a place on the serving line in the cafeteria. As Ryan loaded plates for the homeless with beans and muffins, he noticed the faces of those passing by. Many would not make eye contact, but there seemed to be two main groups of those who did. There was the submissive type that gave a glance and a nod of appreciation, and there were those of a more aggressive nature. One such individual gave him such a piercing stare that it seemed as if Ryan had been run through with a sharp weapon. The man's wild gray eyes blazed from sunken sockets, shadowed under a heavy brow. Against the weathered brown and wrinkled unshaven surface of the man's face, framed by matted and oily unkempt graying brown hair, they seemed to reach out and clutch their victim in a paralyzing grip. Immediately sensing the vulnerability in Ryan, the man stated in a gruff deep voice.

"What are you staring at? You got a problem?"

Regaining his composure, Ryan responded in as strong a tone possible.

"No. What's your problem?"

The man continued his icy glare for a moment, saying nothing. He then moved on to an unoccupied table. After a few minutes, Ryan noticed that only a couple of the homeless men joined him. As the two sat across from the man, they made no eye contact with him.

As he left the cafeteria, Ryan felt a sense of disappointment.

I had hoped for a rewarding experience, or maybe just a sense of spirituality by making a gesture of service at the mission. I found neither.

He walked through the facility and came across a room which was about half the size of the dining area. He quickly recognized that this room functioned as the chapel area. There were rows of metal chairs facing a lectern, and a hymnal rested on every second chair. To the right side of the lectern was an old upright piano, on which was stacked about a dozen Bibles. There was something special about that room. He sat down on one of the metal chairs. Ryan closed his eyes and placed his head in his hands. There was something rich about this plainly adorned place, and he rested in a peace that he had not sensed since the passing of his aunt.

The prayers of many desperate men have passed through the walls of this room on their way to Heaven. It's as if each prayer left a metaphysical form of incense in the pours of the walls during their passing. Not an incense that can be smelled, but something spiritual that may be felt if one was in the right frame of mind and heart.

He felt refreshed as he took in each breath, and he relaxed in the peace that filled the place. Before long, Ryan experienced something even stronger in that room than what he felt when Mary sat beside him on the flight back to Boston. He didn't bother to look at his watch when he rose to leave the building to return home to the condo, so he wasn't sure how long he had been sitting there.

THE NEXT MORNING, he decided to attend a church not far from his condo in Boston. Ryan entered the elegant building, and he found a comfortable area about mid point in the sanctuary. As he took his seat at the end of a partially empty pew, he watched as the people filed in and took their places. He was invisible. No one seemed to see him; no one took notice that a visitor was in their midst. The church organ began. Robed choir members entered from a side door and made their way to their proper section behind the two pulpits. One pulpit was larger than the other, and they were stationed on each side of the raised platform just below the choir. After the opening prelude, the minister entered from the opposite side door, and took a seat near the larger pulpit. With precision, the organist played a classical piece. The choir opened the service with a hymn. They sang each part with elegance and perfection of note and pitch. Announcements of church activities and board meetings were made from the smaller pulpit, and the congregation was led in a couple more hymns. Members of the congregation sang in almost whispers, as the organist played, and the choir sang in precise parts. Expressionless faces sat before the minister as he pronounced his message.

The musicians were very gifted and learned, and Ryan appreciated the talent and hours of practice behind the choir's perfection. The pastor was an eloquent speaker, yet Ryan was untouched. He still felt empty, alone, and unsatisfied. He felt as if a man, who had not eaten for days, was given a tour of a renowned art museum. This somber place felt more like a well-kept cemetery, than a place to heal thirsty souls. The voices of the choir were clear and melodious, but Ryan's soul was uninspired. The minister's mellow voice, correct grammar, and precise diction were tuned to perfection. However, Ryan was felt spiritually dry. Shortly after leaving, Ryan thought to himself.

This man should have been in theater. His ability to speak was profound. What was spoken seemed more like words of a play. In theatre, an actor speaks someone else's words; and they can be spoken without heartfelt understanding of their true basis of meaning. The sermon contained the same rhetoric about social injustice and warnings of judgment against others. They were similar to what I've heard in public service ads on the radio and TV. The words seemed hollow; they seemed to lack true substance; they lacked the Power and unspoken living Presence I felt in the empty and silent mission chapel.

To him, these words seemed to have been spoken for the sake of performance. There appeared to be more emphasis on how the words were pronounced, than reason behind their meaning.

There was nothing from the gut; and the points to be passionately made seemed to be simply intellectually performed as in a skilled debate of facts.

Though Ryan sensed more life and spirituality in the empty chapel at the mission, he felt uncomfortable about attending services there. He left the service in this elegant church almost depressed. Ryan continued his thoughts on the service after returning home. Seated in front of the TV, his mind was entertained by nothing on the screen.

A year ago, I might have been somewhat pleased with that service. At that time, the messages I sought were those able to enhance my career or my position among corporate executives. I would have better appreciated the gifts and hours of practice behind the choir's performance, and I would have been entertained and impressed by the perfected speech from the pulpit.

Now, he sought messages about life, where the wheels of living meet the road we all must travel. He didn't want philosophical lectures on pie-in-the-sky dreams, or ideas about life; he wanted hard answers regarding what to do when we see the frayed edges of the steel belts protruding from the balding tires that move us down an unfamiliar highway.

This road, leading to unknown places, may occasionally contain unexpected sharp curves, a lack of informational signs, and a pothole or two. I needed messages of truths lived and known, not speeches of issues discussed by inexperienced philosophers.

Questions hammered him relentlessly.

What do you do when you meet another soul who may lose a father to a brain tumor, or someone who has watched in desperation the slow and painful death of a child? You certainly don't give a lecture about human rights or social injustice. You don't have a debate as to the point in history for which we may vainly attempt to predict Christ's second return to this earth.

Frustrated, he almost felt anger toward the service he had attended.

How could they waste such an opportunity to address serious life questions?

The beautiful building, well-spoken pastor, and talented choir seemed wasted. To him, it seemed they were doing all this just for the sake of doing it. He even felt disgust for Patsy's and John's discussion. Then he remembered the topic of the sermon given that morning:

Judge not, that ye be not judged.

He was struck hard. It was as if a light had been turned on. The topic of the sermon, and the associated scriptures, cast a spotlight on him. The pastor certainly had no intention of personalizing the sermon for this visitor, and the scriptures in the Bible are written for all.

The spotlight is being drawn to me by my attitudes and thoughts; sort of, like flies being drawn to horse dung. Alright God, maybe the sermon was for me, after all.

Some persons suffering emptiness have a tendency to suck the life out of those with whom they have contact. Still, others find like minded empty souls to join them as they wallow in emptiness. Some retreat away to cry alone; and others try to fill themselves with things or people. Some experiencing emptiness, in frustration, lash out at others around them. Ryan realized that this was what he had done.

Under his breath he issued a soft apology to that church, to the pastor and choir, and to his friends. Yet, he was still frustrated, and still wanted answers. It was at that point that he realized what had occurred during the flight back to Boston. He wasn't supposed to provide answers or words to the woman on the plane. Instead, it was she who had brought a life message to him. Her peace was beyond understanding, and her strength was beyond her small frame. She didn't need him. He needed her message.

As he sat in his chair, not absorbing anything flashing before him on the TV screen, he realized that he had lost interest in life in Boston. He was very good at doing his job, but he felt uncomfortable with his distant relationship with fellow employees. He now cared little for climbing the corporate ladder and making impressions on powerful people. His job was now just his job, and not his life. He decided to return to Brandon Springs the following weekend, and he wanted to share the experience with someone.

He found Larry in the public library, reading a financial journal. His friend glanced up for a moment to acknowledge his presence; and then pointed a finger in the air, as to indicate that he wanted a moment to complete his reading of the article. As the finger lowered, so did the journal. Larry explained to Ryan what seemed so important about the piece, and then the conversation became lighter. After a few minutes Ryan pressed his friend regarding why he had been so adamant about not going to the mission with him. Larry was honest with his friend.

"I want to climb out of my present financial station in life, and currently I'm still too close to the poverty of those at the mission to feel comfortable in helping. Individuals who are doing well, often feel better when they reach down to help another person in need. However, for some of us who are struggling marginally above the state of the homeless, time spent with them serves as a reminder of their own failures and struggles. One screw up, and I could easily fall into that same state. That's me. That's were I am. I just couldn't do it."

"I didn't realize," replied Ryan. "I'm sorry."

"The working poor are often in a more difficult situation than those who are homeless," Larry continued. "For some, it is apparent that the difference between the two states is the fact that those working haven't given up. They're not lazy; they're still responsible individuals, daily facing desperate and difficult financial situations."

Ryan's friend could barely make ends meet with the dishwashing job and had become extremely concerned with his options. He also admitted that he was disgusted with lazy people and believed that he could not go to the mission in the right frame of mind. He tried to make Ryan understand.

"I've found that the working poor can be incredibly generous and willing to sacrifice to help another working man who has fallen on hard times," explained Larry. "However, we can be impatient with those who are just plain lazy. We have too little to squander on those who show little inclination of changing self-defeating lifestyles – like drunks, for example. We're not so far from the situation to be blinded to the reality of it. Some of the homeless people have given up on truly living and have become ungrateful takers from kind and naive hearts. That kind of empty person is like a vacuum, sucking the life out anyone who would spend enough time in contact with them. There are givers and there are takers in this world. I have little use for a self-serving professional taker."

Changing the subject, Ryan told him of his plans to have Larry accompany him to the home in Brandon Springs. Larry explained that he had no money to make the trip, but Ryan told him that he would be glad to pay for the flight. He wanted his friend to see the place that had come to mean so much to him. Larry recognized the sincerity in his friend, and he sensed that this was no act of charity. The trip was Ryan's need, not his. Larry agreed to accompany him to the small Appalachian town.

Chapter 5

OVER THE NEXT FEW MONTHS, Larry traveled with Ryan to Brandon Springs as often as he was able. In October, the hot water heater at the old house had to be replaced; and Ryan felt fortunate to have a friend with so much practical knowledge and ability regarding home repair. At his friend's advice, he decided to replace the old hot water heater with a larger unit. Larry also convinced Ryan to move it within the house. For years it had been on the back porch, but now it would be placed in the kitchen. He built a closet for it, and his craftsmanship was amazing. He ran new piping and wiring under the house so that the new unit provided instant hot water to the kitchen, bath, and laundry area. Larry's father had a violent temper, but he had some redeeming qualities. He had diligently and forcefully taught his son how to make home repairs, and to do neat and thorough work.

Realizing Larry's intelligence, Ryan purchased for his friend used college texts on accounting and finance. He was astounded by Larry's capacity of memorization. In fact, he was a bit envious. Compared to his own, his friend's ability to mentally retrieve almost anything, with which he had ever come in contact, was staggering. Larry's collection of information in his brain was like documents placed within folders, and then filed in an orderly fashion within filing cabinets. In this mental system, any folder, document, page and fact could be easily and quickly retrieved and shared with others at will.

Ryan's mind was different, in that each item of information was more like the colored liquid tint that is squirted into a can of base paint. The colors were quickly shaken and assimilated into the mix, and they became an intricate part of the whole. For him, these colors were difficult to extract and retrieve. The process of pulling things from memory was not an enjoyable experience. At times, it could truly be a painfully impossible effort. Nevertheless, Ryan had disciplined his mind and honed organizational skills to do the best with what he had. Through hard and laborious study, he had received such excellent high school grades that they enabled him to obtain scholarships for college. In order to maintain those grades in college, he had learned to discipline himself even more. It was this discipline that enabled Ryan to function in a highly professional position in his place of work. Larry never had to form traits of discipline and organization, and he often found it difficult to stay with a long-term effort until he saw it through.

There was another difference in the thinking of each. Larry's knowledge sort of floated on the surface, where Ryan's settled into the core of his being and shaped the person he had become. Neither form was any better or worse than the other; they were just very different.

Though the two found little in common regarding how they were raised, they became almost inseparable. It was truly remarkable how they seemed to complement each other. They found themselves to be kindred spirits. Their shared characteristic was the fact that they were both honest individuals, and they deeply appreciated and enjoyed that quality. They also grew in their respect for one another. Ryan had always been in awe of individuals who had a large capacity for memorization, and Larry had envied those who had the discipline he lacked. Honesty, with respect for one another, formed an incredibly strong foundation on which to base a relationship. In addition, they seemed to be on the same wavelength regarding humor. They would often witness the same humorous events and would simultaneously react with the same degree of laughter or silence.

On his third trip to Brandon Springs, Larry was introduced by Ryan to Patsy and John. The introductions among the four were cordial and polite, but within minutes John discovered that Ryan had not exaggerated in his description of his friend's unique intellect. Before long the conversation had become totally dominated by John's prying questions, and Larry's brief and exact answers. From the moment they were introduced, John attempted to size up this fellow who spoke with a slow southern accent and unrefined vocabulary. It was as if John were a fisherman, casting question after question. However, within a half hour it was John who was being reeled in at the end of a fishing line. With each response to a question, Larry's answer was like a hook that became more and more imbedded in the mouth of his inquisitor. It didn't take long for John to become almost mesmerized.

Patsy said little after the first few minutes of meeting Larry. Instead, she was almost captivated by the eyes of this man as he spoke. The longer the conversation wore on, Larry became more comfortable with this couple. Confidence glowed from those clear blue eyes. She had noticed them from the beginning, but they were becoming more and more intense as his sharp mind quickly pulled file after file of information in response to John's questions. Within an hour, she had all but forgotten her fiancé. She wasn't only captivated by his intellect. She was drawn to every aspect of Larry. Whenever she could pull herself away from his eyes, she would move to examine in detail his hair, skin, and muscular frame. Each observed mannerism of his became more endearing. Her real questions for him were not asked, as they were of a more personal nature. In her silence, she was quietly drawn to him by an unseen force. Before long she began to imagine herself in his arms and caressed by his touch.

Realizing what was occurring within herself, Patsy attempted to escape. She eventually excused herself to use the restroom. There she stared at herself in the mirror and asked herself question after question. A debate raged within her, as she attempted to settle the dilemma with reason.

"What are you doing?" she asked herself. *"Are you out of your mind? The guy is a dishwasher; and before that, he worked on a dock in Alabama. His ambition is to be a dock worker in Boston, and he can't even do that. This man isn't even formally educated, and he probably has some horrible disease from some nasty slut. He reads a lot and knows a lot of facts about all kinds of subjects, but he is going nowhere in life. He's good looking. Those eyes are... I have never seen eyes like those before. Not just the color, the look. He is tall and strong, but he probably hangs out with a rough crowd ... No, he hangs out with Ryan. He seems to be Ryan's best friend, or something like that. I've been with John for years; we belong with each other. We have so much together, and I'm in ...."*

She stopped her thoughts in mid-sentence. Deep inside, she knew she didn't love John. She couldn't say it; she couldn't even force herself to honestly think it. It was just comfortable to be with him. Her relationship was a safe one. He couldn't hurt her because she had no strong emotional attachment to him. At once she realized what she had been doing over the last few years. Unknowingly, Larry had stirred something within her. She felt scared. Patsy was no longer comfortable, and she didn't know what to do. She tried to logically reason it out.

"Of course, I don't love Larry," she thought. *"I don't really know him. But now seems obvious that I don't love John either; and I don't know what to do about it."*

During the next few minutes, she began an attempt to convince herself that she really did love John as much as any woman loved a man. After all, she wasn't even sure that being in love was actually a real thing. She had read about it in books. But, she considered most of what she read to be a sort of wild fantasy, conjured up by certain people in order to sell books and movies. She believed Hollywood knew nothing about loving someone because film stars and producers seemed to fall in and out of love on a continual basis. Patsy wasn't sure that her parents were ever in love. But eventually she remembered examples of deep and lasting love between some of the elderly couples at her church. Some of those relationships had lasted over 50 years, and she often watched as they held hands while in church; and they moved as one, as they slowly escorted one another from the church. She remembered watching an older gentleman open a car door for his wife, and then help her frail body into the front seat. The looks they gave each other spoke of mysteries shared only by them over decades lived together.

"This was real love; it had to be," she thought.

This brief encounter with Larry made her think. She could probably learn to love John over time, but she didn't have to find out. They were not yet married. The longer she stayed in the restroom, the more afraid she became to return to the conversation. It wasn't Larry she dreaded seeing, it was John.

There was a knock on the restroom door.

"Are you alright?" Ryan asked.

Because he was virtually left out of the conversation between John and Larry, he realized that Patsy had been absent from the room for a long period of time.

She opened the door and stepped out. At once he noticed that she had been crying, and he again asked, "Are you alright?"

"I'm fine," she responded. "Why do you ask?"

"Well, you were in there for some time, and your eyes are red and swollen," he cautiously explained. "Are you upset? Did someone say something?"

The facts were abundantly clear. It was Ryan at the door, concerned about her welfare, not John. Glancing back to the bathroom mirror, she noticed that Ryan's description of her appearance was true. She had been so introspective that she didn't even realize that she had been crying. Upon seeing her red swollen eyes, she burst into tears again.

"What is going on?" Ryan questioned.

Without saying a word, she buried her head in his chest and sobbed. Ryan said nothing. He placed his arms around her, patted her on her shoulder, and waited. After a couple of minutes, she raised her head. Her vision of him still blurred with tears, she backed away and put up her right hand as if to signify that she wanted him to continue to wait. She reached for several tissues and blotted each eye, and then began blowing her nose. Patiently, he waited. At last, she composed herself well enough to begin an explanation.

"I am just realizing that I don't really love John. I'm sorry. I don't mean to be so weird. I just don't know what to do."

Ryan and Patsy had become close friends, and she felt almost as if he was the brother she never had. Although there was no romance between them, she found it easier to talk with him than with John. She asked Ryan to go back to John and Larry. Patsy assured him that she would soon follow afterwards. She took a deep breath. It was as if some of the pressure within her had been released by her admission to Ryan. She began to relax, and after a few minutes most of the signs of her crying diminished from her face. She made her way back to the three men, but only Ryan seemed to notice her return. A few minutes afterwards, they decided to call it a night and part company. As Patsy left with John, she glanced back over her shoulder and gave Ryan an assuring nod.

Catching a glimpse of the communication between Patsy and Ryan, Larry quietly asked, "What was that all about?"

Looking down at the pavement while walking to his car, Ryan said nothing. A dead silence, filled with expectation, fell between them. Neither made eye contact while Ryan slid his key into the ignition. Before turning the key, Larry bluntly made his point.

"If you are trying to hit up on John's girl, I think it stinks. That fellow seems like a really good guy, and I like him."

"I like John, too," Ryan almost whispered. "Several months ago, I might have tried to go after Patsy, but it's not like that now. We really are just good friends."

"Man, I've heard that line before!" exclaimed Larry.

The intensity and increased volume of his voice boomed through the otherwise quiet night air.

"I'm not sure that it's possible for a guy and girl to be just good friends," Larry continued. "There are too many hormones getting in the way, and they seem to trickle to the surface when you don't expect it. I think you had better talk to me."

"Larry, this has to stay between just you and me," Ryan responded. "While you and John were conquering the world's problems and sharing philosophical entreaties, I found Patsy in the bathroom crying her eyes out. I guess John didn't even notice that she had been gone for such a long time."

"I noticed it, and I noticed that you left and stayed away for awhile too," Larry stated, in an almost reprimanding tone. His face was taking on a stony state of seriousness.

"Cut it out!" barked Ryan. "You know me; you know that I would tell you if something was going on. What is wrong with you? Do you doubt what I am telling you? I have never seen you act like this before."

"OK...OK", Larry said as he took a couple of deep

breathes.

The truth of the matter was that Larry very much noticed when Patsy left, and he very much noticed when she stayed away for the length of time. He had very much noticed everything about her, and he was fighting a desperate battle to keep his eyes off her. Throughout the evening, he repeatedly reminded himself that she and John belonged together. He liked John and would never do something to undermine him. Although Larry at times struggled to hold off violent tendencies when provoked, he was really a kindhearted man. During the conversation, he had purposely focused on John, and avoided making eye contact with Patsy. He truly didn't want to feed the emotions for her that he sensed rising within him that night.

"She told me that she suddenly realized that she doesn't love John with the kind of love a woman should have for someone she is planning to marry," Ryan stated. "This goes nowhere; this stays between you and me. Do you understand? She is my friend, but so is John. This puts me in a bad spot. If she breaks up with him, it may break up the entire friendship. This was not good news, and I really hated to hear it. I am not after her. Is the situation clear to you now?"

"Crystal clear," Larry said staring at the dashboard.

Thoughts and emotions were racing around in his mind and heart. Part of him was thinking that he really didn't need to hear what he just heard. He had struggled during the night to keep his mind off Patsy, and this bit of news was like giving him a giant green light. Little voices within him were almost rejoicing, but then he remembered himself and the situation. Each time thoughts of Patsy becoming available entered his mind, he would condemn himself for selfishly feeling upbeat about it. As they drove down the road, Larry's hopeful visions and emotions regarding Patsy continued to bubble up in his imagination. He instantly beat them down each time. After several minutes he felt almost exhausted.

At last, he couldn't stand it any longer.

"As long as we are being honest, I need to tell you something," Larry muttered. "And this has to stay between only us."

He struggled within himself. He thought that if he confessed to Ryan, his feelings toward Patsy would possibly go away. Sometimes the glue that holds the attraction for a person of the opposite gender is the secrecy of the feeling. Once it comes out into the open, the novelty causing the excitement sometimes goes away. Part of him wanted this to happen, and another part did not. Ryan was his best friend, and he had to tell him.

"I had feelings for Patsy all night long," Larry said, the words stumbling out of this mouth.

"What?" Ryan exclaimed. "You hardly said a word to her, and you and John all but shut her out of the conversation."

"I was purposely trying to ignore her, Ryan," he replied. "She and John are engaged, and I wanted no part of messing that up. Maybe it will pass. Maybe I will wake up tomorrow morning and feel totally turned off by her. Maybe she will change her mind about John. After all, he seems to be a great guy. I'm going to try to forget her, but I just want to be honest with you. I plan to stay away from them both for a while, if you don't mind. I think I need to do that. I'll stay in Boston, and let you come down here on your own. I love this place, but I just can't do this."

"OK, I can see how that might complicate things," said Ryan. "Hey, maybe you will wake up tomorrow totally disgusted with Patsy! Sleep on it before you decide. In fact, I won't need to come here much during the winter. There will be no grass to cut, and most of the repairs have been done. Wait and see what happens."

"You may need to come here," Larry quietly replied. "Patsy trusts you, and she will need a friend. You and I can hang out in Boston."

A sickening sense of disappointment began to rise within Ryan. Earlier that night he was spending time with the three people he enjoyed most. Within a couple of hours that relationship began to unravel and disintegrate before his eyes. Things were not the same, and they never would be.

The flight back to Boston was all but silent. Ryan and Larry were each deep in thought about what had happened during the trip, and about what they expected the future to hold. Larry was the more troubled of the two. Because of his feelings, he needed to avoid both John and Patsy. In doing so, he would no longer travel with Ryan to Brandon Springs. He had begun to love the place. The small-town atmosphere definitely made him feel more at home than Boston. He could have avoided the entire matter by withholding the information from Ryan, but he knew he had done the right thing by being honest with his friend.

Over the next few weeks, the conversations between the two men began to revive. Though they purposely left the couple out of discussions, Patsy and John were often in the minds of both.

BY CHRISTMAS, RYAN CONVINCED Larry to take college classes at night. Because of his low income as a dishwasher, he was able to obtain a government grant for school. Several years had gone by since Larry graduated from high school, and he felt a little intimidated at thoughts of a classroom. He found a small community college that required him to take a battery of tests before being admitted. Larry scored well on the SAT and aced the material for a variety of subjects. The community college offered several CLEP tests, and he took as many as he could. The combination of Larry's reading in public libraries and his unusual ability to remember facts, allowed him to be given credit for most of his freshman classes. Larry decided to major in accounting, and he enrolled in three-night classes that began in January. He consumed the material in each class with very little effort.

Three weeks after beginning classes, Ryan and Larry decided to meet for lunch on a regular basis during each workweek. Mondays, Wednesdays, and Fridays seemed the logical choices. By mid-February, Larry was beginning to have doubts about school.

"I'm not sure if did the right thing with the classes," he began.

"I thought you were doing OK," Ryan replied. "Are your grades slipping?"

"No," Larry responded. "The classes are too easy. This must be a school for flunkies, and I'm not sure if a degree from this place will get me a job. I should have tried a harder school."

"It's supposed to be a pretty good business school for its size," explained Ryan. "I think you'll find the upper-level courses more difficult. If you hang in there and graduate, you should be able to step into an entry level position."

Over the next few weeks Larry excelled in each class, and he continued to be surprised at how easy the courses seemed. One day he decided to reward himself by having lunch at a downtown restaurant. While waiting to be seated, his wandering eyes fell on a familiar couple at the table directly in front of him. The sight produced an icy chill that ran down the length of his tall frame. He was dramatically shaken by the unexpected sight. For a moment, he felt paralyzed and only stood staring in disbelief. However, when Patsy's eyes flashed in recognition of him, adrenaline filled every inch of his body and he quickly bolted out of the establishment. He was only about twenty feet from the restaurant, when he heard her call. He pretended he didn't hear and kept walking. If she had been alone, he might have been more inclined to welcome the sight of her. But he was greatly disturbed by the encounter. It was as if he was on autopilot; and he could do nothing to slow his pace. He was normally not the type to run from a situation, but he was overcome by emotion. He had to leave. Larry felt almost numb as he brushed past nameless individuals walking along the sidewalk. He thought he had made a safe exit, until he heard the footsteps of two people quickly approaching from behind. Thoughts were speeding through his mind, and none of them were good. He could feel rage begin to burn, and the muscles of his body began to tighten.

Catching him by the arm, Patsy yelled, "Stop!"

As he turned, he again caught sight of the fellow beside her. The man was almost out of breath. It was Ryan.

Ryan had seen those wild eyes before, and he knew his friend well. He knew instantly that Larry felt betrayed. Before he could say anything, Patsy interrupted. "Why did you leave?"

Larry didn't know what to say; he just stood there speechless. He wanted to step directly in the face of Ryan and confront him, but he couldn't bring himself to do so in front of Patsy. He turned his attention toward the woman standing beside him. Still holding his arm, her grip began to loosen. She was stunned by the wildness that burned within his eyes, and she sensed a powerful anger building across his lean muscular frame. Patsy suddenly became very uneasy. She had never seen this side of Larry. Upon meeting him, she was impressed by his quick wit, physical stature, and striking eyes. However, this didn't appear to be the same gentle intellect that she admired the night they met.

Catching his breath, Ryan quickly explained, "Patsy called me an hour ago and wanted me to meet her here for lunch. She is in town for a medical convention."

Larry's eyes flashed over to meet Ryan's, and at once he knew his friend was telling the truth. His glare began to soften, and tenseness in his body began to subside. Almost shaking, he spoke to Patsy. "I'm sorry. I didn't mean to be rude. I... I didn't want to interrupt, since I only met you that one time.... "

He was almost at a loss for words, and Ryan quickly rescued him.

"Larry has been working a full-time job and taking three college classes at night. The guy has aced every test, but he is totally exhausted."

With grateful eyes, Larry silently thanked his friend. He was exhausted, but it wasn't due to classes. As the anger escaped his body, he was left drained of energy. He felt very tired.

Patsy was a little confused at what she witnessed, but was relieved to see him return to the state she had remembered seeing when they had first met.

"Hurry," she said. "Our table should still be OK, but they will clear it if we wait much longer. Come have lunch. Please."

She took him by the arm and began to quickly lead him back to the restaurant. He now had no intention of running away, and he seemed to have little choice. Larry glanced over at a smiling Ryan and gave him a look of hopelessness. He totally surrendered to her. She could have led him off the edge of a cliff, and he would have jumped without giving it a second thought. Besides that, he was beginning to feel hungry.

The waiter earlier had been taken aback by their quick departure, and he was a bit bewildered to see them return. Ryan quickly slipped him a $10 bill and announced that Larry would be joining them at the table. The man's demeanor brightened immediately.

At first Larry remained silent and allowed Patsy and Ryan to catch up on their current life experiences. Patsy had broken things off with John, and he had taken it well. However, they rarely spoke afterward. When they did, the conversations were strained. Eventually, John took a job in Knoxville, TN. Patsy had only spoken with him once since the move. Ryan's conversation began with general statements about work, but he quickly moved to updating her on Larry's progress in school. It seemed he was purposely opening the door for his friend.

Larry tried to play down the fact that he so easily conquered the class material, but Patsy was quick to point out the trouble she encountered with her single accounting course in college. Throughout the meal, Larry listened and waited to see if there was a hint of real interest from Patsy. Once the check was paid, Patsy voiced her enjoyment in seeing them both. With those words, she glanced at Larry with a look that spoke volumes to him. There was invitation in her eyes, and he read it clearly. Sensing the betrayal of her feelings, given away by the glance, she quickly looked away and focused her attention again on Ryan.

"I would love to meet for lunch again while I am in town," Patsy announced, as she rose from the table. "I had a great time today. Call me on my cell phone if you can break away."

Purposefully, she addressed her statements to Ryan only. She made sure not to make further eye contact with Larry. She quickly excused herself, and then left the restaurant.

Larry sat in bewildered silence for a moment, and then quietly stated, "That was weird. Did I say or do something?"

Although Patsy's deliberate shun of Larry was clear to Ryan, he was quick to make an excuse. "Oh, I don't think she has been quite the same since she broke it off with John."

Her change in demeanor and sudden departure from the restaurant solidly remained in each man's mind as they concluded their conversation. Ryan discussed several topics with Larry, before they parted ways for the afternoon. However, while they talked, neither could completely shake the thoughts of her odd behavior at lunch.

Ryan did meet with Patsy again for lunch during her stay in Boston, but she changed the subject each time he mentioned Larry. This was the first time Ryan sensed a wall forming between them. From the time they met, she felt comfortable in openly sharing her personal concerns with him. It became clear that the subject of Larry was off limits. Not wanting to jeopardize their friendship, he didn't press the issue.

Over the next few months, Larry threw himself into work and study. Beginning with the following term he increased the number of courses. This left little time to socialize with his friend. Although Ryan made a point to visit the café where Larry worked, Larry spent little time with him and never returned a visit. It was apparent to Ryan that Larry was exhausted, and the few and brief conversations never touched the subject of Patsy. Larry's current focus was to make sure he retained his grade point average. Over time, Ryan's visits became less frequent and the two seemed to drift apart.

Chapter 6

DURING THE NEXT YEAR, Ryan made his bi-monthly pilgrimage to Brandon Springs without the company of his friend. During that time, his boss was promoted to regional manager for the East Coast and one of Ryan's associates became his new manager. He adjusted to the change well, and he reflected on the relative satisfaction he felt at being passed up for the promotion. Two years earlier, he wouldn't have taken it well at all. Ryan would have been furious with himself and with the company. He wanted the job, but he was now totally at peace within himself.

Quarterly, his old boss would meet with her managers. It was on one of those occasions that she popped into his office and asked if he had plans for lunch. Not having any, Ryan accepted the invitation. During the meal, she told him that she planned to open an office in Charlotte, North Carolina and that she wanted him to manage the office. At first, he was stunned, but he readily accepted. She told him that she had considered several candidates for the position, but it was Ryan's experience with people in the South that had placed him at the top of the list. She planned to announce this change in an afternoon meeting and wanted him to attend.

When Ryan returned to his apartment that evening, he

was still dazed by the quick turn of events. It would be an easy move. He had no family, and the company would pay the moving expenses and place him in an extended stay motel until he found a suitable permanent residence. Ryan would be able to purchase a home, if he wished, because he would receive a sizable increase in salary and would be a candidate for a yearly bonus. His mind raced as he considered the qualifications of those he would need to hire. She had given him a list of positions that would be needed, but had asked him to carefully consider qualifications for each and write job descriptions. She had her own in mind, but she wanted to compare his ideas with hers. She would meet with him the following month to finalize the qualifications and job descriptions.

Ryan was intently focused on defining each position, but soon the growling within his abdomen caused him to become keenly aware of his own hunger. Glancing at this watch, he was surprised to see that it was 9:00 PM. He immediately left to pick up supper. Ryan's thoughts moved from one selection of food to another and from one restaurant to another. In the process, he remembered the café where Larry worked. As he considered moving away from his friend, his heart sank. Even though they recently were spending very little time together, Larry was the closest thing to family left in his life. He felt compelled to disclose this recent change to his friend. Although the café was not in his neighborhood, Ryan made his way to it as if he were on a mission. He felt miserable as he neared the café. At last, he pulled up in front of the establishment and spotted Larry through the front window of the café. Ryan felt comforted in seeing him inside, busily clearing a table. He hurried through the front door, as not to allow Larry to make his way to the back before speaking to him.

"I have to talk with you, Larry," Ryan blurted, as he entered the door.

Startled, Larry snapped back.

"What about? I'm pretty busy, and I need to hit the sack early tonight. I have a test tomorrow."

"Six weeks from now, I will be moving to North Carolina," Ryan replied.

Larry stopped his work and made eye contact with his friend. At first, he looked confused; but he then the exhaustion that he carried inside made its way to every facet of his face and body. His strong shoulders drooped, his face became haggard, and he slowly set his tub of dirty dishes atop the table. He said nothing. It was if someone temporarily knocked the wind out him with a sucker punch to the stomach.

"I've been given a management position down there, and the pay will be significantly better," Ryan explained. "I just wanted to tell you. I can see that you are pretty busy. Is there a better time?"

"No. I have no time, anymore," Larry responded. "I've been so busy with school and work that I am running a little ragged. I'm not getting much sleep. We will be closed in fifteen minutes. If you have time, hang around until then and you can tell me all about it."

"Sure, I'll order a burger and fries to go so you won't have to clean up after me," Ryan said.

With that, Larry picked up the tub of dirty dishes and headed for the kitchen. Ryan ordered the food to go, and within twenty minutes they both stepped from the café as the owner locked up.

"Mind if I drive you to your place and eat there?" Ryan asked.

"Sure, that would be great," replied Larry.

Ryan said little about the new job as they made their way to Larry's. He seemed to be more interested in catching up on his friend's progress at school. Larry reminded him that he had finished enough courses to obtain an associate degree in accounting, and he was currently working on a bachelor's degree in finance. As he talked, Ryan's mind was churning. At last, they entered the small apartment, and Ryan began to gobble his lukewarm meal.

As he finished his last bite, Larry questioned his friend.

"You're going to be a big wheel now," he stated with a smile, as he punched Ryan smartly on the shoulder. "OK. Tell me about this job."

"Well, it's a great opportunity," Ryan replied, rubbing his shoulder and wincing a bit. "It pays more, it will be within driving distance to Brandon Springs, and I will get to have a big say as to who will be staffed at the place."

He had been reluctant to say anything until this point, but his calculating mind had brought him to the conclusion that he should place all the cards on the table.

"Look, I can't guarantee anything," he began. "But I will need an entry level accountant. Would you be interested in moving down there with me?"

Larry's tired eyes suddenly narrowed, as if to question the validity of what had just been said. He was quiet for a moment, as he scanned the face of the person before him. Being convinced that the offer was sincere, they slowly widened. Signs of exhaustion were no longer present. It was as if someone had splashed his face with cold water and given him a shot of adrenaline. Fully alert, his eyes were ablaze.

"You can hire someone to be an accountant with just a two-year degree?" Larry questioned. "Besides that, I have a grant to finish school, and I don't want to screw that up. Don't get me wrong, I would take an accounting job over dish washing in a heartbeat! I just don't want to drop out of school."

"Larry, I said I can't guarantee anything," Ryan continued. "I am in the process of writing up the qualifications for each position, and I plan to set that entry level accounting position as requiring at least an associate degree."

Actually, he had not even considered offering him a job

until Larry mentioned his acquiring the associate degree in accounting. Upon hearing it, his mind went to work evaluating the prospects of the regional manager buying into the idea. This wouldn't be the first-time job qualifications had been written with a particular person in mind. By the time they had arrived at the apartment, he felt his notion stood a reasonable chance.

"I don't have the final say, I only have input into the qualifications and the pay grade for each position," Ryan explained. "I have two other accounting positions that would require more experience and a four-year degree, but the entry position might not require a bachelor's degree. You would be reporting to a Lead Accountant if it happened."

"I would love it, but I really need to finish school," Larry said, as he looked down at the floor.

"Our company has a tuition reimbursement program that you might qualify for," Ryan stated. "You would have to pay for the course work up front, and the company reimburses the employee for 75% of the cost for all courses that result in a grade of B or above. It wouldn't cover all of the tuition and the books, like your grant; but you would be making more money than you are now. It would give you experience and a foot in the door. I'm just not positive that I will be able to make you the offer. I need to know if you are interested before I pursue that avenue."

"Absolutely!" Larry snapped.

Over the next three weeks Ryan stayed in contact with Larry and refined the qualifications for each position. He also helped his friend write a resume and had a pretend interview with him to give Larry interviewing tips. Ryan was surprised and delighted to find that the regional manager was pleased with both the qualifications and the pay ranges he proposed. He immediately told Larry of her approval, but warned him that the boss would make the final decision regarding who was hired. The weeks passed, and Ryan moved to an extended stay apartment in Charlotte. He used the pretend interview with Larry as practice for the others. Ryan had been instructed to organize in folders his top two prospects for each position, and to include a one-page summary of his findings and recommendations. He would submit these to the regional manager, and she would select the personnel based on that information and her own perspective.

Within a week, the interviews were completed by Ryan and his summaries were submitted to the regional manager. During his third week in Charlotte, she came to his office with her selections. With each offer to be made, she recommended initial salary offers and a maximum to be offered if there were negotiations. She made it clear he was to secure the personnel for the upper positions first, then fill the lower and entry level ones. If further negotiations were needed, any increase in those top salaries would have to be subtracted from the maximum salary ranges of the lower positions. She began Ryan's managerial training when she allowed him to help establish the qualifications and salary ranges. Now, she would establish his leadership in allowing him to make the offers and negotiations. With those instructions, she left the package of selections in his care.

After he carefully scanned the selections, he sat stunned. All his recommendations had been accepted except for two. One of those rejected was Larry. There was no mistake, as she had thoroughly documented the rationale behind each selection. It was clear that she preferred giving the entry position to Wesley Parks because he had attained a four-year degree in accounting. His grades were good, and Ryan remembered thinking to himself how likeable he was. If not for this friend Larry, he would have made an offer to him. With her decisions, there was now no room for Larry. The accounting group had to begin small, as it would consist of a Lead Accountant and an experienced Accountant with a solid background, and an entry level Accountant. Although Ryan would do all annual evaluations, the Lead Accountant would conduct the daily supervision of the small group. As he reviewed the documents before him, it was easy to see how she had come to her conclusion. Wesley had two years' experience, a four-year degree, an excellent GPA in school, was well spoken, and a likeable young man. He had even been a co-op while in college, making his experience even greater. Ryan felt sick.

The next day he mailed out the offers to each of the upper salaried candidates. He had not yet informed Larry, because he held on to a hope that Wesley would not accept the salary. If he asked for much more, Ryan would feel justified in asking the regional manager to reconsider Larry for the spot. It wasn't to be. The upper-level positions were secured with only the Lead Accountant requiring a negotiated salary. Three days after the second mailing, a smiling Wesley Parks strode in with his signed acceptance. Everyone was to report to work on the following Monday morning.

Ryan couldn't tell Larry with a simple phone call. That Friday afternoon, he caught a flight to Boston and rented a car. With singleness of mind, he went directly to Larry's apartment. He didn't even bother to find a motel or eat supper, before going. Ryan parked the car across the street from his friend's apartment, and silently waited for Larry to show up. Within the hour, he spotted his tall lean frame swiftly moving up the sidewalk. Larry had a distinctive gait in his walk; even his smooth stride quietly spoke of his athleticism. He watched him enter and close the door. Ryan sat for another ten minutes before he left his car for the familiar residence of his friend. Knocking on the thickly painted door, he listened to footsteps as they approached from the other side. At last, the door swung open, and an eager set of eyes met his. Within a couple of silent seconds those same eyes changed to reflect the question that was about to be asked.

"I didn't get the job, did I?" Larry asked as he motioned

with his hand for his friend to come in.

"You were right!" exclaimed Ryan. "There was another fellow that had a four-year degree and experience. I recommended you, but she couldn't pass this guy up."

"It's OK," Larry replied, as he attempted to make light of the situation. "It was a long shot, and it would have complicated the schooling thing."

"I feel sick, I am so sorry…" Ryan mumbled.

Larry asked his friend if he had a motel room for the night, and Ryan confirmed that he did not. Realizing that this visit might be the last for a while, Larry offered him a spot on the couch. Ryan accepted the offer and brought his bag inside. Both men sensed this change could possibly mean the end of a strong friendship. For three hours, the two talked about shared experiences and plans of accomplishments not yet attained. Neither voiced regret, but it was an inescapable fact that things would no longer be the same. Ryan would be very busy establishing the branch office, and most of his free weekends would be consumed with care for the place in Brandon Springs. Larry would continue to have his hands full with school and the mundane job. Being mindful of a test that he would face the next day, Larry reminded his friend of his need for sleep. Ryan apologized for keeping him awake, and Larry slowly headed off for bed. Ryan entertained a sickening and hollow feeling as he sat alone on the couch.

Sleep didn't come to either for several more hours. Ryan lay awake, thinking of possible future job openings. He realized that the chances were remote, and that it would be more than a year before additional positions could even be considered. Although his best friend was in the next room, Larry never felt more alone in his life.

LIFE IN CHARLOTTE proved to be lonely for Ryan. He attended a church there every other Sunday, and he spent the other weekends in Brandon Springs. Without Larry, his life was just not as interesting. It wasn't long before he decided to send his friend airline tickets once a month, which allowed Larry to come to Charlotte for visits. As soon as Ryan picked him up from the airport, they always headed directly for Brandon Springs.

Ryan contacted Patsy, and she invited him for a visit the next time he made it to Brandon Springs. She understood that the visit would include Larry, because Ryan informed her of his making the airline tickets available. Upon hearing of the invitation, Larry was a little apprehensive. However, it wasn't long before he could think of little else than the anticipated visit.

On the next trip made to Brandon Springs, Ryan and Larry attended a service at Patsy's church in the nearby town. During the church service, Larry's sole interest was Patsy. Attempting to divert his attention, he would glance at the preacher from time to time. It didn't help, for he was totally absorbed by thoughts of her. He didn't realize that the same battle was going on within Patsy. Even though her eyes were fixed on the minister, her mind was consumed by thoughts of the man seated next to her. After church, the three went to a local restaurant for lunch. Ryan had not enjoyed this type of gathering since the days of visiting with Patsy and John. It was as if a load was taken off his soul, and he was enjoying every minute of it. Patsy and Larry connected like never before, and they exchanged cell phone numbers before the two men left for Boston.

AS THE YEAR PROGRESSED, Larry adjusted to the demanding hours of work and school. Over time, unexpected changes worked to his advantage. He found the upper-level courses required less effort, so he added an additional class. His years at the public library, and the financial textbooks provided early on by Ryan, had prepared him well for the concentration on subjects dealing directly with finance. Several developments occurred that year. Not long after Ryan's move to Charlotte, Larry was given a tip by a staff member at the community college regarding an entry level position in the accounting department of a Boston firm. With the references of several of his class instructors, he was given the job. During that year the cell phone calls between Larry and Patsy became more frequent.

The visits to Patsy's church became a regular event whenever Ryan and Larry spent a weekend in Brandon Springs. Ryan rarely attended Sally's former church when he was in the area, for it was obvious that Larry had no interest in missing opportunities to be with Patsy.

Although he regularly attended a large church in Charlotte, he missed the tight knit fellowship of Sally's small church. Near the end of the year, Ryan began to visit several smaller churches in the Charlotte area. On one occasion he visited Bent River Church, which was on the outskirts of the city. Before the suburbs spread in its direction, it had been a very small country church made up of locals. An influx of middle-income professional people had begun to mix with the original congregation. His visit happened to be on a Sunday for which a covered dish lunch was held in the Fellowship Hall after the service. The church members quickly and graciously acknowledged him as a visitor. They implored him to stay for the meal, and eventually he was carried along with the flow of the crowd to the large room. After a moment of thanksgiving prayer by the pastor, the people began their selection of foods. The potluck items were arranged in buffet style.

Once his plate was loaded, and with drink in hand, Ryan found an available table. The tables were set in rows; with their ends butted against one another. As the chattering members of the congregation made their way from the serving line, the tables quickly filled. Directly seated across from him was a young woman of twenty-six, Grace Miles.

She was a perfect reflection of the congregation. Grace had grown up in a farming family and had attended the church from birth. After college, she accepted a job with a Charlotte architecture firm. As an entry level architect, she was usually given smaller commercial assignments. Still, she lived in the same community as her parents and attended the same church. Grace was quick to introduce herself and her parents, who were seated to the left of her. She seemed to be entirely comfortable with her environment, and in her conversations with Ryan.

She seemed somewhat captivated by the man seated across from her, as Ryan told her of his inherited home and property in Brandon Springs. Only the discussions regarding his managerial position in Charlotte caused her parents to join the conversation. Until that point, they half-heartedly listened to a few old friends seated at the table. As they overheard aspects about his job, their focus quickly shifted to the man sitting across from their daughter.

After that day, Ryan attended the smaller church when he stayed in Charlotte for the weekends. Although they didn't officially go out on a date, Ryan and Grace would meet for lunch from time to time. Over the next two months, they regularly sat together during church services.

On Ryan's next visit to Boston to see Larry, he discussed with him the budding relationship with Grace. As the conversation progressed, Larry seemed to become more bothered. Ryan felt concerned with the look on his best friend's face.

"Okay, what's your problem with Grace?" Ryan asked, with a sigh.

For a few seconds Larry remained silent, staring motionless at the floor. Lifting his eyes, they expressed a more serious concern. At last, he replied, "It's not you or Grace. It's me. My relationship with Patsy is beginning to be serious, and I need to talk with her about something."

"That's no secret," Ryan responded. "I've never seen a

couple so drawn to each other."

"I haven't been entirely honest with her, or even with you," Larry began. "Neither of you ever asked, so I never mentioned the fact that I've been married before."

Ryan was completely taken off guard. Before he had time to verbally respond, Larry continued.

"The job situation was only one of the reasons I left Alabama. I walked in on my wife and another man. She tried to talk with me, but I had to get out of there. I was so angry. I was afraid of what I might do. In a blind rage, I drove to a deserted beach on the Gulf and slept in my car that night. The next day I had a lawyer draw up papers for the divorce. I stayed with a friend until the divorce was final. I spent most of my time after work in the library in Mobile. The books helped take my mind off my screwed-up marriage, and I usually stayed there until it closed. My living in Mobile seemed to work out, until I ran into her at a grocery store one evening. I was so shaken up. Over the next few days, I found it almost impossible for me to concentrate on the work at the docks. On the docks, a lack of concentration can be dangerous for everyone around you. It's not like sitting at a desk job; someone can get hurt if you're not careful. The next week, I withdrew everything I had in my savings, and I moved to Boston."

Ryan silently listened. As the shock wore off, it was replaced with earnest compassion for his friend. He knew the loss of a loved one due to death, and he imagined divorce might be a similar sort of loss. As he listened to his friend, he began to feel some of the torment Larry had been hiding. As he spoke, pain oozed from Larry like blood from a deep and serious wound. It had been four years since his divorce, but it was obvious that inward flames of sorrow were rekindled as he told the story.

"I have to tell Patsy, and I plan to tell her during my next visit with her," Larry said, with a sigh.

Larry felt somewhat relieved to finally tell Ryan, but he

still felt apprehension in sharing the truth with Patsy. As the conversation wore on, Ryan resumed his original discussion of Grace and Bent River Church. Larry was very interested in hearing of any woman in his friend's life, but he had no interest in the church. Ryan realized this lack of personal spirituality early on in the friendship, and he usually avoided the subject of faith with him. However, he also knew that eventually it would not be so easily avoided in the developing serious romantic relationship between Larry and Patsy.

"Besides your confession of a previous marriage and divorce, I hope you realize that you need to be honest with Patsy regarding your lack of interest in God and the church," Ryan abruptly proclaimed. "You know, she has a very devout faith."

"What we have goes beyond religion," retorted Larry. "I would never get in the way of her church life."

"I think her relationship with God is a larger matter than you think," explained Ryan. "The Bible indicates that a Christian shouldn't marry someone who has no faith."

"My faith and my beliefs are my own, and they are personal," Larry snapped back. "I don't have to pass any spiritual evaluation given by you or anyone else."

For the sake of the rare visit to Boston, the subject was dropped. However, both topics of divorce and faith weighed on Ryan's mind even after he returned to Charlotte. For days he attempted to put the matter behind him, but the issue of Larry's lack of faith nagged his mind continually. It was more than that. It was like it had become a heavy weight upon his own soul; so much that he had difficulty resting at night.

Some weeks later, Ryan placed a call to Patsy. The call began as one of those 'you've been on my mind' conversations. In one sense, he dreaded bringing up the subject of his friend's spiritual vacuum. A part of him wanted to continue the light-weighted chatter. However, like someone sick to one's stomach, it became apparent to him that something must come out in order to begin to feel better. The subject rose from the depth of his heart and made its way through his lips.

"Patsy, do you and Larry discuss God and the church?" he questioned.

It wasn't exactly how he meant to pose the question, but that's how it came out. The conversation had suddenly taken a serious turn.

She paused, and then replied, "Well, Larry doesn't talk about it much, but I believe he has a good heart. He doesn't like to talk to people about it."

There was no immediate response from Ryan, only the gentle and almost silent hum of the call. He immediately felt regret for having addressed the topic. A darkening cloud settled over the remainder of the conversation. With each word spoken by Patsy, he sensed genuine concern. She was in love. The last thing Ryan wanted to do was to hurt her or cause her worry; and it was evident that he had done so.

She shifted the subject of conversation.

"How is Grace?" she asked. "Have you two actually gone out on a date yet?"

Ryan told her that eating hamburgers during lunch every couple of weeks was the closest thing to going on a date. Though the words of the conversation had lightened, the heaviness of Ryan's question still hung throughout the remainder of the call.

Chapter 7

THE LIGHT KNOCKING AT THE DOOR seemed oddly familiar. As he laid his book aside, Ryan peered through the window. Only then did he realize the beauty of that fall morning in Brandon Springs. Opening the door, he saw a face he had somewhat avoided for months.

"Layla," he said, in almost a whisper.

"Could I talk with you for a few minutes?" she nervously asked.

"Sure, please come in," Ryan replied, as he motioned for her to come inside.

His last encounter with Layla had been the day when she greeted him with tears, hugs, and a misunderstanding about who had given her ten thousand dollars in cash. Her apparent emotional volatility, and the complications regarding a large sum of cash being left in her car, had left him uncomfortable. It caused him to avoid her to the point of staying away from the cafe. However, now there seemed to be something very different about her. It wasn't just the fact that she wasn't wearing her waitress uniform, or even the fact that her hair wasn't pulled back in a ponytail. Though it was obvious she was nervous about something, there was an unmistakable enthusiastic gleam in her eyes. The underlying subtle essence of deep sadness, he noticed from the first day he met her, had been replaced by something else.

"I realize that you're not the person who gave me that money," she began. "But I have a feeling that you might know who did."

Before he could interrupt, she continued.

"You don't have to tell me. I just want you to know how much that gift changed my life. That was the first of several blessings. If you know who sent it, please thank them for me. Let them know what it has done for me and let them know how I am doing."

"How are you doing?" Ryan inquired.

"Things have been good, really good," she stated. "Oh, I have already sent a letter of thanks to *Moore, Venicci & Connors*. You don't have to thank them."

Stunned, Ryan explained to her that he knew nothing of *Moore, Venicci & Connors*, or of the source of the money. Layla then went on to elaborate on her good fortunes. She had used a small portion of the money to repair her old car, and she also purchased a couple of pieces of furniture. She placed the rest in an account, and periodically she used the interest gained to supplement her efforts to buy clothes and food for herself, her mother, and her child. She intended to use the majority of the money for "real emergencies," or to do something special for her daughter at a later date. The gift was a huge shot in the arm for her. Though it didn't really change her style of living, it provided a measure of comfort as an emergency fund. It also changed her perception of herself. No longer was she moderately poor, for she had almost eight thousand dollars in a savings account.

Ryan was truly amazed at her self-discipline in handling the funds. He told her that he was really impressed with the wisdom she showed. However, he was very curious to know what *Moore, Venicci & Connors* had to do with her situation.

"You have more cash on hand than most people living

in fine homes and driving expensive cars," Ryan told her. "I honestly know nothing about *Moore, Venicci & Conners*, but I'm glad things are working out for you."

"I thought maybe you knew that the law firm gave me a grant to go to nursing school," she explained in a somewhat surprised manner.

"No!" he exclaimed. "I don't know who gave you the money, and I had never heard of this law firm until now. They gave you a grant for school?"

Layla explained that shortly after getting the money, she received a letter in the mail from the Charlotte law firm. The letter explained that the firm awards a college scholarship yearly to someone they felt deserving, and that she had been selected as a recipient. If she decided to accept the scholarship, she was to respond using the provided self-addressed envelope. In the response, she was to declare a major, send three choices of colleges or universities, and provide the addresses for each. She waited several days before calling because she thought they had confused her with someone else. Layla felt it only fair to inform them of the mistake. Her contact at the law firm assured her that no mistake had been made, and that the scholarships were not reserved only for law students. She was encouraged to make her declaration of major, and to send her selections of schools.

After the call, Layla silently stared at the return envelope. She then dropped to her knees in front of the newly purchased couch. With her face buried in the cushion, she wept and thanked God for miracles and for his Grace. Her eyes still blurred by tears; she wrote a letter of appreciation to the law firm. On the acceptance form, she stated that her major would be nursing, and she listed only the name and address of the nearby community college. She knew it offered a nursing curriculum, and it was the only school within a reasonable driving distance from Brandon Springs. Two weeks later, she received a letter of acceptance from the school notifying her of the date for registration. The letter went on to explain that the tuition had been handled, and that she was to obtain a voucher for textbooks from the business office.

Layla told Ryan that she had earned all A's and B's for the classes taken during the first two quarters, but that she was having a more difficult time with some of the current course work. She explained that she attended school at night, and that she still worked at the café during the day.

"I can't tell you how proud I am of you, and of what you are doing," Ryan emphatically told her. "I can't explain the gift or the grant, but I can't think of anyone more deserving. Because you have done so well in school, the law firm must know that the scholarship was given to the right person. Whoever gave you the cash, selected the right person. This was made apparent by how wisely you have dealt with it. I can't believe you only spent two thousand of it on car repairs and furniture. I'm genuinely impressed!"

"Well, that's not entirely true," she responded. "I spent a little less than two hundred and fifty dollars on the car repairs, and about seven hundred on the new couch and chair. You'll probably think I'm stupid, if I tell you what I did with the other thousand."

"It's your money, to spend how you wish," Ryan replied.

"Okay. I believe in tithing to God," she stated firmly.

She waited for a judgmental response from Ryan before continuing. He stood, shaking his head. A smile grew on his face. She had become accustomed to people's perspective of her being an uneducated and common person, and she began a defense of her decision.

"The way I look at it, everything belongs to God," she said. "I could only keep nine thousand of it. I placed the other thousand in the church collection plate. I mean, I did it in cash over time; bit by bit, so it wouldn't be noticed. I probably shouldn't have told you, and I don't know why I did."

Ryan's smile broadened fully, as he replied.

"You are a surprisingly marvelous woman!"

With a great sense of relief, she returned the smile. At that moment, something changed in Ryan's perspective of this small young woman. It was in that smile, that he sensed a personal attraction for her. Months before, in the café, her eyes were so sad and tired. Now, they were alive and energetic. The two talked a little while longer before Layla revealed to him a recent cause for concern. During the previous month, she spotted a white Lincoln parked in front of her trailer. Through her trailer window, for several minutes she studied the face of the large elderly man seated at the steering wheel. Layla had never seen him before. She thought maybe he was lost, or possibly ill. Layla exited the trailer and approached the car, and immediately the vehicle quickly sped away. Though baffled, she was not yet worried. She thought to herself that the man probably had the wrong address and was too embarrassed to admit it to anyone. However, another incident gave her cause for concern. Two nights prior to her visit with Ryan, she believed she saw the same car parked outside one of her class buildings at the college. Because it was evening, it was too dark for her to be sure that this was the same driver. However, as she approached the vehicle, it again sped away. Since then, she cautiously found herself looking for it. She had become a little frightened.

Ryan told her not to hesitate to call him if the car appeared again. Giving her his cell phone number, he apologized for avoiding her and the café. Before she left, he also volunteered to help her study whenever he came to Brandon Springs for weekends.

After the visit, he attempted to continue reading the book he'd earlier begun. However, he found he couldn't focus on the pages. The visit by her offered too much new and interesting information, and he was captivated by the strange appearances of this stranger in Layla's life. Ryan thought about the fact that she assumed he might know who gave her the money. Though he knew nothing of the matter, he considered the possibility that he might have unknowingly had something to do with her good fortune. He searched his memory for instances in which he may have talked about her to others. He could only remember sharing her need with the Sunday School Class at a church he visited in Boston. He tried to visually picture the faces of each person in the class, but only a couple of individuals stood out in his memory. Ryan could think of no other connection. He was certain there were members of the church who were of moderate means, but he doubted whether any were wealthy enough to provide a stranger with ten thousand dollars. Boston is a long distance from Brandon Springs, so he considered the likelihood of the connection to be remote. Still, he wanted to make an attempt to settle the matter.

ON HIS NEXT VISIT to see Larry in Boston, he visited the church and Sunday school class again. When prayer requests were given, Ryan told the class of the miraculous answers to the prayers given on Layla's behalf. As he told of the money and scholarship, he watched the faces of each class member. He hoped to ascertain clues as to who might have taken a personal interest in her. Though most seemed pleased to hear the story, none offered any such evidence. He scanned the eyes of each, except those of the elderly man who was busily writing down aspects of this story and of current prayer requests in the class prayer log. Bill Thompson was a retired accountant, who performed volunteer work for the church. One such duty of his was to be the Sunday school class scribe, which involved taking notes of all prayer requests issued during the hour. Throughout the class, his head was either bowed in the effort to capture notes or bowed in prayer.

After the class was over, Bill approached Ryan and asked, "That was such an interesting story. Is Layla doing well in school?"

Ryan found it interesting that the older man remembered her name. He didn't remember giving out Layla's name during the class time, but he couldn't be sure. It was possible that he had mentioned it during his previous visit to the church; and it was possible that this retired accountant was detailed enough in his precise notes to have gathered the name from prayer request notes taken on that previous occasion.

"Her grades are good, and her outlook on life is filled with encouragement," Ryan said.

"It sounds like whoever made the gift made a wise choice," replied Bill Thompson.

MONTHS PASSED, and during the summer Ryan and Larry returned to Brandon Springs to help Pete dig the pond. They watched, more than helped. Pete had both the knowledge and equipment to do the job. He just didn't feel right about digging on another man's property without the man being present. Since Ryan could do little to contribute to the effort, he and Larry would just periodically check on Pete's progress.

On one trip to Brandon Springs, Ryan talked Larry into hiking up the mountain and camping at the top. Ryan had enjoyed a memorable spiritual experience while camping alone on the mountain, and he secretly hoped something similar would happen for Larry. The next morning offered a spectacular sunrise. Larry commented on the natural beauty of the sky sand of the property, but that was all there was to it. He made no reference to God, and Ryan began to realize that each person's spiritual experiences are specific to that person.

You can't relive a personal experience of the soul, and

no one else can live it either.

The hike up the mountain was uneventful, but enjoyable. Larry seemed to be completely in his element while in the forest, and Ryan was equally impressed with his friend's outdoor skills. Upon reaching the top, Larry started a campfire using a piece of flint and steel. When he had camped alone, Ryan had eaten trail mix and peanuts while hiking and camping. Larry cooked meals over coals from the fire. Ryan had done some outdoor cooking while a Boy Scout, but he was never very proficient at it. Larry was never a Scout, but his father had taught him outdoor skills while on hunting trips. With each man carrying a backpack, they were able to bring a few cooking supplies and cookware.

Most of the slope on the far side of the mountain was not owned by Ryan, but he wanted to hike it with his friend. After breakfast, Larry covered the hot coals with dirt, and they started down the backside of the mountain. Because it was not as steep as the front side, the hike was much easier. They were shielded from the summer sun by thick foliage in the tree tops above them. As they neared the bottom, Larry let out a yell as he stepped squarely in a hole. The hole was so deep that most of the lower half of his leg disappeared beneath the soil. The leg of his pants was shoved all the way up to his knee, and the downward drop of his foot stopped as his boot slammed onto the back of a copperhead snake at the bottom of the hole. During Larry's slight hesitation to pull his leg out, the angered snake buried its fangs in his calf muscle. The pain made it obvious to Larry that something had bitten or stung him; and he hoped it was from a scorpion or the type of bee that makes its home in the ground. However, when he pulled his leg from the hole, the twisting snake was dangling from it. Filled with fear and adrenaline, Larry promptly pulled the snake off and threw it onto the ground. Before it could slither away to safety, he crushed its head with a large rock. He smashed it repeatedly; even as the lifeless body of the snake wiggled in a synaptic after-death jerky dance. Though the snake's head was totally crushed, he continued to pound it with the rock until he was stopped by Ryan. His eyes were wild with fear, for Larry knew the snake had successfully pumped venom into his now swelling leg. Remembering lessons from his Scouting days, Ryan warned Larry of the importance of calming himself in order to slow the progress of the poison. It was extremely important for his friend to slow the rate of his now speeding heart. Larry dropped to the ground and attempted to calm himself.

After a moment, Ryan realized that his ailing friend needed medical attention soon. Convinced that Larry had now calmed himself, Ryan helped him to his feet and insisted that he carry Larry as they sought help. Even if Ryan ran alone for help, valuable time would be wasted in the effort to bring that help to his friend. With Larry now standing, Ryan squatted down to allow the taller man to drape himself over his back. Larry was lean, but his tall muscular frame caused him to be unexpectedly heavy. Bent under the weight, Ryan made his way down the hill side. He was struggling, as he broke into the clearing at the base of the mountain. Yet, he never slowed. The majority of the time Ryan carefully examined the ground below him, to avoid stumbling with his patient. Glancing up, he caught sight of the small white wooden church. His legs and back were almost locked in pain, and he fought exhaustion as he hurried in the direction of the little building.

Reaching the front door, Ryan found it to be locked. He could hold Larry no longer, and he gently lowered him to the steps of the church. Already, the venom was seriously doing its work. Larry was weak, and his leg was grossly swollen tight against his pants leg. His vision began to blur, and his mouth and tongue were even becoming slightly numb. Ryan desperately screamed for help and beat his fists against the church door.

"I feel like I'm going to puke," Larry said, as nausea

was beginning to set in.

Suddenly, they heard creaking of the old church door hinges. With a last squeak the door opened wide. Standing in the doorway was Alvin Jacobs, a retired church member who did janitorial duties for the church. Gazing down at the man on the steps, he asked Ryan if he could be of help. With a full string of expletives, Larry barked out his need for medical attention. Alvin explained that there was no phone in the Old Ways Church of God, and that he had no cell phone. As Larry continued his barrage of curses, the old man tossed Ryan the keys to his truck.

"Son, take my truck to that parsonage just down the road on the right," Alvin explained. "The pastor has a phone there. Tell the emergency folks to meet us at the corner of Whispery Winds Road and County 115. Then come straight back here for your friend."

Without question, Ryan headed directly for the truck. It started immediately. The old engine purred like a kitten. He could not help admiring how well the old vehicle had been maintained, as he sped down the road in the direction of the parsonage.

Larry still mumbled expletives, as he watched the elderly man bring a large pocketknife from his pocket. When Alvin snapped open the blade with his thumb, Larry became silent. With astounding speed and agility, the man used the razor-sharp blade to rip open the material of Larry's pants leg. His leg was so swollen that the cloth had become tight against the skin. Placing the knife back into his pocket, Alvin asked Larry for his name. Immediately after the answer was given, the old man turned and bolted back into the church. Bewildered by the man's actions, and dazed by the venom, Larry saw himself dying alone on the steps of the old church. He considered this to be fitting, for he considered the church to be nothing more than a group of misguided people, led by clever salesmen of sorts. To him, the church was no more than a taker of hard-earned money from members who could have better used the funds in support of their own families. It was clear to him that the church had never done any good for him or his family.

Just as Larry resolved himself to this pitiful and lonely death, the old man emerged from the church. Opening a small bottle of clear oil, he poured a few drops into his left hand. Before Larry could utter another vile word, Alvin placed the oily hand squarely on the forehead of the ailing man on church steps. Immediately following, he lifted right hand upward to the sky and began calling out to God. Peering out from under the oily hand, Larry saw a younger man step into view from behind Alvin. Just as Larry was about to let out a few more curses, he felt a warming sensation move from his forehead down through his body. This was followed by a tingling that moved from his toes to the top of his head. At that moment Larry accepted the fact that he was dying. He let his soul slide into a peaceful rest. He no longer seemed to care. The anger, fear, and frustration were gone. Those feelings were strangely replaced with a peace he had never experienced.

"Dying isn't so bad," Larry thought. *"I don't know why people are so afraid to die. I don't know why I've been so afraid of it. It's alright. Everything is alright."*

Ryan returned with the truck and quickly explained that he had established the meeting place with the emergency personnel. The two carried Larry, and gently placed him in the bed of the truck. As Alvin climbed into the driver's seat, Larry looked back toward the church. There standing on the church steps was the younger man he had seen earlier. He was puzzled as to why a man of his age would not offer to help.

"Why didn't this guy take the place of the elderly man, when I was being carried to the truck?" Larry thought. *"Why would a stronger and younger fellow leave the job to the ailing back of a much older man? Maybe the guy is retarded, or something."*

Larry's view was blocked as Ryan climbed into the truck. Once he was positioned beside his friend, Ryan placed Larry's head on his knee. His Scout training stressed the need to keep the victim's head elevated above his heart and above the bitten area. He then slapped the roof of the truck cab to indicate that they were ready to go. With that, Alvin sped away with the two friends. Alvin was careful not to hit potholes or rough areas in the old country road. For the most part, the ride was smooth, as Alvin kept his old truck in excellent condition. The cool air blowing across Larry's face was a welcome relief to the growing heat of the day. In fact, within minutes he was feeling better. After a short distance, he expressed to Ryan a desire to sit up on his own. Though cautious, Ryan agreed. Soon Larry's head began to clear, and the two were having a normal conversation about the events of the day.

When they arrived at the designated intersection for meeting, they found the ambulance already waiting. Immediately, the emergency personnel jumped into the bed of the truck and began to examine Larry. To Ryan's surprise, the swelling in the leg had completely gone. They asked Ryan and Larry a battery of questions regarding the appearance of the snake. They then asked Larry more questions about his symptoms and family medical history. It was obvious that the bite had been that of a venomous snake, for the fang marks were still visible. The emergency workers concluded that it was possible that only a minuscule amount of poison had actually been injected into his system. Almost in unison, Ryan and Larry objected. Larry more thoroughly explained his earlier symptoms. After hearing the additional information, the medical personnel agreed that that it sounded like Larry had suffered many of the classic symptoms of hemotoxic snake venom. However, they had little explanation as to why he recovered so quickly. They eventually chalked it up to Larry possibly being one of those rare individuals who have some degree of immunity to the venom.   This was the only logical explanation for his remarkable capacity to overcome the symptoms so quickly. Larry appeared to be in reasonably good shape, and after placing a call to the hospital they decided to release him from their care. However, they emphasized that he should continue to rest and drink plenty of liquids. They instructed Ryan to watch him closely over the next twenty-four hours, and to have medical attention should the bite area become inflamed or change in appearance.

Thinking it unwise for Larry to immediately hike back up the mountain, Ryan convinced Alvin to drive them both to the house in Brandon Springs. After a good night's sleep, Ryan made his way up to retrieve the gear on the following morning. As they drove back to Charlotte that evening, Larry sat in silence, and Ryan thought it was due to his friend's physically and emotionally exhausting weekend. He was partially right, but it was mainly because Larry was deep in thought. He replayed the events of the day over and over in his mind. Finally, Larry spoke.

"Ryan, who was the younger guy at the church?"

"I'm not sure I would call a man in his seventies or eighties a younger guy," Ryan replied.

"No, not the old man," Larry retorted. "I'm talking about the other guy. He was still standing on the church steps as we drove off in the truck."

Ryan attempted to comfort his friend.

"Hey, you were in pretty bad shape for a while. There's no telling what you thought you saw. I was honestly afraid you were going to die, and I have no clue as to why you recovered so fast. That was one of the most amazing things I've ever seen. You've got to have some remarkable genes. Does that kind of thing run in your family? I mean, do you have an uncle who wears a big red cape and runs around in blue tights? Perhaps you've hidden the fact that you are really a superhero. Maybe you're the Incredible Hulk. If you feel a little green tint in your skin coming on, you would warn me, wouldn't you?"

Though he smiled at the thought, Larry's eyes spoke of total seriousness.

"I think I know what happened," Larry softly answered,

Ryan said nothing, allowing his friend the opportunity to finish without interruption.

"That old man prayed for me, and something happened," Larry continued. "He did some pretty odd things, and for a while I thought he was a total nut ball. But something happened. He put some kind of oil on his hand, and then he put his oily hand on my forehead. I haven't a clue about the oil, but I really felt something when he prayed. That was about the same time the younger guy showed up. He stood behind him, staring at me. It wasn't a weird stare, he just looked at me. He didn't say or do anything. I was surprised he didn't help when you and the old man carried me to the truck."

Larry could tell that Ryan was a little unsure as to how he should respond. It was like a role reversal. Normally, it would be Larry not believing Ryan's words about prayer. Larry considered the fact that maybe the old man had some kind of gift.

"Maybe the fellow had some kind of energy that flowed out to other people," Larry said. "Maybe it really did have something to do with God, or maybe it was just a freak coincidence."

Whatever it was, Larry was positive that he had experienced something special. Ryan said nothing in reply.

"Hey, you saw the snake," Larry stated. "You saw my leg swell up. You saw how sick I was getting, and you saw me get better in a hurry. What do you think happened? Do you really think that I am just a freak of nature, able to toss off snake venom after showing such a strong reaction to it? I'm not buying it. I'm telling you that it had something to do with that old man."

"I don't understand what happened," Ryan replied. "I

saw the snake, the swelling, and I saw you recover remarkably fast. The EMT guys said that you could be a rare case, but I just don't know. It was a little weird. I wasn't around to see what the old man did with the prayers and the oil. I just don't know."

"I thought you believed in God, and prayer, and all that stuff in the Bible," Larry replied.

"I do," Ryan quietly responded. "I just don't understand all there is to know about it."

The two drove in silence until they reached the outskirts of Charlotte. At last, Ryan spoke up.

"I never saw a younger man at the church."

Larry didn't respond to the statement, but he had been bothered since the first time he heard Ryan discount the existence of the person. Instead, he chose to change the subject.

"My flight is not for three more hours. Do you want to catch a bite to eat before dropping me off at the airport?"

AFTER RETURNING TO BOSTON, Larry frequented the library when he was not working, attending class, or studying for class. In fact, he slightly neglected both his studies and sleep in favor of researching cases of miraculous healings. Though his study of the subject included healings based on both secular and religious situations, his concentration remained with those involving the Christian faith. He believed his experience was a direct result of Christian prayer. On weekends, he sought out inner city Christian churches promoting spiritual healing. In most, he found uneducated members of a congregation whipping themselves up into emotional states. He failed to find a certified case of having someone in attendance visibly showing a proved healing. Week after week, he researched and attended various forms of worship in the Boston area. Though he found no confirmed healing, he wasn't discouraged.

Within a short period of time Larry gained respect from the individuals with whom he worked, and the company made it clear they planned to reward him with a raise upon graduation. He was now able to pay for some of the flights to Charlotte. When he was only six classes away from obtaining his bachelor's degree in finance, he paid Ryan another visit. Shortly after his arrival in Charlotte, he shocked Ryan with a request to attend a service with him at the small church on the outskirts of the city.

Ryan, Larry, and Grace Miles sat together during the service. At times, when the pastor brought out points for consideration, Ryan would glance over at Larry to see if he showed any reaction. None was given. Larry sat with his eyes intently fixed on the minister. When the service ended, members of the congregation swarmed around the new visitor with greetings and invitations for return visits. In all his visits to churches in the Boston area, Larry had never encountered such a welcome. He seemed appreciative of the gracious congregation. Larry discussed the minister's message with a few. Though Ryan welcomed Larry's interest in the church, he thought it best not to press his friend regarding his personal state of faith.

ON LARRY'S FOLLOWING VISIT to Brandon Springs, he asked Ryan to take him to a service at the Old Ways Church of God. This didn't come as a shock to Ryan, as he had suspected his friend might want to visit Alvin Jacobs again. In fact, he was a little surprised the request had not come sooner.

Sunday morning, Ryan and Larry parked in front of the little Appalachian church building. They quietly sat in the car for a moment, visually taking in the remote setting. The quaint scene of people at the church door giving informal greetings to one another appeared to be out of a Norman

Rockwell painting. As the two ascended the steps of the church, Ryan was stopped by a somewhat familiar voice coming from behind them.

"Ryan!" Layla called out to him. She quickly caught up with the two.

"I didn't know you attended this church," Ryan replied. "This is my friend from Boston, Larry Chatterson. Larry, this is Layla Quick."

Larry greeted her.

"Ryan told me about you and your good fortunes," Larry said, holding out his large muscular hand. "It's nice to finally meet you."

"You don't sound like someone from Boston," she replied.

Ryan quickly explained that Larry was originally from Alabama.

"I've never been to Alabama," Layla said. "Maybe I'll visit there one day. I insist that you both sit with me."

Layla moved between the two men and took them both by the arm. She winked at a couple of friends as she led them to her favorite pew.

When the singing of hymns began, so did the clapping of hands to the beat of the music. Within a couple of stanzas, tambourines blended in. Ryan watched in astonishment, as the fingers of a small elderly woman effortlessly danced across piano keys. Atop her slight frame, she was adorned by white hair pulled back into a tight bun at the back of her head. A pair of glasses rested on the tip of her nose. As each hymn ended, she softly continued to play improvisations until the next hymn began. At last, the minister rose from his seat and stepped behind the pulpit. The once lively congregation became silent. As he started his oration, the pastor's clear and deep voice proclaimed several verses from the New Testament of the Bible. Laying the Bible aside, the man described several examples of sin and corruption.

Occasionally, an "Amen" could be heard from different

parts of the sanctuary. He spoke of miracles of healing, but he emphasized that the greatest miracle occurs when a life is changed by the hand of God. The pastor told of man's opportunity for salvation, provided by the death and resurrection of Jesus Christ.

"When a soul connects and communes with the Creator of the universe, the blending of man's spirit and the Holy Spirit of God takes place in an unseen realm," the minister spoke. "This is the greatest miracle. The world is filled with miracles that usually go unnoticed by man. Our eyes are often so fixed on the things of this world, that we are blinded to things occurring in the spiritual realm. Most aren't even aware of the spiritual condition of the person seated beside them. We usually look no deeper than what we physically perceive externally of the persons with whom we come in contact. God can cut through the outer shell of a man and reach directly into his soul. I believe there is someone here today, who senses God's touch on his heart."

The minister was correct in his assessment. When the invitation for salvation was made, Ryan was stunned to see Larry stand and make his way to the front of the church. At the altar he lowered his tall frame until his knees made contact with the floor. The minister whispered something in the ear of Larry's bowed head, and Ryan watched his friend's head nod in agreement. The pastor placed one hand on Larry's broad shoulder, and the other hand on his head. Looking upward to God, he prayed for his soul and for God's mercy. The hand that was first placed on Larry's shoulder was then raised up into the air. Within seconds, Larry lifted both of his hands high. The congregation erupted into loud enthusiastic praise to God. Ryan was pleased to see his friend in prayer, but the reaction of the congregation caused him great uneasiness. As the shouting became louder, the tension within Ryan grew. Larry stood, and immediately the pastor gave him a big hug. Afterwards, one by one, various church members followed suit.

After the service, Layla invited the two to her humble trailer for lunch. In route, Larry confided in his friend.

"Ryan, God saved me."

Ryan didn't know what to say. He just quietly nodded in agreement.

"The preacher asked me if I wanted God to save me, and I told him that I did," Larry continued. "I really can't explain how I felt when he put his hand on my head. It was similar to what happened that day of the snake bite. I really believe that God saved me, just like the pastor said. Now we are both Christians. I can't explain it, but I believe God is real and I believe in Jesus; just like you."

Ryan smiled faintly, but he still said nothing. He wasn't sure that Larry was just like him in his faith. He hoped Larry had become a Christian, but he was afraid his friend had experienced an emotional break down.

Ryan attempted to counsel himself.

Maybe whatever happened to Larry was a good thing. He sure seems to be at peace with himself.

Still, he couldn't escape felling genuine concern regarding the emotional and mental state of his friend. Larry's recent behavior was unusual, and Ryan wasn't sure about the cause.

After all, Larry had suffered a poisonous snake bite. He's taken on tremendous loads in his studies and new job. His life has been stressful, to say the least.

Ryan decided he should watch his friend more closely than ever, and spend more time in prayer for him. He was very concerned.

Chapter 8

WANTING TO LEARN MORE about the firm that granted Layla a scholarship, Ryan decided to visit *Moore, Venicci & Conners.* It seemed too much of a coincidence that both he and the firm were located in Charlotte, and he had a gut feeling that he had done something to bring Layla to this firm's attention. Her contact regarding the grant was attorney Charles Moore. Ryan made an appointment with him, and left work early to drop by his office. Upon entering the lobby, he approached the desk of the main administrative assistant. He gave her his name and asked to speak with Mr. Moore. She let him know that the attorney was busy in consultation, but that the meeting would end shortly. Ryan said that he would be glad to wait and took a seat in the lobby. Within minutes, he noticed two elderly men step into the lobby. As one of them turned to face Ryan, he was immediately recognized.

It's Bill Thompson, from the Sunday school class in Boston!

As soon as Bill Thompson noticed Ryan, he turned to the other older man and whispered something to him. As they parted, the administrative assistant announced Ryan's visit,

"Mr. Moore. This man has an appointment, he and wishes to speak with you," she began. "His name is Ryan

Walker."

As Ryan stood, he sensed the intensity of the eyes which were upon him. The glare was similar to Larry's, the night they met. Those eyes were anxious, and alive with caution. Ryan approached the older man.

"Charles Moore," the man simply stated. "Please come with me."

As they entered the office, Ryan noticed the brass plate upon the desk, which read:

Charles Moore – Corporate and Financial Law.

The man motioned for him to take a seat.

"What can I do for you, Mr. Walker?" Mr. Moore began.

"I wanted to personally thank you for your firm's grant to Layla Quick," Ryan plainly stated.

"You could have called or written a letter. Is there anything else?" Moore asked.

The attorney had quickly come to the point, and Ryan thought it best that he do the same.

"Shortly before Layla received the scholarship from your firm, she found a package on the front seat of her car containing a large amount of cash," Ryan explained. "Did you have anything to do with that money?"

"I'm not in the habit of randomly tossing money into cars," Moore responded. "Sounds like your friend must have made an impression on several people."

"I don't want to take up much of your time, but I have one more question," Ryan replied. "How do you know Bill Thompson? Boston is a long way from Charlotte."

"Bill and I are old Army buddies from the Korean War," Moore stated rather firmly. "As for why he was here, I hold each of my client's discussions in strict confidence."

With that answer, Charles Moore rose to indicate that the conversation had ended. As he escorted Ryan from the office, he asked, "Do you live here in Charlotte?"

"Yes sir, I do," answered Ryan.

"I hope you will remember us when you do your financial planning," Moore offered, as he politely showed Ryan the door.

Ryan now knew the connection regarding Layla's grant. He told the Sunday school class in Boston of her need, and Bill Thompson was a member of the class. He was an old Army buddy of Charles Moore, an attorney with the Charlotte firm *Moore, Venicci & Conners.* This happened to be a firm which annually gave a scholarship to a deserving individual. Immediately after leaving the office, Ryan called Layla to tell her everything he found about the connection to the grant.

A couple of weeks later, during a visit to see Larry, Ryan decided to attend the Bostonian church of Bill Thompson. Since the day when he experienced a personal spiritual awakening in Brandon Springs, Larry continued to visit a variety of churches. He found the connection interesting, so he accompanied Ryan to Mr. Thompson's Sunday school class. Ryan gently attempted to press Bill about his relationship with Charles Moore, but he could tell the retired accountant was uncomfortable about discussing his friend.

"I doubt you would understand," began Mr. Thompson. "You've never been to war, have you?"

"No sir, I have not," replied Ryan.

"There is a camaraderie that is difficult to put into words, and I really don't believe that I can adequately explain," he simply stated.

Bill Thompson didn't want to appear rude, but it was obvious to Ryan that he wanted an end to the conversation regarding this subject.

Upon returning to Charlotte, Ryan called Layla to let her know that he had found no additional information from Mr. Thompson. Inwardly, he was pleased to have been part of her blessing. However, he felt there was more to the gift than what he had been told by Charles Moore and Bill

Thompson. Over the next few weeks, he tried to put the matter behind him. However, his interest was rekindled when he read an obituary in the Charlotte Observer. The main article was about the recent death of Charles Moore. He couldn't believe his eyes. Within minutes of reading the article in the paper, he called Layla. Over the phone, he read the entire obituary to her. It discussed his military service during the Korean War and listed surviving relatives. Ryan and Layla agreed to attend the service, which would be conducted on the following Saturday in Charlotte.

He took Thursday and Friday off from work, in order to drive to Brandon Springs to pick up Layla. Her car was in no shape to safely make the trip. On Friday, he and Layla made their way to Charlotte. Although the circumstances were unpleasant, their conversations and time spent together were not. Ryan confided with her about the loss of his parents, and he told her of the many years he had hardened his heart to those around him. Layla shared her thoughts on the subject.

"Maybe you weren't so uncaring," she began. "Maybe you had good reason to avoid family members. Some people pass pain to those around them, like roots of a spreading cancerous growth. It's important that a person not allow the pain in his life to infect the lives of others. Pain can be almost contagious, but so can peace and kindness."

Ryan believed she was right about some people passing pain to others, but he knew that his intentions weren't so noble.

"I avoided people because I was self-absorbed," Ryan stated.

Layla stayed in the spare bedroom of his condo Friday night, and they were early for the service the following day. Ryan learned that Charles Moore had suffered a massive heart attack, which took his life within just a couple of minutes. After the service Ryan spotted Bill Thompson speaking with a large elderly man. As he approached them, he felt the firm grasp of a slender hand take hold of his arm. Glancing back, he caught the frightened eyes of Layla. Not fully understanding the gesture, he tried to explain.

"I just want to say something to Bill Thompson regarding the loss of his old friend. I think it would be good for you to meet the man who was instrumental in your obtaining that scholarship."

With fear growing in her eyes, she whispered a reply.

"That's the man who was parked outside my trailer and my classroom!"

"Because of his health, Bill Thompson has a bit of trouble getting around," Ryan explained. "I doubt that this is the same man you saw in Brandon Springs."

"Is Mr. Thompson the large man or the shorter one?" she asked.

"Oh, he's the shorter one," Ryan replied, as he began to realize who might be the source of her fear. "I don't know who the other guy is."

"I do," she whispered. "He is the driver of the car parked outside my trailer."

As their discussion ended, so did the conversation between the two older men. Glancing in the direction of Ryan and Layla, the larger man quickly made his way to a white Lincoln, parked just a short distance away. Though Ryan was not thoroughly convinced this was the same man Layla had seen, the car seemed to be too much of a coincidence. He began to follow this acquaintance of Bill Thompson. Even from a distance, the stranger seemed a bit intimidating. Ryan was unable to catch him, but he wrote down the Georgia license plate of the car before it pulled away from the cemetery.

Joining Layla again, they both watched as Bill Thompson and his wife attempted to console the grieving widow. Charles' wife was limited in her mobility, and for all but very short distances she used a walker. They slowly helped her into the back seat of their car. As he had done for half a century, Mr. Thompson took the hand of his wife and opened the passenger side front door for her. After she was seated, Bill placed Mrs. Moore's walker in the trunk.

As Ryan drove Layla to Brandon Springs, he could tell she was still shaken at seeing the man she believed to have stalked her. He thought it best to steer the conversation away from the subject of the man seen talking with Bill Thompson, but she repeatedly returned to the subject. Along the way they discussed the unusual Boston-Charlotte connection, which allowed the good fortune of her receiving the grant. He told her that Bill appeared to be a kind man, and that it was doubtful that he would associate with anyone capable of doing her harm.

Once Ryan was alone with his thoughts on the return trip to Charlotte, he began to more seriously consider the stranger at the cemetery. He decided to pursue the matter. Since moving there, he had established an acquaintance of an accountant in the local driver license division in Charlotte. Once he returned, he asked this contact if there was a way to identify the owner of the car from Georgia. Though he personally only had access to the North Carolina database, Ryan's acquaintance told him that he would see what he could find out.

SEVERAL DAYS LATER, Ryan learned that the car was owned by a retired Atlanta policeman, Sam Wells. That night, he called Layla to let her know what he had learned. She knew that some retired officers picked up supplemental income doing private investigative work, and she speculated as to why someone would be looking into her personal life. Although she no longer was concerned about her physical safety, she was still deeply bothered. Layla doubted that encounters with the retired policeman had anything to do with the money. She told Ryan of an occasion on which a Social Worker came to the trailer to evaluate her daughter's living condition. She never had a repeat visit, but the thoughts of some agency possibly looking into her relationship with her daughter caused her concern. The child's father had been from a wealthy family, but he had never shown an interest in his daughter. In fact, he even denied being the father. Layla's imagination began to run, and she envisioned the family having a change of heart.

"Maybe they realized Kaylee's true linage, as some of her father's physical characteristics are becoming evident as the child has grown older," she told Ryan. "Perhaps they want to prove me to be an unfit mother, in order to take my daughter away."

It had been clearly obvious to Layla that the family wanted no relationship with her, but she felt it was possible that they now thought differently about the child. She remembered giving her daughter a swat on the behind in a store one day. Layla became afraid his family had someone watching her, looking for an opportunity. The thought of Social Services taking her daughter, was even more horrifying to her than the fear of a stranger stalking her with malicious intents. Ryan tried to calm her fears.

"If someone reported the swat given to your daughter several months ago, Social Services would have visited you long before now," he calmly stated. "I think it probably has more to do with the scholarship. This retired policeman seems to have a close relationship with Bill Thompson and Charles Moore. I think maybe this guy was hired by the firm to determine whether you deserve a second year on the scholarship. That's the only logical connection with these two old men."

The more he talked, the more she believed him to be right in his assessment. Throughout the call, Ryan never confessed his own concerns about the matter. He was unsure as to why Bill Thompson hid his connection with scholarship grant from public knowledge in Charlotte.

It couldn't have been due to a desire to remain

anonymous, for the firm had sent Layla the letter. The letter made the matter open to the public. Why does Mr. Thompson wish to appear disconnected with the charity?

On Ryan's next visit to Thompson's Sunday school class, he pulled the older man aside after class and presented the subject of Layla receiving the grant. Bill Thompson was silent regarding the matter. He simply turned and walked away, saying nothing.

Why would a retired accountant want to remain in secret? The grant wasn't his money.

DURING THE NEXT VISIT with Larry, Ryan again visited Bill Thompson's church. After the service, he again pulled the older man aside.

"At the funeral, I saw you speaking with a man from Georgia," Ryan began. "Was this another old Army buddy?"

Bill studied Ryan's demeanor in an attempt to determine how much he might already know about the relationship.

"He is a mutual friend of Charles and myself," he replied.

"Layla said she saw this man parked outside her trailer on an earlier occasion," Ryan continued. "What was that about?"

"His name is Sam Wells, a retired policeman," Bill admitted. "Charles sometimes used Sam's investigative skills to determine whether a scholarship should continue. If someone is living a life that would reflect poorly on the law firm, Charles would have reason to transfer the scholarship to someone more deserving."

As the statements were being offered, Bill watched to see if his answer satisfied the inquisitive younger man. Ryan had thought out different scenarios during the past several weeks, and he had prepared himself to follow that explanation.

"I don't see why Charles Moore would want an investigator from Atlanta," Ryan stated. "Why not just use a local investigative agency? Charlotte is much closer to Brandon Springs, than Atlanta".

In his question, Ryan had given Bill additional insight. Thompson had not mentioned the city in Georgia, so he knew Ryan had been doing serious investigations of his own. He attempted to put an end to Ryan's questions by revealing personal information.

"Let some old men try to do something good before they die," Bill said, as he took a deep breath. "Charles is dead, and I probably won't be far behind. I have a cancer."

"I'm sorry about your friend, and about your health," Ryan said quietly. "I would still like to know why Mr. Moore would have an aging retired cop drive all the way up from Atlanta to do his investigating. Why not hire someone younger; and why not a local investigator?"

Bill confessed that the three were old Army buddies, and that it was a matter of trust. He also pointed out the fact that the firm granted scholarships to candidates living in various areas of the United States.

"We even award scholarships to individuals who live outside the Southeastern United States, and it wouldn't make much sense to attempt to find a local investigator for each area of the country," Bill explained. "Don't underestimate Sam Wells. He gets around pretty well for a man of his age. Don't be concerned. I feel sure your friend should be awarded a continuance of the grant. She appears to be a diligent individual."

"What about the $10,000 given to her before the scholarship?" Ryan pressed. "Did that money come from the law firm, as well?"

It was at that point that Ryan suddenly became aware that Bill Thompson's calm and pleasant demeanor had run its course. The old man's eyes narrowed, and his face hardened. He had lost patience with the prodding and decided the conversation had come to an end. Within seconds, the glare from the elderly fellow caused Ryan to feel as though he was a small child about to be sent to his room to await a spanking. There was now a presence about this seasoned man that seemed to overpower the younger one. It was one of those intangible experiences in life, and Ryan would have never been able to explain it to anyone. Inside, he was now on the defensive. It happened within a few short seconds, and it was as real as if a giant was standing before him.

"Leave it alone," were the last three words uttered to Ryan that day by Bill Thompson.

It wasn't the words, but the manner in which they were spoken, that caused an unexpected chill to run through Ryan. It was enough.

Larry had been speaking with others during Ryan's conversation with Bill. As the two drove back to Larry's apartment, Ryan informed his friend of all he had learned. Larry advised him to do as Thompson demanded.

"I think you should leave it alone," Larry stated. "If you continue to pressure Mr. Thompson, there is a chance you could jeopardize Layla's scholarship."

Ryan had not considered this aspect, and he told Larry that he would make a conscious effort to put the matter behind him for the time being. However, Larry decided to do some investigating of his own. He had purchased an old Buick for himself, but he had never driven far from his work or school. The following weekend Larry began attending Bill Thompson's church, but he refrained from going to the Sunday school class. After several weeks, he saw Sam Wells seated beside the Thompsons during a church service. He knew him to be the retired policeman, because Ryan had given him a thorough description of the man.

"He's a large man with black hair combed straight back, and he seems to favor his right leg somewhat," Ryan had told him.

Keeping his distance, Larry followed them outside after the service ended. Bill and Sam Wells talked for some time before Mr. Thompson handed the man an envelope. Immediately after the two parted, Bill returned to his wife to help her to the car. Larry continued to watch the retired policeman from a safe distance. Sam Wells tossed the envelope onto the front passenger seat of his white Lincoln, as he lowered his huge frame into the seat behind the steering wheel. For a man of his age, he moved with smooth flowing coordination. He had a way about him that spoke of warning.

Deciding to ignore the signs, Larry followed him in his old car. He was thankful not to have to stop for fuel, for his gas tank was almost full. It was a good thing, because Sam wasn't headed for a local motel in the Boston area. Curious to see if the retired policeman planned to head home to Atlanta, Larry continued to follow. A slight sense of excitement began to come over the younger man, as he secretly kept the white Lincoln in sight. Keeping a reasonable distance behind, he followed him down Interstate 90 and onto Interstate 84.

It was later in the afternoon, when Sam exited Interstate 84 onto Interstate 81. Larry looked at his watch and considered turning back. It had become apparent that Sam wasn't going home to Atlanta, but curiosity had taken a firm hold on Larry. Though he had followed Sam into the state of Pennsylvania, he couldn't force himself to turn around. At last, just outside the city of Wilkes-Barre, Sam exited the interstate onto a busy two-lane highway. After about a half mile, he pulled into the parking lot of an unremarkable motel. Larry continued to drive down the road. About a hundred yards down from the motel, he entered the parking lot of a restaurant. He waited for about twenty minutes; then made his way past the motel and back onto Interstate 81. Within minutes, Larry noticed a Pennsylvania State Trooper closing in from the rear. The trooper followed him for more than fifteen miles, but never turned on the siren or lights. Eventually, the law man exited onto a small rural road.

The next Sunday, Larry decided to follow Bill Thompson and his wife as they returned home after the church service. He kept a safe distance between the two cars, and he returned to his apartment immediately after the couple made it home. Two days later, Larry looked out the window of his apartment to find a Boston city police car parked outside. Any other day, he would have been thankful. He would have experienced a sense of protection. Today, he felt uneasy. Every ten minutes he looked to see if the car was still there. It was. After an hour, a maturing fear began to creep over him. He called Ryan to tell him about the police car and to confess his adventures of following Sam Wells. Ryan reminded him that he had broken no law and encouraged his friend to relax and not be concerned.

Though he told Larry that he had nothing to worry about, Ryan remained uneasy after the conversation ended. Two hours after the conversation with his friend, the phone rang again. Expecting it to be Larry, with news that the police car had departed, Ryan slowly made his way to answer. He was very surprised to hear the voice on the other end.

"Ryan, this is Bill Thompson," the voice firmly announced.

"Yes sir. How are you doing?" Ryan asked.

"I'm going to say this once, and I want you to listen carefully," Bill continued. "You tell your friend that he had best stop doing what he has been doing. I don't intend on giving you an explanation. You just tell him what I said, and he will know exactly what I mean. Do you understand me?"

The chilling tone of the voice coming from the old man stopped Ryan cold. Though tempted, he thought it unwise to act as if he knew nothing about the subject.

"Yes sir, I will tell him," Ryan responded.

He heard the receiver drop on the other end, and the call

was over. Ryan immediately called Larry. The first thing he asked was if the policeman was still outside the apartment. His friend confirmed that it was. Ryan told him exactly what the elderly man had told him to say. Larry was terrified. The conversation continued for a few more minutes before Larry witnessed the police car pull away. He promised Ryan he would never attend that church again, and he swore he would never follow either man again. Ryan could sense the fear in his friend's voice. Larry was intensely shaken and felt more vulnerable than he had at any point in his life.

Once the call with Larry ended, Ryan called Layla. He thought it best to warn her of Larry's experiences, so he told her everything. On Ryan's and Larry's next visit to Brandon Springs the three discussed in detail everything they knew about Charles Moore, Bill Thompson, and Sam Wells. Assured that none of them had been further contacted by the two remaining older men, they came to the conclusion that they would be fairly safe if they took Bill Thompson's advice. The conversation shifted to that of the current status of each.

Larry was in his last quarter in school, and he would graduate with a degree in Finance within a couple of months. Layla was progressing, but at a much slower pace. She had performed well in lower-level nursing course work, but now she was afraid her grades might drop for the more advanced classes. While Ryan continued to encourage her, Larry quietly slipped outside the small trailer. Larry called Patsy on his cell phone and told her about Layla's difficulties in nursing school. Patsy offered to provide tutorage, since she had been a nurse for several years. It was a Saturday, and Larry convinced Ryan and Layla to meet Patsy for supper. At first, Layla refused Patsy's help, for she felt it would be an imposition on someone she had never met. After Ryan reminded her that Patsy had volunteered to help, she agreed to receive the offer.

As they drove to the larger neighboring town to met Patsy, the three discussed the future. Although Larry was guaranteed a promotion and increase in pay immediately after graduation, he considered moving to Charlotte. His best friend lived there, and he knew the cost of living was much better in Charlotte than in Boston. He also still disliked the New England city and he wanted to avoid any situation of running into Bill Thompson or Sam Wells. However, none of those subjects included his primary reason for his wish to leave Boston. Charlotte provided an easy drive to visit Patsy.

Layla's main concern was to finish nursing school, and Ryan had become more comfortable with his role in management. Layla and Patsy hit it off exactly as Larry had hoped. During the conversation at supper, Patsy was able to clearly explain to Layla the answer to one of her nursing difficulties. They enjoyed the visit and planned to get together the following weekend. Over time, Patsy and Layla became friends; and whenever Larry would come down from Boston, all four spent the weekend together.

Ryan was still on the mailing list of the church Charles Moore had attended. Usually, he would scan through the monthly document and quickly drop it in the trash. On this day, his eye caught a familiar name on the prayer list. Charles' widow, Beverly, had been placed in a Charlotte facility due to her suffering the latter stages of Alzheimer's disease. Knowing her husband had passed away, and in light of the fact the Thompson's lived a significant distance from the Charlotte area, Ryan placed a call to Bill Thompson. At first, he was reluctant to contact the man who had caused Larry such concern. However, he knew that once Layla heard about the woman's state of health, she would want to visit her. Layla felt a great deal of gratitude to Charles Moore for the scholarship.

"Mr. Thompson, this is Ryan Walker," he began. "I wanted to let you know that Beverly Moore has been placed in a Charlotte center for the elderly, which specializes in care for those suffering from Alzheimer's."

There was a slight pause; then Bill Thompson replied.

"We knew she was deteriorating fairly quickly, and I appreciate you letting me know."

"Mr. Thompson, Layla Quick will probably want to visit her," Ryan explained. "She feels like she owes a lot to Mr. Moore, and I really believe she will want to periodically check on his widow at the center. Would you have any objections?"

There was silence for a few seconds. Then with a voice filled with sorrow, Bill responded.

"No son. That would be fine."

Due to his own failing health, and his wife's disability, he realized how infrequently he would be able to look in on Beverly Moore.

The call ended quickly. Ryan thought he had never heard such a wary and broken tone from the old man. He could tell Bill Thompson was fighting back tears during the short conversation. Immediately, Ryan called Layla. He told her about the condition of Mrs. Moore, and of the conversation he had with Mr. Thompson.

The following weekend, Layla, Ryan and Patsy paid their first visit to Mrs. Moore. The three were her only visitors that hour. There were a few flowers and cards about the dimly lit room, which was unusually warm. Having a hand and foot each in restraints, she appeared to be very small as she lay quietly in her bed. Beverly Moore remained almost completely still. Her eyes stared blankly into a corner of the room.

"Mrs. Moore?" Layla softly asked, as she stood directly between Mrs. Moore and the observed corner of the room.

"Who are you?" Beverly Moore suddenly replied, almost frightened.

"My name is Layla, and this is Ryan and Patsy," she answered. "Your husband helped me a lot, and I just wanted to come by to tell you how much I appreciate it."

"He helped a lot of people," Mrs. Moore stated with a smile. "Are you one of the young ladies he sent to school, or did he give money to you?"

"He sent me to school," Layla replied.

"Well, he could have given you money, Sweetheart," Beverly continued. "He had it to give. They all had it to give. So many people are dead, but the money is still here."

"I would imagine you've lost several of your friends," Ryan stated in a consoling tone.

"Those men weren't my friends; they were acquaintances of Charles and Bill," she firmly stated. "They're dead, but Charles didn't kill them. He never had a violent bone in his body. Not that he was sorry to hear that Max was dead. He deserved to die. That murdering…"

She stopped in mid-sentence, her eyes wild with distant memories.

"Are you a policeman?" she asked Ryan.

"No Ma'am, I'm not," he replied.

"Well, Sam is and don't you forget it," she charged.

Leaving the center, Ryan and Layla discussed the odd conversation with Patsy. Patsy explained to them that memories and imaginative occurrences sometime fold together in the mind of an Alzheimer's patient. Still, there was something very mysterious about her perceived memories, and each silently wondered about her statements of death and money.

Chapter 9

AFTER THE ENCOUNTER with Sam and Bill, Larry remained afraid while alone in Boston. At night he would close all the blinds so that no one would be able to see if he was at home in the small apartment. One night he found himself in a state of panic, when the sound of car tires screeched to an abrupt stop in front of his building. Creeping over to the window, he was relieved to see a group of teenagers exit the vehicle. Still mindful of being observed on those occasions by policemen, apparently with ties to Sam Wells, he dropped to his knees beside his bed and begged God for protection. He asked for a sign that his prayers had been heard.

The next evening, while walking past a small church cemetery, he noticed a cross that seemed to glow in the dark. He took note of its exact location, and the next day he visited the grave. He was strangely astonished to find that it was the grave of a *Lawrence Chatterson*. Years ago, a coincidence of that nature would have sent a chill up his spine. That evening, he felt no fear.

"Is this a sign from God, or was the glowing marker caused by the ghost of a relative having the same name?" he asked himself.

Two weeks later he passed by the cemetery again at night and witnessed no glow on any of the tombstones. Still unsure as to the reason for the glowing marker, he was confident that it must have been a one-time event.

Larry floated from one church to another, and from one denomination to another. He was like a nomad, in search for a home. One evening he visited a Pentecostal church. During the service, a certain man caught his attention. He tried to focus on the sermon, but he felt compelled to watch the man. It wasn't because there was something odd or strange about the fellow. Larry felt God was placing this person on his heart for some reason. He began to pray fervently that God would bless the man, and he asked God to allow this stranger to sense the presence of God's Spirit. Almost immediately, the man jumped to his feet, waved his arms around, and began speaking loudly in tongues. Afterwards, the man testified before the church that he thought he had felt the hands of Jesus on his head. Larry was convinced that he had been selected by God for a special and divine purpose.

At last, Larry graduated with a bachelor's degree in finance from the community college. Ryan, Patsy, and Layla came to Boston to attend the ceremony, and afterwards they went to dinner to celebrate. It was one the happiest days of Larry's life. A few days after the three friends departed, he heard a television evangelist make a strange proclamation.

The preacher said, "There is a man named Larry, who God has chosen to be His prophet. You know who you are, and in your heart, you know this to be true. You just haven't been willing to accept it."

Larry was stunned. He thought of the glowing cross at the cemetery, the man at the Pentecostal church, and this proclamation. Larry now strongly believed that he had been selected by God to be a prophet. Still, he told no one. He began to pray as to whether God wanted him to remain in finance or quit his job to become a preacher. A short time later, he was given a promotion at work. Larry was given the title of Financial Analyst and was also given the raise in pay he had been promised. For the time being, he accepted this to be a sign that he should remain in finance. With the new financial success, he moved to an apartment in a better part of town and traded his old car in on a newer model. He was careful to spend his money wisely. Larry didn't rent an overly expensive apartment, he just moved to a better one which was in an area of town with a lower rate of crime. He didn't purchase an extravagant car, or even a new one. He selected a late model car, which was known for high reliability. Larry also began investing more of his income.

TWO MONTHS AFTER GRADUATING and settling into his new job and apartment, Larry revisited his family in Alabama. It had been five years since he had even spoken to any of them. Larry was now twenty-eight years old; his sister Heather was twenty-five, and his baby brother was twenty-two. After knocking on the front door, he was greeted coldly by his sister. Standing at her feet was a toddler, her child. He found that she was unmarried, out of work, and was unsure as to which man was the father. His sister lived at the home of her parents, and she spent each day caring for her son and her father. The younger brother had moved into an apartment nearby and worked at a local convenience store. Early in his adult life, Larry's father had been a strong physical specimen. He now was bedridden with cirrhosis of the liver. The old man collected a disability check, and the family had begun to draw Social Security. However, it wasn't enough to take care of all three of them. Larry's mother worked at a restaurant, doing her best to provide for her husband, daughter, and grandson.

The weight of his family situation bore heavy upon Larry's soul. He sat for a few minutes beside his ill father and shared some of his accomplishments with him. Outwardly, the worn older man was almost unrecognizable. His once powerful frame had been reduced to a frail and boney body, and his once trim physique portrayed a bloated belly. The fearsome eyes of a younger man had now become hollow. However, little had changed inwardly. His father gave him little praise, and actually heaped most of the credit upon himself.

"I made you what you are, boy," he began in a weak soft voice. "I was hard on you, and you were tough enough to take on whatever came your way. You might be educated and all, but don't forget where you came from and the people who pushed you along".

After a short conversation with him, and the fact that he was almost ignored by his sister, he decided to see his mother. As he drove to the café, he couldn't help hearing his father's words over and over in his head. He was aware that some of his father's words were true. Larry knew his old man had made him tough. But he knew there were others, besides these family members, who had encouraged him and helped him along the way. Larry also had begun to realize his own gifted intelligence.

As he walked through the front door of the restaurant, he caught his mother's eyes. Quickly cupping her hands over her mouth, in an attempt not to make a scene at her place of employment, she began to weep almost uncontrollably. She quickly pulled him aside into a more private area and threw her arms around him. She continued to cry. His mother stroked the back of his head, just as she had done when he was a small child. At last, she released him and wiped away tears with both hands.

"Where have you been?" she asked. "Why haven't you called?"

Her words tore at his heart, as no one else's could. Fighting back shame, he searched for words to explain. He and his mother had always shared honesty, and still there was no way for him to escape it.

"I was so upset by the divorce, and it was hard for me to look back," he began. "No excuse is a good one. I should have let you know something".

"You surely should have!" she responded, as she dealt his muscular shoulder a loving blow with her hand.

"I found religion, and I have a college degree," he whispered.

She grabbed him again and said, "You've always been a smart one, and you've always been a good boy. You always had a good heart. I shouldn't be surprised. I'm so proud of you."

That evening, when everyone was at home, he told them of he had accomplished. However, he reserved the part about his relationship with God for only his mother. She would be the only one who would truly appreciate it. One of the conversations that night was interrupted by a phone call for his sister. It was one of her ex-boyfriends. The young man was angry because she had listed him as the father of her son, and because she was pressing him for child support. Her response to him consisted of a multitude of foul words.

The following day, his little brother came to visit. Ronnie's manner was even colder than Larry's sister. He said nothing to Larry for the first hour, as though Larry was not even present. It was evident that he came for the sole purpose of sending his brother a frigid message. He was angry.

No one offered Larry a room in the house, and Ronnie certainly made no offer for him to stay at his apartment. Around eleven that night, Larry left in search of a motel. As he walked out to his car, his brother followed him. Larry was unsure whether Ronnie had intentions of hitting him out of anger, but he considered that it would be a welcome break from his brother's silence.

"I guess you had it easy up there in Boston," Ronnie finally spat out.

Larry stood and waited for the next words.

"It wasn't so great here, you jerk!" Ronnie stated emphatically. "He didn't have you to beat anymore, so he started in on me. I finally had enough, and I clobbered him back one night. That was my last night of sleeping in that house. I moved out. Actually, I was kicked out. Dad said that since I was man enough to stand up to him, I was man enough to live on my own. I slept in my car until I could come up with the rent money."

"I'm sorry," Larry mumbled. "I guess I was caught up with my own stuff. I just couldn't stay in the same town with her. I had just had to leave."

"Why didn't you take me with you?" Ronnie blurted out.

"You were too young to work at the docks up there, and I thought maybe you could help Mama out," Larry replied. "It didn't work out, anyway. I couldn't get on up there. I ended up washing dishes in a diner, and I lived in a slummy neighborhood. You would have had to finish school in a rough neighborhood, and I couldn't earn enough to support us both. I hated it there, but I felt I couldn't come back here with my tail tucked between my legs. I washed dishes and cleaned up after people all day, and I went to school at night. I have a good job now, but it wasn't always like it is now. I didn't want to upset Mama with the bad stuff, so I left that out of what I told tonight. I'm telling you because I think you need to know."

"Well, if I were you, I might have done the same thing," Ronnie admitted. "This place is the pits. I don't have much, but I don't have to be around Dad or the stupid crap our sister Heather is always getting herself into. Heather is a stinking slut. She jumps the bones of anything with pants! Dad is not strong enough anymore to beat people. He's just pathetic. That jerk has drunk his stupid self into the grave, he just isn't dead yet. Mama's OK, but I really don't want to hear any of her lectures. Well, she doesn't really lecture. I don't want to make her sad. When she hears of some the stuff I do, it's like those sad eyes are giving me a lecture. I know I don't do what I should. Mama is Mama. She's a saint if there ever was one. But she probably would have done us all a favor if she had kicked Dad's crappy butt out a long time ago."

"I really am sorry, Ronnie," Larry replied. "I won't ever do that again. I'll write, and call, or do whatever I need to do to stay in touch. Same with Mama, I won't do that to her again. Next time I come down, I'll wait until you can take a few days off and I will bring you back up to Boston for a visit."

"I would like that, but you probably ought to take Mama up there first," Ronnie responded. "If I went up there first, she would really bop me when I got back home. She has missed you like you wouldn't believe. She cried for days. People told her that you might never come back, but she wouldn't listen to it."

Ronnie didn't tell Larry about his other activity. He had, indeed, slept in his car before finding work. However, he found an apartment by moving in with Chris, a fellow construction worker. He split the rent with him. What he didn't realize, at first, was that his fellow employee sold drugs on the side. Shortly after Ronnie moved in, he walked in on Chris and a couple of other shady characters in the middle of a drug deal. After being confronted by them, the young Ronnie was afraid not to take part in the business.

The construction crew moved away for another job, and Chris went with the job. Ronnie felt he couldn't leave his mother. He found a job, making less pay, at a local convenience store. After his fellow worker moved out of the apartment, Ronnie was left to be responsible for paying the entire rent. The drug supplier expected him to continue dealing drugs. Ronnie needed the extra income to make the rent and buy food. He could have moved into a smaller apartment, but Ronnie realized he could not escape the drug situation. A cold rough character, Keith Turner, had been the drug supplier for the two. Chris handled most of the transactions with him, and Ronnie had only a minor selling role. Now that he was left as the only seller, he was expected to take the lead participation. He quickly became a major drug dealer in the area. As time passed, he became more comfortable in this new role. However, the risk and peril never lessened.

THE NEXT TIME LARRY TRAVELED TO ALABAMA, he decided to drop by Ronnie's apartment before visiting the rest of the family. With no prior notification by his brother of the visit, Ronnie was caught off guard. Larry found his brother in discussion with Keith regarding the expansion of his role in the organization. Keith was about to introduce him to the "big men". Although the conversation between the two stopped immediately when Larry arrived, it didn't take Larry long to realize what was going on. He had seen Keith's kind in the rough sections of Boston. Keith was not quite as tall as Larry, but he was very muscular and extremely cold in his demeanor. He knew that his brother was dealing with a brutal individual. After Keith departed, a serious brother to brother discussion ensued. Over the next hour, Ronnie confessed the situation to his brother. Ronnie explained to Larry that the drug involvement was the reason he hadn't offered his apartment to his brother during the previous visit. The younger brother expressed a strong desire to get out of the situation, but he was terrified at the consequences of attempting such a thing.

"I would be dead," Ronnie stated. "It's just that simple."

Within a couple of days, Larry and Ryan found a construction job and cheap apartment for Ronnie in Charlotte. Larry gave him money to get started and paid the deposit and the first month's rent. Ronnie wrote home to tell his mother where he had moved, and he gave her the good news of the job. She had been worried about someone robbing the convenience store, and she was glad to know her son was away from a job that carried risk. She knew nothing of the real danger of which he had been a part.

Everything seemed to be going as planned, until Keith paid Heather a visit with questions about her missing brother. Seriously afraid for the safety of herself and her child, she revealed Ronnie's whereabouts. She was too ashamed and afraid to warn her brother. She secretly hoped her brothers wouldn't be found.

A COUPLE OF WEEKS AFTERWARDS, Larry and Ryan treated Ronnie to supper. They selected a local inner-city diner that Ronnie often frequented, for the younger brother wanted to introduce them to his find of such great food. After ordering, Ronnie went out back to smoke a cigarette. He had no clue that Keith had come to Charlotte to find him. Ronnie didn't realize that the drug supplier saw him leave the restaurant for the alley behind the place.

As he sat at the table, Larry had an odd feeling he couldn't shake. He decided he should check on his brother. Actually, he was afraid his brother might be doing drugs out back. As he stepped into the alley, he found Keith confronting Ronnie. In the dimly lit alley, he could see the knife in Keith's hand. This supplier had not come all the way to Charlotte to merely have a discussion. He intended to either have Ronnie back on his payroll or silence him.

Keith held out the knife toward Larry and warned him to stay out of the situation. Realizing that his brother's life would be at risk as long as Keith could find him, the older brother had no intentions of staying out of it. During Keith's threats Larry scanned his surroundings, while still keeping an eye on the man and the knife. Mindful of how he had left his brother at the mercy of their father, Larry's commitment to Ronnie was now steadfast. Larry felt partially responsible for Ronnie's plight, and tonight he saw murder in Keith's eyes.

When threatened, some people run, and some people react in a much more aggressive manner. With the speed and agility of a gifted athlete, Larry pushed his brother aside. Almost in the same motion, he stepped backwards and picked up a lose brick from the alley pavement. As Keith moved toward him, Larry let the brick fly against his assailant's face. Dazed, Keith hesitated for a moment. Like a cat, Larry quickly snatched up the brick again. Keith's hesitation lasted just long enough for Larry to grab the wrist that was holding the knife and push Keith backwards. Tripping over a bag of garbage in the ally, Keith dropped backwards onto the pavement. Larry followed him down, still holding onto the wrist. Once on his back, Keith came back to his senses. Realizing his peril, the drug supplier was filled with a mixture of fear and rage. Adrenaline flowing, his free left fist smashed into the side of Larry's face. Immediately, Larry returned a blow with the brick in his hand. Keith's head slammed back against the pavement and bounced back toward the man on top of him. Larry continued to bash his face with the brick repeatedly, until he felt the hand of his brother on his shoulder. With the brick still poised for another blow, he recognized his brother's shouts.

"Larry, stop…man! He's down… he's down now!"

Larry looked down at the crushed face beneath him. It no longer looked like the face of the man Ronnie once feared. Most of the front teeth were gone, and there was blood oozing from several large gashes on his face. Keith's forehead had taken on a slightly concave shape, and blood flowed onto the pavement beneath his head. Larry heard the gurgling sound of blood mixed with struggling shallow breaths, and he saw a bubble of blood form from one swelling nostril.

Finally, Larry released the brick from his hand. He glanced down and found that blood covered most of his lower right arm. The front of his shirt was covered in blood splatter. He looked up into the wild eyes of his brother. Larry rose to his feet and realized what just occurred. He remembered the rage of his father, and he began to shake violently. Ronnie led him over to a set of steps in the ally, and suggested he sit down. Just as he was seated, another customer walked into the alley for a smoke. He took a look at the bleeding man on the pavement. Stunned, he glanced in the direction of the blood splattered fellow seated on the steps. He quickly retreated back into the restaurant. Within seconds, the manager and several men rushed out into the ally. They began asking Ronnie and Larry questions. One voice began shouting for an ambulance and another announced he would call the police.

Ryan stepped out into the ally to see what the commotion was about, and immediately saw a small group of men examining the man on the pavement. As women began to come out into the ally, other men uttered warnings and ushered them back into the restaurant. Glancing to his right, he recognized his bloody friend seated on the steps. He caught Ronnie's eye, and he was motioned to come over. Ryan had never seen Larry in such a state. The wild eyes were familiar, but his friend's entire body shook intensely as every part of him was overcome by emotion.

Within minutes, police and paramedics arrived. The emergency crew frantically worked on Keith, and the police began their tasks. Some asked questions of Larry and Ronnie, another gathered Keith's wallet from his pants and examined the contents. Still other policemen gathered the knife, brick, and other objects from the alley. One by one, they were placed in bags and the bags were labeled. Soon reports came back to the police that Keith was wanted on drug charges in Alabama. He was also a suspect in a murder. Larry was instructed not to leave town for a couple of days. He immediately called his boss, to let him know why he would need to miss a few days of work. Throughout the conversation, he felt nauseated from embarrassment, guilt, and fear. By the end of the following day, word spread throughout his workplace.

Two days later, the police visited Larry and his brother at Ronnie's small apartment. Keith had suffered extensive brain damage and was not expected to live. Larry was released, as the police report indicated that he acted in self-defense and in defense of his brother. After the policemen left the apartment, Larry departed for the drive back to Boston. No longer did he view himself as God's prophet. During the drive back, he felt confused, frightened, and alone.

WHEN LARRY RETURNED TO WORK, most of his fellow employees avoided him. Most of the men gave him cautious glances, and the women made no eye contact with him. Away from the others, while in the men's restroom, a couple of other men gave him unwanted slaps on the back and told him that he was a real stud and that they would have liked to have "kicked a drug dealer's butt" the way he did. Larry politely nodded and returned to his office. He knew that it was all talk, for they showed no signs of support among the other employees. His boss told him the incident would have no negative effect on his position or his future with the company. However, the man's demeanor indicated otherwise. Larry decided to send out a few resumes. He sent some to Atlanta and Knoxville. Because of Ryan, he sent a couple to firms in Charlotte. Almost immediately after sending it, he partially regretted the submission. Though Charlotte was a fairly large town, he absolutely wanted to avoid running into anyone who was present the night he dealt with Keith. However, Larry also hoped it would be an opportunity to move nearer Ryan, Ronnie, and Patsy. He was unsure as to what he should say to Patsy when he next saw her. Larry was afraid of what she might think of him, as he was sincerely unsure as to what he thought of himself.

However, on his first visit with her after the incident, she immediately wrapped her arms around his neck and told him that she was in love with him. He sobbed like a baby."

Two days after he returned to Boston, he got the word that Keith died. He received offers for job interviews in Atlanta and Knoxville. He never realized that his boss had given rave reviews of him, when contacted by those firms. Personally, his boss in Boston liked him and thought he was an excellent employee. However, he wanted the chilled atmosphere in the office to go away. He knew that meant Larry would have to leave.

Before interviewing in Knoxville, Larry visited Ryan and Layla for encouragement. Ryan enjoyed the opportunity to see Larry. However, it was obvious that Layla was initially uncomfortable when being around his best friend. By the time the visit ended, she had begun to remember what a good man Larry had always been. Just before he left, she took him aside and told him so. For some strange reason, this meant more to Larry than he anticipated. In days ahead, that conversation would play over in his mind as he encountered difficult times of adjustment. It helped him go on with his life.

After the incident with Keith, Ronnie hung on to his older brother like glue whenever he could be with him. Larry sent him money to attend tech school, so that he could become certified in printer repairs. Eventually, Ronnie landed a job with a company servicing printers at corporations with maintenance contracts. Larry received an offer from a Knoxville bank, but he turned it down after thoughtful consideration. It would have taken him much closer to Ronnie and Ryan, but he really didn't want to work in banking. Deep down, he hoped for a job in Charlotte. After deciding against the offer, he realized that his heart was set on being near his brother and his friends.

"If I really want to be with my brother and my best friend, then I should put my effort into going there," he

thought. *"I should consider going elsewhere, only if it doesn't work out."*

After sending the letter of refusal to the bank, he sent out several more resumes to firms in Charlotte. By the end of the month, an interview was set up with a brokerage firm which had an office in Charlotte. Knowing that Ryan would be able to drive him to the interview, he decided to fly down from Boston. He called to first confirm the plan with his friend. Throughout the phone call, he found it difficult to not to become excited. He remembered the time when Ryan attempted to make him an offer, and he didn't want another let down like that again. It was even more difficult when he called his brother Ronnie. He decided against calling Patsy because he thought it would just be too much.

TWO WEEKS LATER he received the offer from the brokerage firm in Charlotte, and he immediately sent his letter of acceptance. He could hardly believe it. Though he had never worked for a brokerage firm, the interviewer quickly picked up on his knowledge of the stock market. Larry wasted no time informing family and friends of the job. He first called Ronnie, then Ryan, and he lastly called Patsy. Though he maintained his cool during the conversations, as he ended the last call he exploded with emotion. He leapt into the air, while spinning around and releasing a loud shout. He vigorously danced through the living room, and into the kitchen. There, he danced with a gallon jug of milk before pouring the contents into a bowl of cereal. He had finally done it, and it seemed an enormous load had been lifted from him.

"I couldn't stand being alone in Boston much longer," he thought. *"I need to be with my bother and true friends."*

Shortly before making the move to Charlotte, Larry had an unexpected visit from someone he thought he would never see again. He was terrified when he opened the front door of his Boston apartment. Sam Wells stood outside the door. Initially, he stood motionless and silent.

"Have you got few minutes for an old man?' Sam asked. "We can just sit on the porch steps, if you like."

Astonished, Larry invited him in before he could think it through.

"What do you want with me?" he asked sheepishly. "I haven't gone near Mr. Thompson, I swear."

"It's not about any of that," Sam assured.

"How did you find me?" Larry gasped. "I don't live in the same place."

"I used to be a pretty good cop, at one time," Sam replied.

The older man explained he had heard, through the grapevine, that Larry had an incident in Charlotte. At first Larry was afraid Sam thought he had been dealing drugs with Keith, and that a deal had gone bad. However, he was very wrong about his assumption. Sam had come to share. He didn't go into details of the circumstances, but he told Larry about a time when he had killed a man. He told him about his own grief, and of his own struggles with guilt. For about two hours, they both shared of the internal battles raging within each man; battles only they understood. Larry felt it was almost like a father and son discussion. After that visit, he never feared Sam again. He had found a true friend in a most unlikely man. As they shook hands when parting, he was unsure as to whether he had grasped the hand of a saint or a killer. Nevertheless, it was clear that a bond was sealed with that visit.

Shortly after moving into the apartment in Charlotte, and settling into the new job, he received word from his mother that his father had passed away. Larry wasn't sure whether he felt sorrow. He just felt a little numb. He called Ronnie, Ryan and Patsy. Ryan then passed the word to Layla. They all met in Mobile for the funeral. Though his death was not a surprise, Larry's mother's eyes remained red and swollen from two days of constant weeping. Regardless of the abuse and her hard life, she truly loved the man. None of the children could understand why. As Larry peered down into the coffin, he thought how much smaller his father's body seemed in death than in life. He placed his hand upon his father's cold hard hand, and then quickly pulled his own hand away. Relatives from all over came for the funeral, but the crowd consisted only of about forty people. Afterwards, Larry met with the funeral director and wrote a check for the balance owed.

When Larry's friends and immediate family reached the house, he felt exhausted. It was only when he sat on his mother's couch that he realized how neglected the home had become. He couldn't afford it now, but he determined that he would help his mother better her living conditions. The entire afternoon, Heather overtly tried to hit up on Ryan. Her actions were almost to the point of being lewd. In words she hinted of sexual interest, and in manner she openly called attention to her body. She ignored the fact that he brought Layla to the funeral. To her, he wasn't married, and he was considered free game. Ryan found it astonishing that she acted in such a manner, in light of the fact that her father had been buried earlier in the day. He focused his attention on the members of the family who seemed to suffer grief, and he made sure that he didn't ignore Layla. He had no clue as to what was actually going on inside Larry's sister, for people handle loss in a variety of ways. Though she almost hated the old man, he had been the only constant male in her life. Her brothers were away in Charlotte, and she was unsure as to the father of her child. She very much felt a sense of loss, and this was her way of reaching out for comfort. Larry wasn't embarrassed by the state of the old home, but he was sickened by the behavior of his sister.

"Ronnie was right," he thought to himself, *"Heather is just a slut!"*

Chapter 10

OCTOBER AND NOVEMBER 1950, the American Army pushed deeper into North Korea. Sergeant Max Cunningham's line of trucks came across acres of debris left from a North Korean convoy, which had recently come under heavy bombardment and strafing from United Nations forces. Before the American trucks rolled through, infantry mopped up the remnants of the North Korean personnel manning that convoy. All that was left were Chinese made trucks, or rather pieces of trucks, and bodies covered with a light dusting of snow.

Max Cunningham, Tom Richards and Henry Pope were tightly squeezed in the cab of a truck containing ammunition bound for the front lines. Max spotted the spinning tires of another truck that had slid off the road and was stuck in the snow. One guy was behind the wheel, another was standing beside the truck shouting instructions, and a third man busily attempted to shovel snow away from the rear wheels.

Pulling alongside the truck, he instructed the men there to stop what they were doing. Max was a seasoned veteran of World War II, and he knew exactly what to do. Within just a few minutes, the once floundering truck was back on the road. Before continuing with the rest of the convoy, the men introduced themselves and took the opportunity to enjoy cigarettes. In the rescued truck were Sam Wells, Louis

Simpson, and Charles Moore.

Max asked Sam, "What made you leave the road? Are you nuts?"

Sam and Louis looked at each other for a couple of seconds, and then Sam began.

"See that shot up Chinese truck over there?"

"Yeah," replied Max. "What about it?"

"Notice anything different from it and the other trucks?" Sam asked again.

"You mean, besides the fact that there is a ton of dead North Koreans lying around the thing?" Max replied.

"Why do you think so many are around that truck?" Sam continued. "I mean, the truck doesn't hold that many men."

"How should I know?" Max responded.

Sam had a gift for noticing details of his surroundings, and he was quick to accurately size up a situation. He was a large athletic individual, and most people expected him to be just another dumb jock. Sam was anything but dumb.

Sam and Louis escorted the other three to the Chinese truck, while Charles stayed with his own truck. Looking in the rear of the damaged Chinese truck, they found it filled with boxes of Chinese made ammunition. Several boxes were riddled with bullet holes from the strafing, and one box had burst open. Behind the fragments of the wooden container, something glittered. Max immediately jumped inside the truck to examine more closely. It was North Korean gold from a bank in Pyongyang. Apparently, as the United Nations forces moved in, the North Koreans tried to move some of the gold to a more secure location.

Sticking his head out from the truck, Max almost whispered, "We can't leave this stuff here."

Within seconds he had devised a plan, and the men were busy at work. There was a break in the line of trucks heading north. Quickly the men loaded the wooden containers of gold into the rear of both trucks. Afterwards, they positioned one man riding in the rear of each truck to rearrange the cargo. While continuing the journey with the rest of the convoy, the men in the rear shoved the gold up close to the cab and covered it with a tarp. The ammunition to be delivered was placed directly against the tarp covering the gold, to keep the Chinese containers hidden. When the convoy stopped to regroup, the men in the rear returned to the cab of their respective vehicles.

As the trucks made their way to the appointed base, men in each cab busily discussed various ideas of how to avoid having the loot discovered. Soldiers at the base waved the trucks in for unloading, and soon both trucks were being relieved of their loads of US ammunition. As this began, Charles and Max quietly agreed on a plan. After the cases of ammunition were unloaded in Max's truck, a soldier reached for the tarp covering the gold.

"That's all you get!" Max shouted to the man. "Take a look at your paperwork. The rest is supposed to be taken elsewhere."

"Yes sir," the soldier replied to the Sergeant.

Before leaving the base, to return to the ammunition depot, Max ordered the other five truckers to load empty ammunition cases into the rear of both trucks. That night, they unloaded the gold from the Chinese wooden cases and reloaded the contents into the US ammunition cases.

They were exhausted when they reached the ammunition depot, but Max directed them to continue on to the main ammunition storage building. Bill Thompson was a young officer in charge of inventory at the building. Upon inspection of the trucks, he questioned the Sergeant.

"Why didn't you deliver all of the ammo, Sergeant?" Bill asked.

"Sir, we found it to be bad ammunition," Max replied. "Come in here and take a look, Sir."

Bill and Max climbed into the back of the truck, and Max slid the tarp from the cases. He handed a case to Bill and advised that he examine the contents. After opening the case, the young officer was speechless.

"There's enough of this North Korean crap to make us all pretty rich, Sir," Max suggested. "Counting you, there would be seven of us. I know how to exchange this for currency, but I need you to help us store it here for a while."

Bill Thompson studied the North Korean markings on the gold, and quietly shook his head. It didn't take him long to size up the situation. He could either turn in these men and the gold or come home with a sizable amount of currency. He knew that turning the men and gold over to his superiors by the book was the right thing to do, but he also realized that the gold would probably just end up in the hands of others. If this became public knowledge, the gold would come back to the States and be used by the government. If he turned them in, he would be known as a "rat" by fellow servicemen. Bill was a shrewd accountant, and over the next week he found a way to have it placed in inventory. He made sure that none of it was loaded into ammunition trucks bound for bases.

OVER A PERIOD OF SIX MONTHS, Max was able to fence the gold on the Korean black market through a South Korean businessman. Each of the seven men received US currency in exchange for the gold. The plan was for each of them to rent lockers at train stations to store the money, once back in the states. They would spend the money in small quantities, as not to be noticed. The loot was equally cut between each of the servicemen and the Korean businessman. Evenly split eight ways, each retained an enormous amount of cash.

Although most of the men were from Virginia, after the war they decided to locate in different states. Once honorably discharged from the Army, and with the help of the Korean businessman, Max Cunningham opened a branch of the South Korean business in Los Angles. Having served in World War II and in Korea, he was the oldest of the bunch. Before leaving for Korea, he had become engaged to be married. However, he cancelled the wedding shortly after returning to the States. He was now free to do as he pleased, and he spent a great deal of time traveling between the United States and the business headquarters in South Korea.

Charles Moore was probably the most intelligent of the group. He went to college on the GI Bill, and then went to law school. He set up a law practice in Charlotte, and shortly afterwards married his wife, Beverly. She was from one of the aristocratic families in the city and was considered "old money". Charles's success in the law firm quickly made him acceptable with her crowd. They had a son and a daughter.

Although they had decided to live in different states, Tom Richards eventually moved to Los Angeles. Shortly, he was made an executive for a shipping business. He remained single and enjoyed a very active bachelor's life.

Sam Wells became a policeman in Atlanta. He and his wife, Nancy, had two sons who later played high school football. One was talented enough to win a scholarship to play in college.

Henry Pope never went to college, and he decided to stay in his hometown of Richmond, Virginia. He was doing just about the same thing he had done in Korea; he remained a truck driver. Henry married, became the father of two daughters, and lived in a modest home. No one, in a million years, could have guessed his actual wealth.

Louis Simpson obtained a degree in Business from a community college and managed a department store in a small town outside New York City. He was a devout Catholic, and at one time considered becoming a priest. However, his marriage to Ellen put an end to that idea.

Bill Thompson also remained in his hometown of Boston, and he became a CPA. He was a faithful husband to his wife Mary, and they had three daughters and a son.

In 1957, the Korean businessman was found shot to death in Seoul. No one was surprised, due to his years of dealing with shady people. Tragedy struck in 1958, as Henry Pope was the first of the servicemen to die. An investigation found that the brake lines of his truck had been cut, and it was apparent that his death was not an accident. Two months later, Louis Simpson and Tom Richards were both found executed in a Chicago alley. They had gone there under the pretense of attending a Bears football game, but the others were sure they each had money stored in lockers at the Chicago train station. This was first suspected when they became big Chicago Bears football fans shortly after the war. Both were from Virginia and had never lived in Illinois. They became year-round Chicago sports fans, and often went to the city in the summer to see the Cubs play. Their murder was too much for the other men to believe it to be a random crime. Max and Charles discussed the idea that someone else in the South Korean business must have gotten wind of what occurred during the war and was systematically picking each of them off. It made sense because the South Korean businessman was the first to be found dead.

Afterwards Charles talked with Sam Wells about his suspicions, and Sam decided to secretly check it out. As a policeman, he had resources at his disposal. He found that both Simpson and Richards had lockers rented in their names at the train station in Chicago. However, upon inspecting the lockers, he found them empty. Someone else had found out about the lockers and the money. This person had either lured them to Chicago or waited for them to arrive. Their periodic traveling to Chicago was known mainly by the other "war buddies" and their families. It was possible that the two were simply followed by the killers of the South Korean businessman. However, Sam could not escape the logical possibility that one of the remaining four partners could have lured them to Chicago.

"It's unlikely that they could have been brought there by South Koreans," Sam considered. *"They wouldn't have trusted anyone outside the group of fellow soldiers."*

FOR TWO WEEKS, Sam was at a loss regarding who it might be. Then it hit him, as if it were by inspiration. He decided to check out the passport information of Max Cunningham. It took him several days, but he found that Max had been in South Korea at the time of the Korean businessman's death. He decided it best not to contact Bill and Charles just in case they were in on it. After all, both men adamantly insisted that the deaths must be related to the South Korean business.

Sam placed a call to Max in Los Angeles. He told him that he had a few clues relating to the deaths of Simpson and Richards, and he wanted to meet to discuss his findings with him in Los Angeles. He figured that Max would be overconfident on his own turf, and he hoped to use that against him. Sam took a week's vacation and told his wife and the department that he wanted to spend a little time fishing and resting. He had fished in Missouri a few years back and made arrangements to rent a cabin there for the week. He did drive to Missouri, and he did rent the cabin for a week. However, the next day he headed for Los Angeles. It took him a day and a half to reach the city, where he rented a motel room to rest. That evening, he arrived at Max's house at about 8:00 PM. For the most part, Max lived alone in an upper middle-income suburb. The yards were large, and the homes were ample.

Max invited him in for a drink, and to discuss the information Sam found about the killings.

"I bet you could use a drink, after that drive," Max began. "You must have found some pretty interesting evidence to come all the way out here."

He led Sam to the den, which was often used to throw

parties for singles. Max stepped behind the bar and began to mix drinks.

"I found that the guys from the South Korean business you were associated with, just happened to be in Chicago the night Louis and Tom were killed," Sam stated, attempting to extract a reaction from the man across the bar. "Don't you think that is something we ought to look into?"

Sam watched as Max's eyes narrowed and his face hardened.

"So, you must be actively investigating this yourself?" Max questioned. "What else do you know?"

Max placed the two drinks on the bar, and lowered his hands so they were no longer visible to his guest. His eyes seemed to burn holes through the air, like lasers. Sam knew what was coming, and he attempted to move the conversation in a more truthful direction.

"I know that you were in Korea when the South Korean businessman was killed," he said slowly. "I want in on it. I know you're sitting on a lot of money".

Max brought a revolver from behind the bar, and pointed it at Sam.

"Do you, now?" Max asked, in almost a whisper. "What makes you think I'm the type to share?"

Sam had anticipated the gun, but as he stared down the barrel he was almost at a loss for words. Finally, in a somewhat awkward tone, he answered.

"Max, we've always shared. From the beginning, I was the one who let you in on the Korean gold. Louis, Charles and I could have kept it all to ourselves."

"You really have been the sharing sort of individual, but that wasn't my question," Max replied, still pointing the gun at Sam. "Well, I think you and I should go for a drive and talk it over."

He stepped from behind the bar and headed straight in Sam's direction. Wells knew that he had only a small chance to get out of this situation, and that it required no hesitation on his part. He slowly turned his back to the aggressor and moving very slowly for the door.

"OK, let's talk," Sam said.

Sam waited to feel the pressure of the gun barrel against his back. He had known Max for more than eight years, and Sam had a gift for picking up on small mannerisms of people. He focused his attention on one thing. Sam waited to sense a measure of relaxation in the fingers holding the gun. As quick as a cat, the large man spun around to his right, using his forearm to shove the gun aside just far enough for the shot to miss. The bullet splintered the door facing just behind him. Before another shot could be fired, he grabbed the wrist of the hand holding the pistol with his left hand and pulled it straight above his head. His powerful right fist slammed into the face of his attacker. Max struggled to bring the gun down, attempting to point it again at the huge policeman. Immediately, Sam punched him again in the chin.

Now almost in a blind rage, all Sam could see were the coffins of three Army buddies, and the agonizing grief of the families left behind.

Dazed by the blow to the chin, Max stepped back a couple of feet. At that instance, Sam took hold of Max's left wrist with his massive right hand. Though Max still held the gun, both of his hands where under the controlling strength of the policeman, and he was no match physically against Sam. He was four inches shorter and was outweighed by at least eighty pounds. Max struggled desperately to free the hand holding the gun, but slowly Sam forced that hand down against Max's own chest. With the gun now positioned below the face of his adversary, Sam slowly and methodically twisted the gun so that the barrel pointed upward toward Max's chin. With every ounce of strength he could muster, Max continued to struggle for the next couple of minutes. As Sam forced the revolver to slowly slide up Max's chest, the hammer caught against his jacket, so that it was pulled back into firing position. Eventually, the gun was positioned with the barrel shoved under the chin of Max.

At that moment, the one-time aggressor realized he was completely at the mercy of Sam. As a gesture of surrender, or possibly a willingness to deal, Max ceased the struggle. Sam wasn't ready to accept a deal, or even surrender. Only moments before the gun had been fired in his direction. His muscular long finger stretched over the relaxed finger curled over the trigger. The hammer of the gun slammed against the cartridge in the chamber, causing an almost deafening explosion. A portion of the top of Max's head burst open, as the bullet exited; and blood spattered across the ceiling. As the limp body dropped to the floor, Sam was now willing to accept Max's surrender.

Sam stood over the corpse for a couple of minutes, as if to study it for rejuvenating signs of life. None appeared. The lifeless form before him didn't seem to be the man he thought he knew. For eight years, Sam considered him to be a loyal Army buddy, a man for whom he would have put his life on the line. Now this was the shell of an executed killer, a man who had coldly taken the lives of trusting friends. This was a stranger. Warm memories of a man with whom laughter and trust had been shared would return during years to come, but not in this hour.

He reached into his own rear pants pocket and brought out a handkerchief. With the handkerchief placed over his hand, he reached into Max's right front pants pocket and brought out a set of keys. None appeared to be a key to a locker, but the set contained a desk key. With his muscles now beginning to ache from the struggle, he quickly moved toward the study. A key fit the desk, and in the top middle drawer he found a locker key. He took the key using the handkerchief, and quickly read the writing printed across the attached tag. After sliding it into his left pants pocket, he used the handkerchief to move aside various items in the drawer. The sight of one object caused him to immediately stop his meticulous search. Lying in the same drawer was an old envelope, on which was inscribed a familiar name of someone he knew from South Korea. Memories flooded his mind as he stared at the name. Breathing a deep sigh, by use of the handkerchief he picked it up. Carefully, he slowly removed items from the envelope and methodically placed them on top of the desk for examination. After reviewing the contents, he replaced the items back inside the envelope and slid it into his coat pocket. He then locked the desk drawer.

Returning to the den, he found Max's body just as he had left it. Using the handkerchief, he placed the set of keys back in the victim's pants pocket. Sam used the handkerchief to remove any possible prints of his own from the handgun, careful to leave only those of Max's. He glanced over to the two glasses sitting on the bar, and he immediately began to move towards them. Careful not to step in the blood, now being absorbed by the carpet, he stepped behind the bar. Wrapping a glass with his handkerchief, he raised one of the drinks and thought of the victims of the man now lying before him. He lowered the glass, but stopped momentarily before placing it against his lips. Sam closed his eyes in reverence to those slain men for a moment, and then poured the drink into the sink. Sam washed the glass and carefully dried it with a bar towel, before placing it with the other empty glasses. As he had entered the home, he had made a point to remember each item he had touched. On his way out, he wiped each item thoroughly with the handkerchief. In those years the study of DNA was not yet a tool used in investigations of murder scenes, so his only concern was that of leaving fingerprints. He locked the front door on his way out.

It took him about an hour to reach the train station, but only another ten minutes to find the locker. Sam opened it using the handkerchief, and inside he found four gym bags. Each one was filled with stacks of one-hundred-dollar bills.

The money from each victim was not even placed in a single larger bag. It was if they were kept as trophies from the kills. Sam continued to use the handkerchief to handle the locker and everything touched. Taking all four bags, he wiped the key with the handkerchief and left it in the locker door.

As he drove to Nevada that night, images of Max flooded his mind. He reflected on pleasant experiences from the past; both of camaraderie during the war and of times afterwards. Before long, the oncoming headlights were blurred by tears.

"Why did it have to come to this?" he questioned. *"Why had Max taken a turn for the worse?"*

He thought about the life he had just ended, and contemplated possibilities of how it could have been handled differently. There was no escaping the fact that he had done what had to be done. Sam had acted in self-defense, and none of the others would have been safe as long as Max lived. Those men had been murdered by Max. He had purposefully taken the lives of those men from their families. They were all supposed to be buddies, sealed by the bond of wartime sacrifice and trust. There, he determined to find a way to honor the three men who were killed. Within several hours, he found himself exhausted. He was exhausted by the struggle, exhausted by the emotional tension, and exhausted by the lack of sleep. Using cash, he rented a room at a small motel. The next day, he didn't stop until he made it to the cabin in Missouri. Once there, he slept for hours. Afterwards, he spent the remainder of the vacation resting and fishing.

TWO WEEKS LATER, Sam called both Bill and Charles to tell them it was imperative that they visit him in Atlanta. When they arrived the following weekend, he invited them into his den and began to explain everything.

"I had to kill Max," he began.

Both Bill and Charles were stunned beyond belief, and very frightened. They were both white collar men with successful businesses, and each knew the physical strength of the man speaking to them. Each knew the powerful policeman had the capability to take them both, if he wished. They sat in silence.

"Max was in Korea when the South Korean businessman was killed," he continued. "I saw the records of him using his passport. He killed that man, and in cold blood he executed Louis and Tom. I know for a fact that he had something to do with Henry's accident."

"How do you know that he killed them?" Bill asked, in almost a whisper.

Sam said nothing. He moved to his gun safe, spun the dial several times, and opened the door. The two men seated in his den became exceptionally nervous. They looked at each other, in an effort to ascertain whether the other man was in on a set up by the policeman. Reaching in gun safe, Sam brought out the four bags of money.

"I found these in his locker," he replied. "Not to mention the fact that he pulled a gun on me after I told him that I was personally investigating the murders. Unzip those bags and take a look. One belonged to Max, and the others belonged to Henry, Louis, and Tom. I believe he killed the Korean business partner, but I would guess he hid that money in Korea."

The two each took a bag and examined the contents.

"Those bags in your hands are yours," Sam spoke. "The other two are mine. I took the risk in confronting Max, and I am very lucky to be alive. I think that should be fair enough, don't you?"

Bill and Charles agreed with the logic of the offer, and the conversation later moved to the subject of how the money should be spent. An agreement was reached before the two left Sam's company. The cash should be spent in small amounts on small items. They discussed the fact that periodically, new bills should be obtained to replace older bills. Spending several one hundred dollar's worth of old bills would be certain to call more attention than spending newer ones. They would take cash out of their personal bank accounts for vacations or expenditures, but each would use money from the bags instead. They would then replace the money used from the bags with money withdrawn from their accounts. Over time, the bills would be cycled and remain somewhat fresh.

Louis and Henry were both family men, leaving widows and children. Tom had been single. Of the money he kept, Sam filled each of three envelopes with ten thousand dollars. Over the next six months, he found ways to deposit two of the envelopes in places where the widows of Louis and Henry would find them. He left the third envelope in the mailbox of Tom's ailing mother. He found a great deal of joy in the gifts of cash.

FOR THE REMAINDER OF THE YEAR, Bill and Charles avoided Sam. They were somewhat afraid to be in contact with a man who was able to kill with such predetermination and ability, and they were afraid to be linked with him should the authorities connect him with the death of Max. They were also grateful to Sam. Both knew that if it hadn't been for him, they both would have been in danger of Max. They had no idea of how their avoidance of Sam impacted him, but Bill was ever mindful of what Sam had given them. He tried to imagine how Sam might feel. Bill considered that Sam probably struggled within himself, reconciling the fact that he had killed a man. He made sure that he placed a call to Sam at least once a month.

By 1961, they realized the chance of Sam being linked to Max's death by the authorities had diminished. During the mid-sixties, the three men grew close. They learned to trust one another completely and began to spend weekends going hunting or fishing. They actually spent less time hunting, as each kill in the woods reminded them of the deaths of old acquaintances. Nevertheless, they felt a need to stay in touch, so they used the excuse of hunting trips when addressing family and friends.

Eventually, the three men pooled some of their funds to purchase a cabin in the mountains of western Virginia. Year round, it was a pleasant escape for each man. Since it was atop a mountain and surrounded thickly by forest, it stayed fairly cool during the summer. Wildflowers were abundant in the spring, and the resident bird population often exploded in song during that season. In the fall, the hardwoods around the rustic building provided a spectacular show of color. A small fireplace provided the only heat during winter snows, but it provided sufficient comfort within a couple of hours after starting a fire. Although little hunting was done, they purchased a large gun safe and stocked the cabin with a few guns.

BY THE EARLY SEVENTIES, they made a decision which formed an even stronger bond between them. They decided to pool their money from the Korean gold, and each month they selected a worthy recipient of a ten-thousand-dollar donation. They pledged among themselves that all of the money would be used solely for that purpose until all of it was given away. A solemn vow was made to each other and to God. Standing facing each other in the cabin, they raised glasses of beer in honor of Tom, Louis, and Henry. A toast was made to each, and each toast consisted of considerable quantities of brew. A charitable practice had begun on a continual basis.

Soon afterwards, they made a list of worthy candidates for consideration. Each would make a selection from the list, so that recipients were selected for gifts covering the first three months. Bill selected John O'Reilly, a young Viet Nam veteran. He had been disfigured from wounds received in combat, and Bill wanted to provide money for plastic surgery. Veteran's benefits covered some of the cost for surgeries of physical need, but there was no coverage regarding cosmetic surgery. Mr. O'Reilly had been awarded the Purple Heart and sited for bravery. Due to the disfiguring of his face, he felt more like a freak rather than a hero. Anonymously, Bill contacted a plastic surgeon and told him of the situation. The surgeon agreed to do several surgeries for less than eight thousand dollars. With the packet of cash, Bill left a note of instruction regarding the contact information of the surgeon.

Charles selected a young law student, Donald Stewart. He was doing very well in school, but was having great difficulties paying for classes. Charles researched the matter and found him to be an honest young man working long hours to support himself and school. His grades were adequate, but not exceptional. Therefore, he had passed under the radar of most beneficiaries. Charles happened upon him while providing legal consultations to a Charlotte business. He met Donald on an elevator, and afterwards he often found himself mindful of the young fellow. He believed the gift was to be for him, for he felt God had placed Donald in his thoughts.

Sam chose Agape Ministries, a struggling New York mission attempting to help troubled young men. It concentrated on drug users and members of gangs and proved to have a phenomenal success rate. The ministry helped the young men form stronger character regarding work habits, and then placed them in jobs. The men spent two years in the program, reported weekly to the ministry for counseling, and had to attend spiritual services twice during each week. They were not spoken of as clients, but rather as students. Successful and stable upper-level students were termed "upper classmen", and they had responsibilities of checking on the lower level students almost daily.

Over time, all of the money was kept in the fireproof gun safe at the cabin. This allowed the cash to be accessed by all, at any time. The combined total was still worth almost five million dollars. At least every three months, they would meet at the cabin for a "hunting trip" to discuss worthy causes for the monthly ten-thousand-dollar cash gifts. In a sense, they were "hunting" for candidates. The money pulled from the gun safe for each donation was always placed in large envelopes. Everything was handled with gloves, as not to leave fingerprints.

Ten years into the practice, an agreement was made among the three. The last remaining partner would give it all away in ten-thousand-dollar allotments. This was to be done within the first three months of the cash falling into the hands of the last survivor. While more than one partner lived, there was a degree of accountability. Dispersing the last of the money quickly, would help ensure the agreement was kept by the last man. Sam's wife passed away several years before Charles died, and prior to her death Sam confided in her. He told her everything. Sam even told her about killing Max. He couldn't let her go with secrets kept from her. As he opened up this last private portion of his life to her, they both wept.

Upon her passing, Sam was chosen to be the man to make the "deposits" on behalf of the selected recipients. He had no one left to care for, and he was the most robust of the men. In confiding to his wife, Sam had done what Charles and Bill had desperately wanted to do for years. Each man had total trust in his wife, and shortly after the death of Sam's wife the other two shared with their wives the existence of the money. They confessed how the cash came about, and what they had chosen to do with it. Both wives were told of how Max murdered the old Army buddies, and of how Sam had saved them from the same fate by killing Max. They felt it right to be honest with the women who knew them so well.

By the time of Charles' death, the majority of the cash

had been given away. Much death was associated with the money. The deaths of North Korean soldiers during the war, the death of the South Korean businessman, and the deaths of fellow war buddies had dirtied the money. This cash had turned the heart and mind of one who had been trusted; so much, that he murdered three of their own. Even with the good that was being now being done with the cash, it was tainted with murder. It had become blood money. None of the three felt good about passing the cash on to children, and they knew of no one outside of family who could be trusted. Their children, and those on the outside, should never be told. They determined that the knowledge of the money would die with the last man or spouse. The years passed, and events would cause this decision to be reconsidered.

Chapter 11

IT RAINED SATURDAY AFTERNOON in Charlotte, and the sound of a knock on the door interrupted Larry's napping on the couch. He sat up for a moment, his head still in the hazy state of being between the world of dreams and the realm of the awake. Another set of knocks at the door helped clear his mind. Slowly, he made his way across the room and opened the door. Standing on the front porch was an elderly man he had not seen for some time.

"It's damp, and I'm a little chilled," Bill Thompson complained. "Can I come in?"

"I'm sorry, of course," Larry replied, as he opened the door more fully.

Bill stepped inside and removed his overcoat. As Larry reached out to take it, the owner of the coat explained.

"I won't be here long, so there is no need to put it in a closet. I just didn't want to sit on your furniture with a wet overcoat."

With those instructions, Larry simply hung the coat on a set of hooks mounted beside the front door. He invited Bill to take a seat on the couch, and asked if he would like a cup of coffee.

After pouring a cup for each of them, he finally asked,

"What brings you around? Are you OK?"

I've been better, but I'm doing alright," Bill answered. "However, Sam had a stroke. I've been visiting him in Atlanta."

The older man stopped for a moment and glanced down at the floor. As memories of his friend, and current events cycled through Bill's mind, Larry took note of how frail he had become. After a few seconds the visitor raised his head. Looking intently into Larry's eyes, he continued.

"He has a lot of trouble speaking, but he made it clear that he wanted you to know about his condition. My health is not very good, and there are very few people for whom I would travel. Sam would be at the top of my list. Apart from my wife, there is no one I trust more. At his request, I flew directly from Atlanta to see you."

Larry had not spoken with the retired policeman since the time of Sam's unexpected visit to his apartment. Still, the bond that was fixed between them that day held firm. He thought of him often and remained thankful for the visit.

"You probably might not understand it, but I am not surprised that he asked you to contact me," Larry replied. "I can't really explain it to anyone else, but I have great respect for Sam. I...."

Larry paused, not knowing exactly how to put his emotions and thoughts into words. The silence was short lived, as Bill continued.

"I understand probably better than you know. Sam told me of his visit with you, and of your conversation. He asked me to make a request of you. I've had my doubts, but he trusts you. Trust does not come easy with Sam, and I respect his judgment. For that reason, I am confident that I can trust you as well. You should seriously think about what I am about to ask before answering."

"Mr. Thompson, what does he want?" Larry asked.

"Sam, Charles, and I had a practice of making anonymous monetary donations to deserving individuals, as you probably know," Bill began. "Ryan's friend, Layla, was a recipient. Since Charles' death, Sam took sole responsibility of delivering the envelopes of cash. Although his mind is still sharp enough to make decisions regarding the candidates for our donations, he's now physically unable to deliver our packages. Charles is gone. My wife is not well enough to be left very often for long periods of time, and I'm not so sure that I am strong enough to travel often outside the Boston area. Sam and I don't believe candidates should be limited to the immediate Boston area."

"So, you want me to deliver the money to the people you select?" Larry questioned. "I could…"

Bill quickly interrupted him.

"Don't commit yourself so soon. There is more to it than that."

"OK, go on," Larry cautiously stated.

"Are you sure you want to know?" Bill asked. "The knowledge I am prepared to share could pose legal issues for you."

Surprised somewhat, Larry agreed to listen. However, Bill was in no hurry to leave the information with only Larry.

"I want you and Ryan to visit me at my home," Bill requested. "Sam wanted me to personally contact you, but I want to include Ryan in this conversation. I believe this is too serious a commitment for you to bear alone. Sam and I found the need for multiple person accountability, a long time ago. Here's my phone number and address. Will you contact your friend? Warn him that there may be serious consequences from having this knowledge and participating in our gift giving."

With that, Bill slowly departed for the airport. As he flew home, he felt comfortable with the limited success of the visit. Though a final commitment had not yet been obtained from Larry, he knew his time of handling the money was coming to an end. He felt relieved.

DURING THE MEMORABLE VISIT with Larry, Sam had seen a unique quality in the younger man that only comes from suffering and a sense of humbling guilt. Sam carried a similar burden, and he knew it well. Though he saved the rest of the group from a killer, the blood of Max's death was always felt in his hands and heart. Late at night, when tired from the work of the day, his killing of Max would often replay in his mind. He would second guess himself and wonder if there could have been another way of handling the problem. Though he always came to the same conclusion, the question would repeatedly arise from time to time. He saw the same suffering and guilt in Larry. The purpose of that visit was to help relieve the younger man of this burden,

There was a bond of unexplainable trust between Sam and the younger man. Evil had attempted to capture Larry's heart and mind after he killed Keith, by false accusations that he was no better than his cruel and brutal father. Guilt had cast a line in an attempt to reel in a soul, for guilt loves nothing more than despair and loss of self-worth. It was as if the hook had penetrated Larry's soul. Through prayer and the friendship of charitable friends Larry was able to cut the line. However, in a spiritual sense, the barb was imbedded, and the hook was left hanging. Sam knew that Larry would find the task of delivering the donations to be a means to relieve his inner wounds. The most powerful way to reclaim self-worth is to realize God's love and view of our worth. The Creator of the universe would not have given up His Son to abuse and death on the cross for our sake, without counting us worthy of that sacrifice. The second most powerful method is to spend effort participating in a worthy activity which benefits others. Simply put, selfless actions for a worthy cause promote a sense of self-worth.

Upon finally arriving home, Bill shared with his wife the aspects of his meeting with Larry. Outside of her husband, she had no greater respect for any individual than for Sam. She also felt relief that the effort of making donations might soon pass to others, and she looked forward to the meeting with the younger men.

Immediately after Bill Thompson's visit, Larry contacted Ryan to tell him all he had learned and of the request being made of them. Prior to meeting with Bill to formally obtain the details, they tentatively agreed between themselves to help in the effort. Having seen the positive impact on Layla's life, Ryan felt the risk was worth taking. Larry had grown up somewhat poor and could easily see the benefit to those on the receiving end of the gifts. However, it was his relationship with Sam that gave him the real motivation to make the commitment. Each man spent time in prayer before making the visit, and they believed it to be the right thing to do. However, they were not yet aware of all the legal risks.

TWO WEEKS PASSED before Larry and Ryan were able to visit Bill and his wife. Mary greeted them with a warm smile, but Ryan felt her eyes as she scanned them during her initial evaluation of the two. Once they were seated, their host wasted no time in explaining the facts. Bill shared with them the source of the money, how it was found, and how it had been transferred to the United States. He didn't tell them of how the others met their fate; he simply told them that they were dead. The only living souls with credible knowledge of the story were himself, his wife, and Sam. Charles' wife, Beverly, would sometimes recall bits of the facts. However, her mental state had deteriorated to the point where very few seriously listened to her ramblings. The two younger men listened intently as Bill explained how the system of selection worked. Bill and Sam would continue to make the selections of those receiving the donations, and Ryan and Larry were only needed to physically deliver the packages. Before asking for the verbal commitment from each, Bill stressed the fact that they would be taking risk.

"This effort does great good for deserving people, but you must realize that you'll be becoming part of something that is basically outside the law," Bill firmly stated. "The government doesn't know about this money, and certainly does not know how it was obtained. Its discovery would certainly place you in legal jeopardy and could cause international consequences for the United States government."

After hearing what Bill had to say, they took little time before promising to make the deliveries. Both younger men believed the good outweighed the risk and felt a spiritual peace concerning their relationship with God. Once the promises were made, Bill told them about the location of the money.

"I want to emphasize the importance of leaving the bulk of the money in the safe at the cabin and removing only the amount to be given for each donation of ten thousand dollars," he began. "This will require monthly drives to the cabin in Virginia. I keep very accurate accounts of the money left in the safe, and Sam and I traveled to the cabin twice a year to take inventory and to confirm the total. My figures show that one million two hundred and eighty thousand dollars remain in the safe."

Ryan was speechless, but Larry's financial mind almost immediately calculated what this meant.

"Good Lord!" Larry gasped. "I had no idea so much would be left after all these years. It would take… it would take over ten years to finish giving this all away, at the rate and amounts the donations have been made!"

"I wanted a firm commitment from you before revealing those details to you," Bill explained. "Does the amount or the required length of commitment cause you serious concern? Have you changed your mind?"

"No, there is no change in my commitment," Ryan firmly stated. Looking over to Larry, he waited for his answer.

"I'm in also," Larry replied. "I have no intention of going back on my word. I was just surprised, that's all."

The bond between Larry and Sam was strong; and his commitment to the effort was just as firm.

"I'll be just a moment," the older man stated.

Bill rose from his chair and slowly made his way to a desk in the study. During her husband's conversation with Larry and Ryan, Bill's wife had remained silent. Now that she was alone with the two younger men, she issued a warning.

"It is very important that you both remain honest with each other and make sure this continues to be a joint effort. This amount of money can cause negative changes even in the best of people. The money can be viewed as personal power, or a burden of personal responsibility. The capacity for temptation can be extremely great, and mutual accountability will help you ward off some of the evil influence this kind of money tends to bring. Sam trusts you, and so does my husband. It is the judgment of those two great men that allows me to do the same."

Her eyes were filled with reverence for Bill and Sam, yet the younger men sensed a particular sadness in her words. Within a couple of minutes Bill returned with a small briefcase. He placed it on the coffee table that was located between him and the younger men. Opening the case, he pulled a key from one of the inner compartments. An old thin leather strap had been looped through the hole in the key and tied at the ends. Years of handling had caused the leather to be darkened by the oil and sweat transferred to it from palms of men.

"This is the key to the cabin," he softly spoke. "It will open both the front and rear doors."

Bill returned it to its proper place in the case and pulled out a current map of Virginia. Slowly he unfolded it, and then refolded it to display the main roads leading to the cabin. He placed it beside the case on the coffee table and reached back inside for a yellowed sheet of paper.

"You can see the general location of the cabin on this map, but the smaller gravel roads are not shown," he explained. "This hand drawn map can be followed to bring you to the exact location of the place. It's not to scale, but you can see that mileage indications have been written for stretches of road between the specified landmarks. I suggest you make a special trip to the cabin prior to the first delivery, to make sure you can easily find it. The timing of a delivery can be crucial. You must make sure you are not seen by the person or other individuals. You should take the proper time to ensure this. It would be better to call off the drop and reschedule it for another time, than to risk being seen. Do you understand?"

Larry and Ryan both voiced their understanding. At last Bill produced two manila envelopes containing information regarding each of the next two recipients of the money. He explained the need for the person making the delivery to study the information well and be keenly aware of details. This would reduce the risk of being seen and would give them understanding of the worthiness of the cause.

"After making each delivery, you are to write down the time and date of the event and note any unusual observations," Bill explained. "Place this in a marked envelope, and then put that in the safe at the cabin. There is a second briefcase for that purpose, and it is kept on the bottom shelf. We often monitor the persons receiving the donation for three months afterwards. When you are satisfied that the gift resulted in no adverse side effects, the information must be totally destroyed. I suggest the pages be removed from the envelopes and burned in the cabin's fireplace. Make sure gloves are worn when handling the money and the envelopes in which the money is placed. Use plain common envelopes for that effort and leave no trace that can be used to track the gift's origin or participants. Any letter of explanation left with the donation should be typed, rather than handwritten, even when gloves are used. You should leave no indication for handwriting analysis, should the letters be turned over to the police or the government. Are there any questions?"

Neither Larry nor Ryan had questions, but they promised to call if questions came to mind later. Although both seemed sincere in their commitment, Bill could easily see that both were tense and uneasy. He decided to help with the initial undertaking.

"I have a question for you," Bill said. "Which of you will be making the first delivery?"

"I will," Larry responded.

After placing all the contents back into the briefcase, he handed it to Larry.

"I am placing this in your care, but I would suggest that you accompany each other for a while until you become more accustomed to the task," Bill offered.

The older man gave each a firm handshake and a smile, but it was the actions of Bill's wife that gave them comfort. She slowly struggled to her feet and gave each one a loving hug and a kiss. She then took a hand of theirs into hers and began to pray.

"Lord God, please be with each of these young men. We send them out to accomplish good in Your name, and we ask for Your guidance. Place Your protective hand on each and cause them to know that You are with them. Grant them the peace that passes understanding and give them strength and wisdom inspired by Your Holy Spirit."

Both immediately felt at ease, as she sent them out to shoulder these new responsibilities. It was a lot like a mother comforting a young boy before sending him to school for the first time. As they drove away, apprehensiveness was replaced with a sense of adventure and excitement. They had become a part of a secret mission for good and would be involved in a slightly illegal service in the name of God.

They talked of those smuggling Bibles behind the Iron Curtain prior to the fall of Communism in the Soviet Union, and they sensed a connection.

"I believe there are certain times when it seems God accepts illegal activity into His work," Ryan said. "For the most part, Jesus instructed His followers to abide by the laws of man."

They discussed the Bible verse Matthew 22:21.

"Render unto Caesar the things which are Caesar's, and unto God the things that are God's."

They talked about Daniel's placement in the lion's den after choosing to disobey the pagan laws of the land rather than refrain from doing what he believed God wanted. Although both knew what they were doing was not as clearly ordained by God as the situation in which Daniel found himself, they were convinced they would be able to do good with the illegally obtained funds. This would not be the last time they would find cause to examine and evaluate the spiritual merit of this activity.

THE FOLLOWING WEEK, Larry paid Sam a visit in the nursing home. This once powerful man was restrained in a large chair, as to protect him from taking a spill. Due to the stroke, the left side of his face drooped with paralysis. His once muscular left arm was now motionless, and it lifelessly lay across his lap. Though the left side of Sam's face showed no response, Larry recognized a sparkle in the older man's eyes. Sam was more than pleased at the visit. He quickly put out his right hand to take Larry's. His speech slowed and slurred; he welcomed him.

"So good to see you, son."

Without going into details, Larry pledged to not let Sam down in the matter of being charitable. Little was said on the matter, but all was communicated and understood. The remainder of the visit was spent by Larry sharing with

Sam the other aspects of his life. Before leaving, the younger man promised regular visits.

IT WAS ON A COOL AND CRISP FALL DAY when Ryan and Larry first arrived at the cabin in Virginia. The leaves were brilliant in color, and the sky shown bold blue in the absence of polluted city air. The surrounding hardwoods gave an unforgettable earthy fragrance to the afternoon's slight breeze, and the only sound was that of rustling leaves in the trees. As he ascended the steps, Larry noticed a stack of aged firewood at the end of the front porch. He stood for a moment, soaking in the peaceful setting, as Ryan moved past him to the cabin door. The key smoothly slid into the lock on the door, but he had to jiggle it a bit before allowing entrance into the rustic building.

This was an older one room cabin, built in the late forties and remodeled during the following decade. On the left front wall were two sets of bunk beds, accommodating the overnight stay of four. The floor consisted of oak planking, except for the right rear corner where ceramic tile had been laid over the oak flooring. In this corner, the building had been equipped with running water. A bathtub sat against the wall, with only a hanging curtain to provide privacy. To the left of the tub was counter space with a sink and a stove to allow for kitchen activities. In the left rear corner, between the bunks and stove, was an old wooden table and four wooden chairs. A couch and two chairs were placed in front of the tub area, facing the fireplace situated on the front wall. Both men quietly inspected the arrangements, and immediately came to the same conclusion.

"OK, there must be a small facility out back," Ryan stated.

With that, they both turned and made a hasty run down the steps and around to the rear of the cabin. In somewhat disrepair, a wood framed outhouse stood directly behind the cabin. The door hung open and slightly down, as loosened top hinges allowed the bottom of the door to rest on the ground.

"I can fix that," Larry assured his friend.

"Well, I don't plan to spend a great deal of time in there," Ryan replied.

Larry was already standing on the outside of the outhouse, looking in and examining the interior of the facility.

"Got to get rid of the spiders before doing any serious business in there," he concluded.

"I was a Boy Scout," Ryan stated. "I'll take my chances behind a tree, thank you,"

The two returned to the interior of the cabin to look for the object of most importance. There in the front right corner was a large and sturdy gun safe.

"Turn on a light," Larry requested.

Hanging from the ceiling of the cabin were four wires suspending simple unadorned light bulb fixtures from each. Each fixture was operated by a pull chain. Pulling the chain of the fixture nearest the safe, Ryan was surprised to see that the light worked. The gun cabinet was secured by a substantial pad lock. As soon as the light provided its yellow glow, Larry was ready with the second key. The lock opened easily and was removed and placed on the floor beside the safe.

"Are you ready?" asked Larry.

"Go for it," Ryan replied.

Larry slowly swung open the heavy steel doors, revealing a sight each had only seen in the movies. To the left were two high powered rifles with boxes of ammunition. However, the remainder of the cabinet had been fitted with wooden shelving. All but two shelves supported stacks upon stacks of money, in the form of one-hundred-dollar bills. Resting upon the second from the bottom shelf, were stacks of both legal and large envelopes and a box of latex gloves. A briefcase was positioned on the bottom shelf.

"Don't touch any of that money, without first putting on gloves," Ryan reminded his friend.

"Those guys brought back a fortune from the Korean War," Larry said. "Originally, there must have been at least five times the amount still on hand in the cabinet; and in those days it would have been worth much more than today. I would guess we're talking probably around seven million dollars in the 1950's."

Each stretched a pair of latex gloves over their hands and began the work they had been set to do. Still somewhat stunned, they placed $10,000 in each of the two envelopes given to them by Bill. They placed the filled envelopes in the briefcase and dropped in a couple of pairs of latex gloves for future handling. They agreed to have Ryan keep the briefcase at his place for the first drop, and that Larry should keep it with him for the second delivery.

Though the cabin contained bunk beds, the two decided to place sleeping bags on top of the bedding instead of using the sheets and blankets found in trunks stationed at the end of each set of bunk beds. Ryan brought sandwich meat, cheese, and soft drinks in a cooler. He also had bread, chips, and paper plates in a bag. As they sat at the table eating and talking over the events of the day, they planned for the following day. Upon first arriving at the cabin, they noted they had weak cell phone coverage. Due to this, and the fact that the cabin had no phone, they would wait to call Bill during on their return trip on the following day. The two decided against starting a fire in the fireplace, as they felt they should obtain permission from the cabin owners prior to using the firewood on the front porch. They also were uncertain as to the condition of the chimney. Soon, their eyes became heavy. Larry turned out the lights and both men slipped into their respective sleeping bags. The silence was almost deafening, as they lay without speaking. The still night air offered not even the sounds of rustling tree leaves.

The morning brought a noticeable chill in the air, and both men voiced regret over not making a fire during the previous night. After making sure the cabin was secure, they wasted no time in departing with the briefcase and everything else brought with them. Once in a stronger cell phone range, and before stopping for breakfast, Larry called Bill to let him know how things were going. The older man instructed them to keep the key and to call him again after making the second delivery. The drive home seemed short, as conversation was rich concerning the adventure they were beginning.

Chapter 12

TWO WEEKS LATER, Ryan and Larry met at a hotel in Charleston, West Virginia. Forty miles away was the hometown of the recipient of the first package. Kathy Harris was the widow of a local firefighter, who had lost his life five years previous while saving a family in an apartment complex fire. He had gone back in for the family dog, and never made it back out. She had two children, a boy 10 and a daughter 8. Immediately after the loss, the small town had raised a minimal amount of money to initially help the family. However, that money had long been spent and Kathy was now financially living on the edge.

"How in the world did Bill hear about this woman and her kids?" Larry asked his friend. "I mean, this is really a rural area."

"I have no clue," Ryan responded. "I guess he's a pretty good listener. He found out about Layla when I visited his Sunday school class, and he seemed to have no trouble finding her. Sam's experience in law enforcement probably helped, but I have no idea how he found out about this woman."

As they drove passed her home, they spotted the two children playing in the front yard. By this time of the year, the weather had become somewhat cold in West Virginia. It was apparent that the coats worn by the children had been purchased the previous year, as the sleeves on both children failed to cover their wrists. They decided they would have to return later, hoping the kids would be back inside. No such luck occurred, for on each pass the children were still in the yard. Finally, they decided they would have to park the car in a safe place and walk to the wooded area across the road from the home. The two determined to wait in the woods for the kids to go inside the home. They then could take the opportunity to place the envelope on the front seat of the car.

The town had a small park near Kathy's home, which offered a small parking lot. After parking the car, they walked about a half mile to the wooded area across from her house. They were careful to enter the woods from a side road, as to not allow the children to see them. It was decided that Ryan would deposit the donation, so the envelope had been safely placed inside his coat. Though they each had ample winter coats, they began to become uncomfortable as the temperature quickly dropped.

Eventually, they heard Kathy call the children inside. Ryan was about to make his move for the car, when he was stopped by the sight of the mail truck coming down the road. The mail was delivered to Kathy's mailbox, which was stationed on the edge of the road. He compared the relative short distance to the mailbox, against that of the car in the driveway. Ryan became uneasy; for he knew she could come out to collect the mail at any time. He decided it would be safer to place the package in the mailbox, rather than try to make it to the car and back to the woods. But he still had no idea as to when she would check the mail. Within a couple of minutes, his fear turned to perfect calm. He sensed this to be the right time. As he slipped on his gloves, Larry questioned him.

"Are you sure you want to do this right now?"

"I'm going," Ryan replied.

He stepped out of the woods, removing the envelope

from inside his coat as he walked. He quickly opened the mailbox and slid the envelope inside. Though she had a large mailbox, the package barely fit. As he entered the woods again, he heard Larry whisper.

"Man, I thought you would be caught for sure."

As they quietly discussed the success of the mission, they saw the front door open. Kathy was quickly making her way to collect the mail.

"Stay still," Larry advised. "Don't move, and don't make a sound."

Both men froze. Kathy pulled the envelope out of the mailbox, and then collected the few smaller pieces of mail. Sliding the smaller envelopes into her coat pocket, she examined the larger package. There was no address written on it, only a typed note that stated, *"For Kathy Harris – use it well"*

Ryan and Larry remained motionless, taking shallow breaths, hoping not to be seen within the trees. Kathy looked down the street in both directions, curious as to who could have placed the package in her mailbox. It was obvious it had not been delivered by the mail carrier, for it contained no address, stamp or post mark. Knowing the mail had been delivered only within the last few minutes, the deliverer of the package could not have gotten far. She had heard no vehicle traveling down her street since she had heard the engine of the mail truck, so she doubted anyone had left by car. Slowly, she opened the package. Gingerly spreading the sides of the package apart, she caught her first glimpse of its contents. She took a quick glance down both ends of the street again and slipped her right hand into the large envelope. Stunned at what she brought out, she accidentally dropped the package containing the rest of the cash onto the street. She quickly picked it up and shoved the discovered cash back inside the envelope with the rest of the money. She placed her hand over her mouth and closed her eyes in disbelief. Kathy stood by the side of the mailbox for several seconds, and then quickly made her way back inside her home.

Once the door of the house was shut, the two men caught the grin on the face of the other. Quietly and slowly, they traveled through the woods in the opposite direction from Kathy's house. After exiting the trees, a block away, they quickly walked several blocks out of their way before making it back to the car. Neither said a word until they were well out of the small town. Ryan eventually let out a whoop, and Larry offered a high-five. Over the next hour they relived the experience over and over.

Throughout the next several days, the two called each other and eagerly discussed the next drop. Two days before meeting to make the next delivery, Ryan received a call from Bill's wife. She informed him that her husband's cancer was in the late stages of development and that he was not expected to live out the month. Ryan called Larry immediately to let him know of the situation. Both agreed that Layla and Patsy should be told. Ryan was sure that Layla would want to attend the funeral. She was extremely grateful for the money Bill had sent her way. The gift had been a turning point in her life. The two men considered telling Layla and Patsy about the money, but they decided not to bring them into the precarious situation. This was a new effort for them, and they were not yet entirely comfortable with the responsibility and the risk. Ryan called Layla and Patsy to let them know of Bill's impending death, and he offered to pick them up on the way from Charlotte to Boston. Both women felt strongly about attending the funeral.

Earlier in the day, from the hospital, Bill's wife had mailed a large envelope to Ryan containing the list of the next two recipients of cash. Mary had full access to her husband's documentation regarding candidate recipients. She was careful to include maps to both locations and a synopsis of each person's basis of selection. In the letter, she expressed her and Bill's appreciation for both men and of their faith in the younger men's commitment. No longer was Bill able to play an active role in the endeavor. Full responsibility was being turned over to them. The large envelope also contained a smaller one. After thoroughly reading the other material, Ryan opened the smaller envelope. It contained the notarized deed to the cabin and the 200 acres of Virginia property surrounding the small building. All was now placed in the legal names of both Ryan and Larry. A note explained the agreement between Bill and Sam of this transfer of property and advised that the utilities for the property should be placed in one of their names. The legal transfer had been arranged a few months earlier, while Bill was still able to travel. He and Sam agreed to wait until after Larry and Ryan had shown success in carrying out the first delivery before physically handing over the deed to the men.

Ryan first called Larry to share the news, and then called Bill's wife to let her know he had received the deed and the list. He pledged to her his intent to finish the effort of delivering the remaining cash to deserving individuals, and he thanked her for Bill's trust in both Larry and himself. Ryan asked that she contact him if her husband passed away, and she assured him that she would do so. Her voice quivered at the thought of her expected loss, but Ryan also sensed relief that the weight of the charity work had passed from her husband's shoulders.

THE CALL CAME eight days after the next delivery of money. Before traveling to Boston to attend Bill's funeral, Ryan and Larry visited Sam in Atlanta. Though Sam had expected the news, he couldn't contain his grief. His eyes overflowed, and tears ran freely down both cheeks. Due to a series of other small strokes, he was now unable to speak. This once physically powerful man had lost his last old friend and had become physically crippled. He motioned for a pad and pencil, which lay on the nightstand. Larry held the pad steady, as Sam slowly and painfully wrote instructions.

"Take keys out of nightstand. Go to house at 211 Boulevard South. Top right desk drawer in living room. Take envelope. Trust you to handle."

Larry took the old man's right hand in his, and with a firm squeeze he assured him that he would personally handle the situation. Sam's breathing calmed, and right side of his face partially formed a faint smile. This unexplainable bond between the two was solid, and Larry felt almost a reverence for the older man. He had never felt anything similar to this, even for his father. Perhaps, when he was very young there had been forgotten respect and love for his dad, but those days had long passed. A lifetime of cruelty by his father had squeezed those feelings completely out of him.

Before leaving Atlanta, Larry and Ryan made their way to 211 Boulevard South. Except for a few overgrown bushes, it was a well-kept wood frame home. Once in the living room, the desk was plainly in sight. It was small and was plainly built. It probably would have been the last piece of furniture to be noticed, if it had not been the object of importance noted by Sam. A small reading lamp rested on the desk. Searching the key ring given to him by the suffering old policeman, Larry spotted a key which seemed to be made for the old desk. He was correct in his assessment, for the key easily slid into the lock and turned. With the desk unlocked, Larry pulled open the top right drawer. The envelope was in plain sight, as it was only accompanied by two wooden pencils and a small magnifying glass. Upon the yellowed old envelope was written an unfamiliar name, *"Park Min Yon"*.

The envelope was not sealed. After glancing at Ryan, Larry proceeded to remove the contents. There were two typed documents. The first was a notarized legal will and testament. The first paragraph specified instructions to transfer the entire holdings of a South Korean bank account to another South Korean account owned by Cunningham Min Yon. Both account numbers were given. It went on to say that if the account no longer existed, the money would go to Cunningham Min Yon in any fashion that she desired. If she was no longer living, the entire account holdings would go to her eldest son.

"Why don't the names match?" Ryan asked. "Why would the outside of the envelope show the name *Park*, and the letter inside state *Cunningham*?"

"How should I know?" Larry responded. "This Min Yon sounds like a female name, and she apparently lives in South Korea. Bill told us the money originated there."

"What's the other document?" Ryan questioned.

The other article was an official document written in both English and Korean from a South Korean bank, detailing aspects of an account owned by Sam Wells. Folded neatly within the document, was a handwritten note specifying other instructions. Annually, on the second Monday in January, $10,000 is to be transferred to the account owned by Cunningham Min Yon until the account of Sam Wells is exhausted. The account numbers matched those in the first document. A newer slip of paper detailed how the transfer of money could be made online using a personal computer.

"These old guys are giving away money all over the world!" Ryan exclaimed.

"Sam never said anything about this stuff," replied Larry.

"I wonder how many accounts he has," said Ryan. "He must be filthy rich."

"It's not my business," Larry responded. "I promised Sam I would handle this, and that is exactly what I intend to do."

"Hey! I'm not arguing," Ryan continued. "But aren't you a bit surprised at this second stash of money? This account in Korea must have been a huge one, to be able to give away $10,000 a year for over half a century. Good grief!"

"On the way out of town, I want to stop and see Sam again," Larry firmly stated. "He looks bad, and I don't know how much longer he'll be around. I just want to let him know that we found everything, and I want to ask him if he has specific requests for handling this."

"I'm not going to ask him, but I wouldn't mind an explanation," replied Ryan. "Don't worry, I'm not going to ask."

Upon returning to the nursing home, Larry provided Sam assurance they had found what they were sent to find. He again promised to take care of the situation, and asked Sam if there were any specific instructions in carrying out this second charitable mission. Slowly and purposefully, Sam sketched out fragments of sentences to convey his wishes. Taking a deep breath, the old man slowly wrote the following on the pad.

"Min Yon is Max's first wife – left her in Korea – they had son – Max planned to send money until boy reached 21 – Max dead - I continued spending – don't stop till account exhausted."

Just before Larry turned to leave, the old man reached out with his right hand and took hold of the younger man's wrist. With the eye contact made, Larry understood the deep appreciation Sam had for him in taking on this duty. Nothing needed to be said verbally, for this communication surpassed anything words could state.

WHAT SAM DIDN'T TELL THEM, was that Park Min Yon had been special to him. As the two younger men departed the room, Sam thought back to an eighteen-year-old Korean girl he met during the war. Moisture filed his eyes as thoughts of the past filled his mind. Those events seemed as vivid that day, as they had occurred more than a half century before. The closing of his eye lids forced tears to overflow and spill down his cheek. The reality of the quiet and lonely nursing home room was replaced by memories of a time long ago, and of Min Yon.

During the Korean War, she worked in her father's restaurant in Seoul. She was only eighteen when she first caught Sam's eye, while cleaning tables and carrying used plates to the back for washing. The Army had given soldiers implicit warnings regarding eating at Korean establishments, due to the high likelihood of dysentery. Sam saw her through the window of the restaurant as he passed by on the street and decided to ignore the warning. Actually, it wasn't really a conscious decision. It was if he was on autopilot as he opened the door and was seated at a table. He didn't even remember the warnings until he was halfway through the meal, and he was extremely relieved to find that no abdominal issues were suffered after eating there. Every chance he had, he would visit the restaurant; each time, he managed to catch a glance from her. Though nothing was said, he eventually was greeted by a silent smile from her on a regular basis.

His regularity of dining there was noticed by her father, and eventually the older man came to his table to make sure the service pleased this persistent customer. This personal attention was a good business practice. Over time, Sam learned that Min Yon was the owner's daughter. Mr. Park, the owner, quickly noticed Sam's interest in his daughter. He began to allow her to take Sam's order, although she understood very little English. Sam would point to an item on the menu and try to pronounce the name of the dish. Min Yon found his feeble attempts funny. Initially, she contained her amusement. She enjoyed taking orders much more than the cleanup work, and she wanted no part in offending one of her father's regulars. Before long, she was able to read in Sam's manner the affection he held for her. Min Yon began to loosen up, and eventually the terrible pronunciations caused smiles to spread across her face. Her eyes danced with amusement, and Sam often became the highlight of an otherwise long and exhausting day. Day by day, Sam taught her more words in English, and she began to communicate with short, chopped sentences.

After finding the gold, the men holding that secret spent a great deal of time together. Whether it was due to this newfound camaraderie, or the fact that they initially lacked complete trust in each other, they were often found together. It was Sam's idea that they visit Mr. Park's restaurant, and he went to great lengths to assure the other men that the food was safe to eat. It was on that occasion that Max learned that Min Yon was the owner's daughter. Sam's affection grew for Yon Min, but so did Max's awareness of a business opportunity. Sam was a natural leader among men, but he was not as comfortable with women. Max had no hesitation in taking advantage of any situation. Within a month after meeting Min Yon, Max made friends with her father in hopes of getting in on his profitable business. He realized that he had to be part of the family in order to become part owner, so he eventually gained a commitment from Mr. Park to allow him to marry his daughter. Sam loved her, but he had been slow to act.

Shortly after the marriage of Max and Min Yon, she became pregnant. After the son was born, Mr. Park made it clear to Max that the family business would be passed down to Min Yon's oldest brother. When the cease fire was signed for the Korean War, Max was sent back to the United States. He left his wife and son, with a promise to send for them later. Each month, he sent her money from his Korean account to hers. However, he never made good on his promise to bring them to the States. Eventually, the transfer of money became an annual event and the letters to her ceased. For two years she continued to write Max, but the letters were not answered. Max only intended to send the money until his son reached the age of twenty-one. His interest in Min Yon was based only on the hopes of business, but he felt compelled to help fund the raising of his son.

Sam didn't know of the money sent to Korea until the night he killed Max. He expected to find the keys to the safe deposit boxes in the desk drawer that night, but he had not counted on seeing the envelope marked with Park Min Yon's name. He reviewed the contents and found the records of transfer from one account to the other. The envelope contained a black and white photo of Min Yon and her baby. As Sam held it, his hands began to shake. He had just killed the husband of a woman he had once loved, and he had just removed all chances of a son ever knowing his father. The envelope contained the legal documentation and identification concerning the accounts. He realized that he had all the information needed for him to continue the transactions. She never had to know, and he could make sure all the money in the account became hers.

Over time he learned the address of Min Yon, and later that year he went to South Korea to see her. For two days he watched her in secret. Sam witnessed her leave and re-enter her home. From a distance, he followed her to the old restaurant. Her father had passed away, and the place was now in the hands of her oldest brother. As he took note of her familiar mannerisms and the way she carried herself, his heart was warmed. Though she was now older, the inner pain of being forsaken by her husband and the outer shame visited upon her by family and associates had not taken away her unique ways from her. She openly showed love to her son, whom Sam had not seen since he was an infant. The boy seemed remarkably well adjusted, and Sam attributed that to this gracious mother. He had no intent of talking with her, or even letting her know of Max's death. He just wanted to see her. Sam watched her and her son from a distance on several occasions before returning to the States. He just wanted to see if she and the boy were all right.

Upon returning home, Sam was more determined than ever to make sure that every dime of the account be sent to Max's widow over time. He would move the money exactly as it had been during years past. Sam had earlier sent a change of address to the Korean bank, so that information would be mailed to a post office box in Atlanta. In the beginning, he had to take great care in forging the dead man's signature in order to make the transaction. In the last years, he was able to transfer the money electronically over the internet. He believed that if the amount remained constant, it would be questioned by no one.

EN ROUTE TO BOSTON, Ryan and Larry picked up Layla and Patsy. Unable to make the entire trip in one day, they stopped at a roadside motel to catch some rest before continuing the next day. The women and men stayed in separate rooms, but the guys visited Layla and Patsy in their room until 1:00 AM. They talked about a multitude of subjects that came to mind. Layla could tell that Ryan was not entirely himself.

"Is there something wrong?" she quietly asked, not allowing Patsy and Larry to hear the question.

"I've got a lot on my mind, but everything is OK," he responded. "Bill is gone, and Sam probably won't be far behind him."

"Is Sam that bad off?" she asked. "I know he is in a nursing home, but I didn't know it was serious."

This time, the discussion between the two was heard by Larry and Patsy. The conversation shifted to Sam's health, and then to Bill's widow. By the time the men left to return to their room, the conversation had become serious and solemn. The excitement of the day had worn down, and everyone began to feel the weight of the long journey. Exhausted, all four fell asleep within half an hour of locking the doors to the rooms.

As Ryan drove the next day, he felt Layla's eyes. She scanned him periodically, sensing that he was holding something back. In the back seat, Larry tried to keep the conversation focused on work and Sam. Larry was never one to play games, and the more he talked the more obvious it was to both women that something was up.

At Bill's funeral, Ryan discreetly assured his widow that they felt honored to have known Bill, and that he was an inspiration to them. Without directly stating so, he communicated their commitment to the charitable effort.

"Mrs. Thompson, Larry and I hope to live our lives as courageously and charitably as your husband lived his," Ryan solemnly spoke.

Though her physical health was deteriorating at a hastened pace, her mental acuity was still intact. Her slight smile and wink told him she understood perfectly. They watched as her children helped her into a car. As the car pulled away, she made eye contact with Larry through the window of the vehicle. This look was that of a stern mother when conveying an unspoken message to a child. She expected them to continue to exercise wisdom and discretion in carrying on the risky matter. A very strong woman lived within that frail body. She had just buried the love of her life, but she was determined that his charitable venture continue until it ran its intended course.

That look given to Larry was picked up by Patsy, as women are generally far more sensitive to unspoken communication than men. As soon as the four were seated in Ryan's car for the trip home, she laid into Larry.

"I want to know what is going on," she pressed.

He immediately recognized the tone in her voice. Larry had heard a similar frankness in his mother's voice many times while growing up, and he knew it was difficult to get anything past his mother. He looked at Ryan for help. There was a deafening quiet that seemed to last forever, but after a couple of seconds Ryan replied.

"OK, we probably need to tell you about something," he began. "We didn't really want to involve you, because it is serious, and it carries a risk."

With those words, it became impossible to conceal the situation from the two women. Ryan now had their complete attention, and he knew he would not be able to only partially tell the story. He first gained promises of secrecy from the women. Larry warned them that if they agreed to hearing the matter, they would become part of a situation that could cause legal risks for them. The two men told them everything; the money, the Korean connection, the cabin, and the way in which the cash had to be given. By the time they returned Layla and Patsy to their homes, the effort had become a partnership of four. The women would come along on the next charitable delivery.

Within three months of Bill's passing, Larry received word that Sam died. The older man had left strict instructions that Larry be contacted immediately after the notification of the next of kin. Larry called Ryan and Patsy, and Ryan contacted Layla. The old man's funeral was different than any the four had previously attended. Larry had never seen so many policemen in one place in his life. Rifles were fired in a salute to Sam's service. The crowd knew nothing of the extended charitable service Sam had practiced for years. This work was known only to those directly involved in the effort. Yet, the four heard people talk of heroic things he had done while on the police force. No one spoke a negative word concerning him. Several of the men in uniform had witnessed questionable actions conducted over the years by Sam while gaining information about criminal activity, but those secrets would die with his burial.

Those men practiced loyalty and secrecy to the death; just as the manner of Max's death was now known only to Bill's widow. She was unable to make it to the funeral, due to her failing health. However, she was loyal to the man she credited with protecting the life of her husband. Mary

Thompson believed strongly that Max deserved to die. She didn't care whether his death was a result of a court sentence, or at the hands of a strong man. It needed to be done. The killings had to stop. Because of the circumstances, it had to be done in secret. Max was nothing like her kind and generous husband, and she felt nothing but relief when Sam confided in her and Bill of what he had done.

FIVE WEEKS AFTER the four attended Sam's funeral, it was time to make the transaction of the South Korean account. Ryan and Larry were not as patient as Sam. Dreading being linked to a dead man's account, they decided to move all of the money at once. They had no intention of changing the American address of the account to one of their own. The two felt they were taking a big enough risk just to handle it for Sam. The charity involving paper money was different. If they were careful to leave no fingerprints and remain unseen, chances were remote that they would be tied to it. However, Ryan was not at all comfortable with dealing with foreign accounts. He convinced Larry of the need to make an electronic transfer of the remainder of the money using Sam's home computer. The family was still in discussion as to what to do with the home in Atlanta, and six months had to pass before Sam's will was to be finalized by a Probate Judge.

Ryan called Layla and Patsy to let them know of the plan, and he and Larry drove down to Atlanta the following weekend. They parked the car several blocks down the street at the parking lot of a city park and walked to Sam's house. The two entered the home for the last time to make the transfer of money. Any trace of the transaction would be linked to Sam's computer, and he was now dead. Because of his death, this entry was much different than the last. No permission had been granted to them to enter the second time. If found, Sam would be unable to vouch for them. Due to the nature of the involvement with illegally obtained money, Sam's close relationship with the two younger men was unknown by his family. Ryan and Larry could not afford to be seen inside the house by family members or neighbors.

Before long, the transaction was made. Both breathed a sigh of relief, as Larry placed the envelope containing the account information into a pocket of his coat. They commented on how they had done the right thing. Just as they stood to leave, they heard the unlocking of the front door. They had no time to exit the house. In a state of panic, they carefully hid in the hall closet behind hanging coats and clothes. They quickly and quietly hid their feet and legs with an unused laundry basket. Just as quietly, Larry removed some of the clothes from their hangers and placed them in the basket. Almost afraid to breathe, they heard the sound of shoes meeting the hardwood floors throughout the house as someone visited different rooms. They listened as furniture drawers were opened in the living room and a bedroom. Each time they heard a drawer close, they wondered where the person would next go. By the slamming of the drawers, it was apparent that the individual was becoming frustrated in their search. Fear flowed through both men as they heard the creaking of bedroom closet doors open and close. As the steps came down the hall from the bedrooms, Larry and Ryan stood motionless and breathed shallow breaths. The knob to the door of their hiding place turned, and the door partially opened. The two captives tried to be as small and still as possible. Within a couple of seconds, the door closed, leaving the hall closet undisturbed.

After hearing the closing and locking of the front door, the two remained motionless and quiet for minutes. Opening the door of the hall closet, they slowly and cautiously made their way to the living room. Nothing appeared disturbed. This person was careful to leave the home exactly as it had been found. Cautiously, Ryan and Larry went to the living room window and looked for any signs of outside activity. Only the cars passing down the street showed movement. They decided to leave using the front door. The key only fit the locks in the front door, front door dead bolt, and rear door. Exiting from the back of the house would have meant leaving the dead bolt lock on the rear door unlocked. They made their move to the front porch, and Larry quickly locked both front door locks. The men wasted no time in departing the premise, but they were careful not to draw attention from anyone in the area. They walked down the street at a normal pace to the waiting car.

Nothing was said until they were traveling on the interstate highway through downtown. Finally, Ryan looked over to Larry and shouted.

"Good grief! I'm still not so good at this sneaky stuff!"

"Well, we aren't in jail," Larry responded. "That's good."

Then suddenly, it was as if a dam broke under the pressure of flooding waters. Both men suddenly broke open into nervous laughter. Neither had realized the internal pressure which had been building. There was more than the initial pressure of assuming partnership with Bill and Sam to carry out the footwork on an illegal and secret charitable effort. The older men passed away, leaving the entire burden on the shoulders of the younger men. The secretive and illegal additional duty of handling the Korean account was unexpected. By using Sam's home computer to move the total balance of the Korean account to the account of Ming Yon, the two had just come within inches of being caught. They had come close to blowing open the entire risky charitable effort. As a means of self-healing from the intense emotional pressure, their heavy souls exploded into laughter. Ryan was reminded of a verse in the Bible.

Proverbs 17:22 *"A merry heart doeth good like a medicine: but a broken spirit drieth the bones."*

After the laughter died down, and their nerves settled,

they called Layla and Patsy to let them know the money had been transferred. Shortly after Ryan dropped his friend off at his apartment, Larry began unpacking. Before hanging his coat in the closet, he reached into the pocket to clear the contents. There was the last evidence of his link to the Korean account and Ming Yon. Holding the envelope in his hand, he read the name over and over. He thought about Sam, and of the years he had taken care to make sure she was funded by the account. Larry tried to imagine Sam as a younger man in Korea, and of the relationship the soldiers must have had. He imagined the relationship of Sam and the Korean woman.

She must have meant more to him than just the widow of a friend.

Though more than a generation apart in age, Larry and Sam knew and understood each other remarkably well. Opening the envelope, he examined the address on the yellowing parchment. He hesitated only for a few seconds before making his last gesture in behave of his deceased friend. Taking a pen and sheet of paper, he wrote the following:

"Mrs. Ming Yon Cunningham,

I consider myself a friend of Sam Wells. I regret to inform you that Sam recently passed away. For many years, he served on the police force in Atlanta, Georgia, and he was given an honorable burial. I simply wanted to let you know of his passing.

I wish you well. A friend of Sam's"

He placed the simple note in an envelope. From the ancient paper before him, Larry carefully copied the address onto the new envelope for Ming Yon. The next day, he placed several stamps on it and dropped the letter into a post box not far from where he worked. It was the best he could do for Sam.

Chapter 13

THE FOLLOWING MONTH, Ryan and Larry decided to have Layla and Patsy accompany them on the next charitable delivery. Besides this being an excuse to visit with the women, the recipient of the next donation lived in Bristol, Tennessee. Bristol is within two hours' drive from Brandon Springs, making it somewhat convenient to pick up Layla and Patsy. Immediately after making the selection, Ryan and Larry called to inform them of the plan. Excitement built during the discussion over the phone, as the two men went into detail regarding the delivery of the money. Neither of the men noticed Larry's brother, Ronnie, enter the house during the conversation. He opened the front door and heard his brother and Ryan talking in the den. Interested, he quickly made his way to them. Larry turned to find his stunned brother standing in the doorway of the den. At first, the older brother was unsure as to how much Ronnie had overheard. The answer came within seconds.

"You're giving away $10,000?" Ronnie blurted out.

"It's not exactly what you think," Larry stammered, as he glanced over to Ryan for help.

"I don't think we have a choice," Ryan quietly responded. "We are going to have to pull Ronnie in."

The thrilled mood of excitement quickly changed to that of a much more serious and sober tone. Over the next hour, the two carefully detailed the history of the charity they had inherited. Ryan expected Ronnie to become interested in participating in the endeavor, but Larry had a far better understanding of his brother. Still, he tried to hold out some slight hope as Ryan explained the situation. Immediately after Ryan told him of the huge amount contained within the gun safe, Ronnie angrily turned to his brother.

"You have been handing out sacks of $10,000 to strangers, but you never once considered your brother?" he furiously complained. "What about our messed-up sister? Have you done anything for her with this money?"

Ronnie wasn't really concerned about the lack of attention for his sister. He only brought that subject up to enforce his position, and to angrily strike out at Larry. Hearing of the money, flames of resentment began to erupt into an all-encompassing fire within the younger brother. Ronnie had only recently shaken off the feeling that Larry had abandoned him in his move to Boston, and it only took minutes for the anger and resentment to gain a firm hold again. This time, it came with more vengeance than ever. Outwardly, the younger brother let out a chaotic string of curses. Inwardly, he decided that he would not allow himself to trust Larry again. If his brother chose to treat him as a stranger, he would do the same in return. He had always been without money, and the only time he had felt financial relief was while selling drugs. He quickly forgot the fear and desperation he experienced during those days, and he totally overlooked the job Larry found for him. Blinded by the thoughts of Larry keeping this secret from him and not sharing the large sum of money, his emotions caused him to ignore a great many things. Gone from his mind was the fact that Larry had beaten a man to death, in the process of saving Ronnie's life. Gone from his mind was the realization that the past several months had been the happiest of his life. He was relatively free from the dangers of the drug world; he now had a better income with a better future; he now spent enjoyable time with Larry on a weekly basis. It only took minutes for Ronnie to be taken over by a sense of betrayal from his brother.

"I'll tell you what you're going to do!" Ronnie threatened. "You will give me $50,000 in cash, or I am going to the police. I'm going with you to that cabin, and you are going to help out your own blood family before you deal out any more of that stinking money to strangers you have never even met! You've cared more for these strangers than your own mother. What have you done for her?"

Ronnie had no intentions of giving any of the $50,000 to his mother. This statement was just a means of getting what he thought he deserved. In the drug world, he had lived among cons for years, and he thought he knew how to manipulate others to get his way. He was in the process of slipping back into the person he had been before becoming reacquainted with his brother.

Ryan and Larry attempted to explain how they were carrying out the wishes of the men who had begun the charity, and they tried to offer him one of the $10,000 monthly gifts. Ronnie wouldn't hear of it. He continued to only offer threats and insisted on the $50,000. Reluctantly, they agreed to meet his demands. Larry warned his brother to be very careful as how he spent the money. He asked that the money not be spent in a manner which would draw attention to himself, or to the charitable work being done. Ronnie pushed for an immediate trip to the cabin for the money, and he was emphatic about not having any part of the charitable work.

ON THE FOLLOWING WEEKEND, the three made the drive to the cabin in Virginia. Ryan had wanted only himself and Larry to make the trip for the money, because he didn't trust Ronnie with the knowledge of the cabin's location. Larry felt the only way to repair the strained relationship with his brother was to extend trust to him. The first leg of the trip was made in silence, but the tension slightly eased once they stopped for lunch. Larry reminded his brother of the only family vacation they had shared as children. On that excursion, an unusual situation arose when the family stopped for a rest room break. Larry obtained a key from the store clerk to the men's restroom located on the exterior of the building. He and his brother attempted unsuccessfully to open the rest room door. After turning the key, they tried to push the door open. Immediately, it slammed shut after opening only about an inch. They tried twice more, and each time the exact same thing happened. Returning to the car, they explained the strange occurrence to their mother. She followed them back to the rest room and gave them the plan for opening the door.

"Let's all put our shoulders to the door; and when Larry turns the key, we will force the door open," she explained. Larry turned the key. With a loud voice, she shouted, "Heave ho!"

The combined effort forced the door to open about eighteen inches. It was just enough for them to catch a glimpse of a man seated on the toilet with his feet pressed against the inside of the door.

"No lady, no!" he screamed out.

Her face turning a brilliant shade of red, Larry's mother quickly retreated to the car. It turned out that there were two keys to the men's rest room, and the man had picked up the first key without notifying the store clerk. It was one of the few times, when the brothers and their father had a thoroughly enjoyable time at their mother's expense. The three laughed and shouted, "Heave Ho!" periodically over the next fifty miles.

The shared telling of the story to Ryan by the brothers broke the ice. The air of tension was eased during the remainder of the trip. Once they arrived at the cabin, Larry stressed to his brother again the importance of secrecy. They wasted no time in handling the affairs, as this would not be a relaxed extraction of money this time. They would make the return trip back to Charlotte that night. Ryan opened the gun safe door, revealing the entirety of its contents. Stunned at first, Ronnie was left wide eyed.

"Good God," he whispered.

It was then that he began visualizing the many things he would do with the money. Larry removed a total of $80,000 from the safe, as the breakdown would be $50,000 for Ronnie and $30,000 to cover the next three donations. He stressed to his brother the need to be very conservative in his use of the money. Larry repeatedly warned him not to be extravagant or do anything to call attention to himself or the charitable cause.

Neither Larry nor Ryan felt comfortable with staying in the cabin with Ronnie overnight. His reaction to hearing of the money indicated how emotionally volatile he had become. The return trip was long and tiring, as they returned to Charlotte at about 1:00 AM the following morning.

OVER THE NEXT TWO WEEKS, Larry witnessed reckless behavior in his brother that he had never seen. Ronnie bought a new car, and paid cash for it. The following weekend, he drove it to south Alabama to show it to family and friends. He pretended he had become successful in his new job in Charlotte, and he began to throw money around. He didn't fool his sister, and she called Larry to tell him of Ronnie's actions. She thought he might be back in the drug dealing business. Larry assured her that he was not, but Ronnie's openness with his newfound wealth brought concern to others. Word of his apparent success traveled fast. It wasn't long before his behavior attracted the attention of a couple of the bigger drug dealers in the area for whom Keith had worked.

The initial excitement for the trip to Brandon Springs

and Bristol was replaced with dread and tension. Ryan called Layla and Patsy to warn them of the recent encounter with Ronnie. He told them of the money given to him, and of his foolish behavior. Larry's brother had paid no attention to the warnings given him. The attention, brought on himself by his reckless actions, increased the risk to others who continued the charitable effort. Ryan and Larry suggested to Layla and Patsy that they should consider dropping out of the partnership. Nevertheless, the two women insisted on participating in the donations.

On the appointed day, Ryan picked up Larry to begin the excursion to Brandon Springs. The entire drive was dominated by discussion of Ronnie, and it continued well after they picked up Layla and Patsy. This had now gone past the excitement of performing charitable work in secrecy. The four were now moving into a territory of increased risk of being found with a vast amount of illegally obtained wealth. If caught, they could no longer mount a defense based on the fact that all of the money had been used for noble and charitable work, as $50,000 had now been spent as "hush money". "Hush money" is almost always an indicator that those paying it are fully aware of illegality. That act forced innocence to the sidelines.

"THE CAUSE IN BRISTOL IS A GOOD ONE," explained Larry. "A couple with four children is having financial problems caused by the mother enduring the latter stages of multiple sclerosis. She now requires a lot of care, due to lack of mobility and loss of bladder control. Her husband has done his best to provide for the family by working as many hours as possible at a tire store. I understand the increase in hours has caused him to feel guilty for not being with his wife. Neighbors and church members are taking time to check on her and the children, but it didn't stop him from feeling bad about leaving her for so long. The family is doing without, in order to pay the co-pay for medications partially covered by insurance. The children had to do with the minimum of new school clothes, and they've become used to having small Christmas gifts. After school, the children rotate hours to care for her."

The plan had been carefully constructed to almost every detail. Larry and Patsy had visited the store the previous month to examine the both the tire store and the habits of the husband of the next recipient of the money. On that occasion, Larry explained to the man that he didn't quite have the money saved for the tires for his wife's car (pretending that he and Patsy were married), but that he believed he would have the money the following month. Once the man realized there would be no immediate business done with them, he excused himself to make a call to his wife. Patsy watched as he walked back to the area of the restrooms and watched him pull a cell phone from a jacket hanging on a hook on a wall. The call was interrupted when the front door was opened by another customer. As the man began speaking with the customer, Patsy walked back to the area of the restrooms to discretely examine the jacket. She returned to Larry and let him know that she knew how to deliver the cash.

The following month the four arrived at the tire store shortly after 3:00 PM that Saturday. Ryan pretended he was looking for tires for his wife's car, and Layla played the role of the wife. Larry would ask questions from time to time, supposedly about the needed tires for his wife's car. Meanwhile, Patsy found the ideal opportunity to slip the envelope containing the money into the man's jacket hanging on the on the hook on the wall near the restrooms. There was no mistaking the owner of the coat, for the first name of the man was written as a monogrammed label stitched to the front of the jacket. The envelope was much too large to fit in a jacket pocket, so she attached it to the inside of the coat using a large safety pin. She used a handkerchief to avoid leaving fingerprints. Patsy left the store as soon as the money was delivered, and Larry followed soon after. Around 3:30 PM, Ryan and Layla departed in Ryan's car. Larry and Patsy had walked several blocks away and were later picked up by Ryan.

This was the first occasion for which they did not stay around to witness the envelope being found. As they left Bristol, each of the four told imaginary tales of his reaction to finding the money pinned to the coat. Each guessed how the money would be used. They decided to spend the night in Ryan's inherited house in Brandon Springs that Saturday night. They could not have imagined what would happen later that evening.

AROUND 1:00AM, Larry was awakened by a call from Ronnie on his cell phone. The younger brother was terrified. Earlier that evening he had been visited by two of the heavy hitting drug suppliers, for whom Keith had worked. They had heard of his recent spending habits, and the new car parked outside Ronnie's apartment confirmed the fact that he had come upon additional income. Unknown to Ronnie, Keith had died owing the two a rather large sum of cash from drugs delivered to him for selling. Keith died, never making the drug sell. Neither the drugs nor the money ever turned up. Before that evening, Ronnie had never met Lee Turner and Randy Calhoun.

Ronnie told his brother that he had been surprised by the two when he answered the door to his apartment. Prior to that night he had only heard Keith mention the names of Lee and Randy, when conducting arrangements for deals. He had never even mentioned the last name of either. Standing on Ronnie's front porch, Lee invited him outside to discuss a matter concerning Keith. Knowing that it would be impossible to hide from the two, he stepped out.

"Enjoying your money?" Lee asked Ronnie.

"I've got a new job, and I bought a new car," Ronnie coolly responded.

"New job?" asked Lee. "I think I know where your money came from."

Lee explained how they had supplied Keith with a large amount of drugs, and that he believed Ronnie found the drugs on Keith after Larry beat him up.

"I think that was pretty smart how you waited a while before selling the drugs," Randy began. "Or maybe you just didn't spend the money until recently. Anyway, those were not your drugs to sell, and the money really isn't yours either. Just give us the $20,000 Keith owed us and we're cool."

Randy's large left hand quickly rose and took Ronnie by the throat. His right hand immediately followed with a heavy blow to Ronnie's abdomen. The wind quickly exited his lungs, and the left hand of his assailant squeezed tight allowing no air to return. After a couple of seconds, he released Ronnie's neck. He gasped as the air returned. Once he was able to breathe, he repeated his earlier story. Ronnie tried to convince the two men that he had not found or sold any drugs, but it was to no avail.

"I came up here to start a new life," Ronnie explained. "I don't want anything to do with drug business anymore, and I don't know anything about what went on between you and Keith. I'm telling you that I don't know anything about drugs that he might have had. If he messed you over, I had nothing to do with it."

Before the men left the front porch, he had gotten the message. He would have to produce the $20,000 or he would suffer greatly. Ronnie had behaved like a fool, and now he was in trouble.

The phone call to Larry lasted about fifteen minutes, and neither was able to sleep during the remainder of the night. Larry waited for the others to wake before sharing the news of the call. The four had planned to spend most of the day together, but the seriousness of the call caused Larry to ask that they quickly return to Charlotte. Before dropping off the women, the four stopped for breakfast at the café where Layla worked. She was proud to be seen with Ryan by those who knew her, and for a few minutes she forgot about the dangerous situation facing Ronnie. Larry was exhausted, physically from the lack of sleep and emotionally from the stressful news.

During the drive back to Charlotte, Larry periodically called his brother to assure him that he was on his way. Once back in town, Ryan stayed home while Larry drove his car to Ronnie's apartment. He had never heard such fear in his brother's voice. Even during the days of dealing drugs with Keith, Ronnie was able to keep his cool. This was different. Keith had always maintained the face-to-face contact with Lee and Randy, so that he was the only one who carried the risk of knowing them. For this, he had always received the larger cut of the profits. Keith was a rough guy, and Ronnie had sensed an element of fear in him during occasions when he overheard cell phone calls between him and the two men.

Larry entered Ronnie's apartment and found him quietly seated on the couch. He wasn't watching TV, or listening to music, or playing a video game. This was totally unlike him. At first Larry wondered if his brother had been doing a drug before he arrived. As their eyes met, he could tell that his brother was fully alert. After the last call to Larry, Ronnie spent time reflecting on his situation and his life. The encounter with the two men had initially sent Ronnie into a panic, but afterwards it had a powerfully sobering effect. The recent events pointed to a life-threatening situation, but Ronnie realized this was not just a one-time threat. His life would probably be in serious danger from that day forward. Keith had been a cold-hearted individual, but these two were further up the food chain. Ronnie had seen their faces, and he knew the only value of his life to them would be his service to them in selling drugs.

He seriously doubted they would allow him to walk away, even after giving them money. He was like a man on death row. But even a man on death row has opportunities for years of appeals before a fair judicial system. These men were anything but fair.

After several apologies from Ronnie for not taking heed to his brother's warnings, Larry asked him if he wanted to pray about the situation. Ordinarily, an offer of this nature would have been met by a string of curses. This time Ronnie eagerly agreed. Larry prayed that God would guide them in their actions, and that God's hand would be on the situation. Thinking the prayer session had come to an end with his prayers, Larry lifted his head and was about to give his brother advice. However, he was surprised to see Ronnie's head still bowed. With his eyes still fixed on his brother, Larry sat quietly and waited. Within a few seconds, Ronnie began his first attempt at prayer since saying nightly prayers with his mother as a child before bedtime.

"God, help me," he prayed. "I know I've been pretty bad, and for a long time I really haven't had anything to do with You. I'm in trouble. I'm in trouble because I've been stupid and done stupid things. I've not been the kind of guy You would like. To be honest, I've not really even been the kind of person I would like. You have every right to toss me out of the door, and I would understand if You did. I don't know if You would even want to stop those two guys from hurting me, but there is a real chance they might kill me. I've pretty much lived like the devil, and I haven't even treated my brother right. I know where I would go if they did get rid of me. I'm asking You to forgive me and let me go to heaven. I've messed up everything in my life, and I sure don't want to mess it up even worse by ending up in hell. I can't promise You that I'll be perfect, but I am going to try to live like You would want me to live. I know my brother can help me learn how, because I see the kind of man he has become. He is a good man, and I should have never jumped at him the way I did. I'm really lucky to have Larry for my brother. God, these two guys are bad. I guess You know them better than I do. I know I don't deserve anything. I got myself into this situation. If you don't want to help me, I am asking You to protect my dumb sister from these guys. There is a chance they could come after her, since she knew Keith pretty well. Help me to be the right kind of person and help me to understand how to make things right with You. Please protect my sister and her kid."

Before lifting his eyes, Ronnie posed a question to his brother.

"Do you think I prayed OK?"

There was no immediate verbal response from his brother. The tension, involving the threat to his bother's life, suddenly broke. Larry was bawling like a baby, and he was unable to speak. Taken by surprise by the change in Ronnie's attitude and by the sincerity of the prayer, he was overcome with emotion. He knew Ronnie's heart was sincere because his prayer was really unlike him. There was no attempt to make a deal with God, and there was no focus on God getting him out of the mess he was in. He only asked God how to make things right between them, and he asked protection for his "dumb sister".

"I want to start going to church with you," Ronnie stated. "And I want to go ahead and get baptized. Do you think your preacher would do that? Is there something I need to do before getting baptized? I mean, do I have to attend some class or take a pledge, or something?"

OVER THE NEXT FEW DAYS, Ronnie hardly left his brother's side. After work, they ate supper together each evening, and they would find something to do together afterwards. Ronnie went to church with Larry. When it came time for prayer, he went to the altar. After the service, Ronnie talked with the pastor about being baptized. Larry's brother would not go into detail, but he made it clear that he wanted to be baptized as soon as he was allowed. The pastor told him that there were classes which could be taken explaining the meaning of baptism, but he instead gave him a couple of pamphlets on the subject. He gave Ronnie his phone number and told him that he would be available should he have questions.

The following Tuesday night, long after Ronnie went to bed, he awakened to the sound of the bedroom window breaking. He jumped to his feet as a hand reached inside to unlatch the window. Ronnie grabbed a pair of blue jeans from the foot of his bed and ran from the bedroom toward the front door of the apartment. Once at the door, he quickly slid the jeans on and began unlocking the deadbolt and chain lock. Throwing the door open he came face to face with Lee, who slammed his fist squarely on his jaw. The blow sent him reeling backwards into the hands of Randy, who had just come through the bedroom window and had moved into the living room. Held by Randy, Lee pounded him repeatedly in the abdomen. Gasping for breath, Randy allowed him to drop to the floor.

"Have you decided to give me the $20,000 Keith owed us?" Lee calmly asked.

Ronnie attempted to rise to his feet, but was quickly kicked back to the floor by Randy. Dazed by the boot which had landed heavily to the side of his head, he attempted to answer.

"Not yet," Ronnie whispered. This time he stayed on the floor, but still turned to face his attacker. "That's a lot of money that I don't have. You've got to believe me. I didn't take any drugs from Keith, and I don't have that kind of money."

"Well, you have just a few days to find that kind of money," Lee warned. "We'll be back. You won't know where or when, but we'll be back. And I will expect the cash."

"How can I pay you, if I don't know when or where you will turn up again?" Ronnie pleaded. "Even if I can find a way to get hold of that amount of cash, do you expect me to just leave it lying around until you show up?"

He had bought himself some time. No other blow would be landed that night, as he had earned the right to a conversation. Lee told him that he would call in a week to verify that Ronnie had the money and would arrange a place to meet. Lee's voice took on a softer tone, and he began to assure Ronnie that the money was all that was required.

Ronnie waited until the two had driven away before calling Larry. Larry immediately came over to see about his brother. It was very apparent that Ronnie's life was in serious jeopardy unless the money was paid. Larry called Ryan on his cell phone to discuss the situation.

"Ryan, the situation with Ronnie has become more serious," Larry began. "Unless he gives them $20,000, there is a good chance they will kill him next time."

Ryan reminded Larry that they still had the $20,000 in cash to give to the next two recipients of donations. They discussed the coincidence of the amounts of cash being the same, and how it seemed possible that God wanted the money to go to Ronnie. The thought of the money getting into the hands of drug dealing thugs was repugnant, but Ronnie's life was on the line. There was no chance they would withhold the money. They discussed going to the police, but decided it would not be a good idea. Too many questions would be asked regarding where Ronnie had gotten the money for his new car, and too many questions could be asked about Ronnie's drug dealing past.

The next day, Ryan arrived at Ronnie's with an envelope containing the $20,000. Ronnie believed the two would want him to meet them somewhere for the delivery of cash. The plan was for Larry and Ryan to be contacted immediately after Ronnie received the phone call from Lee. Ronnie would give Larry the location of the drop off. The younger brother would stall for a few minutes before leaving to meet with the two suppliers. Ryan and Larry would drive to the area and would already be in hiding, waiting for Ronnie to show up. They decided to park some distance away and walk to the location, in order not to be detected by Lee or Randy. The two would watch to make sure the delivery went down without Ronnie being harmed. There was no guarantee, but it was the best plan they could think of.

The following Sunday, Ronnie assured the pastor that he had read and understood the pamphlets he had given him. Satisfied that Larry's brother had made a personal commitment to God, and that he understood the sacrament of baptism, he agreed to baptize him on the following Sunday.

Ronnie received the call from Rick on Thursday night of the following week. He was to meet them at a city park, at a pavilion. After the call, he immediately called Larry and informed him of the call and the location. The plan was for Ronnie to give them the $20,000, explain to them that there was no more money to give, and let them know that he was through with drug dealing. Ronnie waited for about fifteen minutes before leaving, as he wanted to make sure Larry and Ryan had enough time to make it to the park before he arrived. Both of them were familiar with the pavilion and knew of a good place to park the car and of a hiding place allowing full view of the pavilion. With the envelope tucked under his arm, Ronnie walked from the apartment to his car. Just as he unlocked the car door, he felt a hand on his shoulder. Ronnie turned to face Randy.

"Going somewhere?" Randy asked.

Almost stuttering, Ronnie answered. "Yeah, I'm supposed to meet you and Lee at the park."

Suddenly, Ronnie's face went pale, and his heart sank. He knew what was about to happen. Only about a half second passed before the knife blade ripped into his stomach.

Dropping the envelope, he bent over in pain. Repeatedly the blade of the knife entered his body until Ronnie dropped to the pavement from the loss of blood. Randy then sliced open the throat of his victim and watched as a large red pool spread across the concrete from beneath Ronnie. The abdominal pain subsided, as Ronnie's vision began to dim. Slipping into unconsciousness, he thought about his older brother. Unfortunately, Larry and Ryan were dutifully stationed in place at the park.

Assured there were no signs of life left in the pale form that lay at his feet, Randy calmly slid the knife into the pocket of this jacket and picked up the envelope. Walking down the sidewalk, he pulled out his cell phone.

"I have it, and I'll be at the corner," he confirmed.

After about forty-five minutes, Larry knew something was dreadfully wrong. He and Ryan made a hasty drive back to Ronnie's apartment, where his worst fears were realized. There lying beside his new car was Ronnie. Ryan called 911 and requested an ambulance, as Larry bolted from the car. As Ryan approached, he saw Larry sitting on the pavement holding his brother's lifeless body. His eyes stared distantly into the star filled sky, as he rocked his brother back and forth. He was in a state of shock. After the police arrived, Ryan told them about Lee and Randy. The police confirmed that they had been tracking the two on drug related suspicions for some time. Ryan didn't tell them of the charity work or the $20,000. He told them that Ronnie had been connected with the two in the past regarding drug use, but that he had recently turned over a new leaf and was leading a good life. He left it at that. Larry said nothing, until the paramedics attempted to pry the lifeless body from his arms. It took close to a half hour to convince him to give them Ronnie's body.

Chapter 14

AFTER THE PARAMEDICS TOOK RONNIE from the scene, Larry remained seated on the pavement where his brother had lain. Saying nothing, he stared with tear filled eyes into the clear night sky. Ryan tried repeatedly to talk to him, but there was no response. He called Layla and Patsy, and then called Larry's pastor. Within a half hour the pastor arrived. Larry still giving no response, the pastor assured Ryan that he would handle the funeral situations until Larry was able to deal with things. He warned Ryan not to leave his friend alone that night and promised to check back with them later. Ryan pulled upward on the muscular shoulders of this man seated on the pavement, and eventually obtained a sorrowful glance from him. Once Larry stood to his feet, streetlights revealed the massive bloodstains which covered the front of his shirt and pants. With his friend still silent, he took him by the arm and led him over to his car. In almost a trance-like manner, Larry seated himself in the passenger side of his friend's car; his eyes still locked in a distant world of thought.

Realizing that he had no clothes to fit his larger friend, Ryan drove to Larry's apartment. He had to lead him the entire way inside the apartment. There, he helped him remove the blood-stained clothes and washed the blood from his hands and arms. Even the right side of Larry's face contained areas of dried blood. Ryan gave him a wet washcloth and pointed out areas of his neck and chest where Ronnie's blood had soaked through his friend's shirt. It was at that point, Larry seemed to notice the real world around him. He quietly glanced around the room, moved to the dresser, and changed his underwear. Standing at the side of his bed, he dropped to his knees and bellowed out in agony.

"Why did God let this happen?" he yelled out, as he looked up at the empty ceiling.

"I don't know," Ryan quietly stated. "Ronnie didn't listen to you… you tried to warn him, but he did stuff that attracted the attention of those jerks."

Larry said nothing in reply. Instead, he thanked his friend for being there, and climbed into bed. Ryan took his friend's bloodstained clothes to the kitchen sink and did his best to scrub out the stains. After squeezing water from them, he hung them over chairs at the kitchen table. Exhausted emotionally from the events of the evening, Ryan made his way to the living room of the apartment. He removed his shoes and laid down on the couch. Within seconds he was fast asleep.

"WHAT ARE YOU DOING HERE?" Larry asked.

Ryan was sleeping soundly, but he became fully alert when awakened by the question. Not wanting to admit that he had stayed the night out of concern for his friend, he answered.

"I was really tired last night. Do you mind?"

"No, it's OK," Larry snapped.

For a couple of minutes, Ryan silently observed his friend's body language. Larry behaved as if his friend was not present in the apartment, and Ryan easily read the message. Understanding that Larry wanted to be left alone, he excused himself.

"Larry, I have some things to do today," he began. "I'll give you a call later."

Larry nodded in response, and Ryan immediately left. As he had promised, he called his friend two hours later. Larry informed him of the arrangements.

"The funeral will be day after tomorrow near Mobile, at the church my mother attends," Larry plainly stated. "It will begin at 1:00PM, and the service will be held jointly by my preacher and my mother's pastor".

"Do you have pall bearers for the graveside?" Ryan asked.

"Oh, yeah; the preacher wanted me to look into that," he responded, with a deep sigh. "I haven't gotten around to it, but I will get some of the distant relatives down there together. The preacher will probably have a hard time finding the church. I'll need to help with that."

"Reading a sense of dread in Larry's voice, Ryan offered to help.

"I can let the preacher follow me down."

"Sure… OK," Larry replied in a slight relieved tone.

"How is your sister?" Ryan asked.

"She's OK; she's just mad as hell," he replied.

Ryan was a little taken back by the statement, but he understood the terrible loss. Larry continued.

"My mother is really taking it in a bad way," he explained. "I guess, Ronnie being the baby of the family and all. She was always fearful that something would happen to him, but she was pretty shocked when it finally did. I'm leaving this afternoon, to drive down to south Alabama."

Ryan offered to go with him, but Larry refused any need of help in the matter. He reminded Ryan that he had offered to lead the pastor to the church in the Mobile area, and that effort would require him going separately. The call ended with Ryan feeling a sense of separation from his friend. He reminded himself of how difficult the situation was for Larry.

AS PROMISED, Ryan later led the pastor to the south Alabama church. In fact, the minister stayed at the same motel as Ryan, Layla, and Patsy. Ryan paid for all four rooms, for he felt he had done little to help his friend during this time of suffering. He wanted to do something. After checking in, the four went to Larry's mother's home to check on the family. Larry's assessment of his sister had been correct. Ryan couldn't help but notice the anger in her eyes. Ronnie's mother was devastated. Her face drawn, she seemed to have aged fifteen years since the last time Ryan had seen her. Larry spent his time on the phone with locals or trying to console his mother. Every so often, he would glance over to his sister. He knew her to be unpredictable. He acknowledged the presence of Ryan, Layla, and Patsy when they arrived. However, he seemed to ignore them afterwards.

Larry soon left to meet with the two pastors and finalize the arrangements. In Larry's absence, Ryan attempted to comfort Ronnie's mother.

Moving next to her, he caught her attention.

"Ronnie changed a lot during the days leading up to when he died," he began. "He prayed to become a Christian with Larry and had made plans with the pastor up there to be baptized. It was very apparent that he was serious. I wanted you to know that."

"Thank you, Ryan," she whispered.

He wasn't sure whether he had helped, for her countenance remained the same. Her swollen eyes, from hours of crying and sleepless nights, caused her to appear her age for the first time to him. The usual spark of intelligence in her eyes had now given way to despair and grief. All the hopes she had carried for her youngest child were being put to rest with her son's body. Memories of his childhood danced through her mind, and all the worries she bore for him now seemed meaningless. It didn't show, but Ryan's assurances were a source of comfort.

"When we pass from this life to the next, the all-important thing is that we be prepared for it," Ryan told her.

Those words let her know that Ronnie made preparation for the afterlife. Eternity is a very long time. In fact, it is timeless. A small flame within began to warm her soul, and this moment was the first step of her overcoming the grief.

After the service, Ryan assured Larry that he would see him back in Charlotte before driving Layla and Patsy back home. Layla was quiet, but she knew what Patsy was thinking. After about fifteen minutes of silence, her thoughts were confirmed.

"Larry is really going through it," Patsy began. "It was all he could do to make sure his family was cared for, and to make sure the funeral went as best as it possibly could. I have no idea what must be going on inside of him, because he hardly spoke to me. I hope he's going to be OK."

Ryan told her that it might take a little while for Larry to handle the loss, but that Larry was a strong individual. In truth, he was seriously concerned for his friend's welfare. He had never seen him like this.

ON THE NIGHT OF RONNIE'S MURDER the police conducted a thorough investigation of the scene. They were successful in lifting a set of fingerprints from the bedroom window. Later that night, they located a bloody jacket with the knife in a dumpster behind a nearby convenience store. The following day, they impounded Lee's car and picked both him and Randy up for questioning. They found a small bloodstain in the impounded car, and it gave them grounds to hold the two. The fingerprint on the window matched Randy, and the small amount of blood in the car matched Ronnie's blood type. Over the next three weeks, they found evidence of several crimes in Lee's apartment. Before long, a strong case was built against them both.

"It's good that the police have the two in custody," Ryan thought. *"For weeks, Larry's been extremely volatile. It's possible that he might have sought them out to take revenge."*

Ryan tried to call and visit Larry, but he hardly acknowledged his presence or words. It was the same when Patsy tried to call. More and more, Larry began to isolate himself from his friends. At the same time, he steadily drifted away from God. At first, he was angry with God for allowing Ronnie's murder. He questioned God on every conceivable issue for which he could think. Then the anger melted away into apathy regarding his spiritual needs and his relationship with his Maker.

Ryan called his friend to set up the delivery to the recipient of the next donation of money. However, Larry informed him that he would no longer take part in the monthly donations. He told Ryan to do what he liked with the money. Larry said it would be fine with him if Ryan gave it all away or spent it on whatever he liked. He knew his involvement in the money was a direct contributor to his brother's death. It no longer mattered to him, and he made it clear to his friend that he no longer wanted anything to do with the money or the charitable cause. He was completely absorbed in thoughts about his brother. Larry was consumed with questions regarding whether he could have done some things differently that would have resulted in a different outcome. It was as if his walk with God had stopped in its tracks, and he refused to take another step in that direction. Larry couldn't bring himself to move beyond his pain. Partly because he unconsciously felt it would be disrespectful of the memories of Ronnie, to simply get over it and move on. However, the primary reason was due to his conscious anger towards God for allowing the tragedy to happen.

Deeply concerned, Ryan called Sally's old pastor for

advice.

"It might take some time for Larry to get over his bother's murder, but that it's important for people to get to a place where they can let the past die," the old man told him. "It's all right to reflect on the past from time to time, to remind ourselves of where we've been and where we are going but it is unhealthy to live there. We should learn whatever lessons we can from a situation, but we must make the decision to go forward in life. We need to stay on the road God has placed before us. Regardless of situations and inner pain, we need to stay mindful of where He may be leading us. It may feel good for a moment to drive off road and spin our wheels around in the mud. But if we stay there long, we can easily become stuck. If we remain in that place and continue to spin our tires, we may begin to sink lower and lower. It may initially seem to be a safe place because we are not faced with the unfamiliar surroundings of new places God may take us. However, it is also true that we will not experience the wonder of some of those places. If we cease to move from a place and refuse to proceed in the direction God has laid before us, life can eventually seem to become meaningless."

The delivery of donations fell on the shoulders of Ryan, Patsy, and Layla. Though they enjoyed the act of giving, thoughts of Larry dominated each mind. The group seemed a bit like a chair with a missing leg. They were ever conscious of the loss. For weeks Ryan attempted to call, but Larry would say very little, and the conversations were brief. Patsy called almost every day during the two weeks following Ronnie's funeral, but Larry's tone of voice and lack of response in conversation became almost unbearable for her. She had fallen deeply in love with a man, who had all but totally shut himself off from her. Sorrow gripped her, and the calls became less frequent.

It was in response to intense inner torment that Larry shut them out. Little did they know, but each conversation with them rekindled the pain of Ronnie's death. It was like someone ripping open the scabs from a heavy wound. Pain flowed, as blood from a deep open wound, each time they called. It would take a couple of days after each call for the pain to subside. In truth, his friends could have been agents of healing if he had let them. Larry told himself that if he stayed away from them his hurt would scab over. In truth, his wounds were spiritually festering with infection below the scab. This painful area in his life needed to be opened up and thoroughly scrubbed clean before it could properly heal. Each time God would attempt to bring this healing to Larry through his friends, he would snatch his painful wound from their presence and protect it. We've often seen a child run away from a doctor, when the caring physician pulled out a syringe to inject the child with a lifesaving drug. A small child can be somewhat short sighted, and adults have their own way of doing the same. Each time God's Spirit reminded him of His concern for him, his tormented soul would shout out, *"No – I'm not going to let You jerk me around anymore. I've had enough of Your games."*

Larry now viewed God as a cruel puppeteer; gently guiding the puppet across the stage, only to slam it into a wall when it was least expected.

On one occasion of making the monthly charitable delivery, Patsy wept most of the time. Each delivery reminded her of her loss of Larry. Still, she viewed the pain to be worth encountering for the sake of those helped by the venture. The situation even began to impact Ryan's and Layla's relationship, as they sensed the heaviness in Patsy during each donation. In the past, the delivery had the added bonus of giving Ryan and Layla an opportunity to enjoy one another's company. Now, it was difficult to shake the burden in Patsy's heart and the loss of a friend. Larry's misery was spreading to those who loved him.

THE WEEK FOLLOWING THE DELIVERY, Patsy could take it no more. That Friday night she drove to Charlotte, and at 2:00 AM Larry was awakened by her pounding on his door. Still somewhat in a walking slumber, Larry opened the door and invited her in. She immediately slammed the door behind her and began a verbal assault.

"What do you think you are doing?" she questioned, in a rather loud voice. "You don't want to talk to Ryan. You don't want to help other people in need, and you don't even seem to want to talk to me…"

She stopped in mid-sentence, and tears began to pour from her eyes. Larry moved towards her, but she stopped him cold with a sure blow from her fist to his muscular chest. She then placed both hands over her eyes and began to weep almost uncontrollably. His chest still smarting a little from her pounding, he moved in and wrapped his arms around her. It was if her warm tears ran across the apathetic ice that covered his heart, and it began to melt. For the first time in weeks, he began to focus on someone other than himself or his dead brother.

Larry said nothing. The way he held her said it all. For several minutes she wept in his arms, as he caressed her hair and shoulders. At last, she lifted her head. Eyes swollen and red, looking directly into his, she quietly spoke.

"I love you, Larry. I really love you."

Her words ended as if there was more to be said, but she gave him no more. They hung in silence for about a minute; then he replied.

"I love you too, and I need you," he began. "I've just never had anything hit me so hard. My father's death was expected, and in my mind, I knew Ronnie's actions were probably going to cause him serious trouble. After years of separation, we finally had a relationship again, and I opened myself up to it. In the back of my mind, I sort of expected God to protect him and step into the situation."

"Things happen," she responded. "Life sometimes

comes at you with unexpected situations and unexpected results from actions taken. Please don't push me away. Please don't throw away everything."

"OK, I'm sorry," he said tenderly.

On the couch, they held each other and talked for over an hour before falling asleep. They awoke about 7:00 AM, and Larry prepared breakfast while she showered. During her shower, Larry also took the opportunity to call Ryan and apologize for his behavior. Before hanging up, they discussed the charitable venture. Larry let his friend know that he would rejoin the effort. He had begun to mend the horizontal relationships in his life, those with his friends and loved ones. However, he inwardly remained angry at God for failing to protect his brother. His vertical relationship continued to be seriously damaged to the point that it was all but nonexistent.

Weeks went by, and Larry continued his work with his friends to give out large sums of money to deserving people. The four worked out a plan to meet each quarter to select three recipients for the charitable donations. They would still deliver the money on a monthly basis, but the quarterly meeting would allow them more time to research candidates. Larry felt better about life, in general, but he still sensed an unsettling in his soul. In his mind, he tried to pretend the vertical relationship in his life didn't matter. However, he sometimes found himself still talking to God in an unfriendly manner under his breath. As he was alone driving in his car, on rare occasions he allowed his anger to be more verbal. He found himself audibly yelling at God.

As the weeks passed, the verbal abuse of his Creator subsided into a spiritually numbed state. Larry concentrated on his work, his friends, the donations made in secret, and Patsy. He had stopped attending church the week after Ronnie's funeral, and he began to fill his life with other activities. Often, situations would arise that reminded him of God. But each time the Spirit of God reached into his heart, he consciously shoved God aside. On one occasion, he played tennis with a fellow employee from his workplace. The man was an avid atheist. After Larry beat the man soundly in the match, the man let out a string of expletives which included several instances of taking God's name in vain. After the outburst, the man apologized.

"I'm sorry," he began. "I forgot you're a church guy. You probably didn't appreciate the language. Although I think religion is a load of crap, I don't intentionally mean to offend those who are believers."

"No big deal," Larry replied. "I don't care".

In truth, for an instance, he did find it offensive. When the words were first spoken, he felt very uncomfortable. However, he quickly brushed the uneasiness aside. He felt even more uncomfortable when the man apologized. It reminded him of his deteriorated relationship with his Creator. As he stated that he didn't care about the cursing of God, he felt an inward ache deep within him. Larry still believed in the existence of God. However, he was deeply disappointed in what God had allowed to happen to his brother. The anger toward God had created such friction within him that it had begun to wear a spiritual callus on his heart.

On another occasion, he was about to enter a downtown pornography shop, when he spotted a Salvation Army bell ringer just across the street. A shiver went through his heart, as God attempted to speak to him. However, he shoved the emotion aside and entered the shop and purchased a couple of movies. He told himself that it was all right, because he was lonely due to the long-distance relationship with Patsy. He tried to convince himself that it wasn't really hurting her because he believed she would never know. It seemed like God was constantly trying to remind him of His continual presence. It was as if God was saying, *"Remember Me? I'm still here. I'm not going away, because I love you."*

Each time he felt that reminder from God, he shoved it

aside. Eventually, the reminders were sensed less and less. Each effort to toss aside the Spirit of God, led to less emotions felt and less consideration of the event.

He reminded himself that he was doing a great charitable work, in secretly given away large sums of money to deserving people. However, there was little peace within him. Larry was recognized for his success in his work, but he didn't feel much self-worth. He had once sensed the Hand of the Creator of the universe on his life, but he purposefully walked away from it. He had tasted the Spiritual waters flowing from Heaven, and he now refused to drink. Larry could not help but feel thirsty. This was not a thirst that could be satisfied by accolades or accomplishment, nor could it be quenched by anything in this world. If he had never known God, he would have never missed His presence. As time passed, and as he continued to push aside every reminder from God, the uneasiness in his spirit was replaced with a dulled state of internal discontent.

THE TIME CAME AGAIN for Ryan and Larry to visit the Virginia cabin to collect money to cover the next three deliveries. They enjoyed the company of each other, but both sensed the spiritual gap which lay between them. The following week Patsy drove Layla to Charlotte, because the next donation was to be in the area of Dalton, GA. The money was to be given to a couple, who spent a great deal of time taking care of a handicapped daughter. The son and daughter of Allen and Rebecca Wilson were involved in an accident while returning to college in Atlanta, GA. Paul was a junior, and his sister, Heather, was a freshman at the school. He was killed, but the accident resulted in her being wheelchair bound due to paralysis. Heather planned to continue her study in Secondary Education, but she had need for a van with a wheelchair lift and controls on the steering wheel.

Her small church had begun to raise money to help with the cost of the co-pay of her father's insurance, but the cost of the handicapped equipped van was out of reach. This struck a personal chord with Larry, since he had lost his own brother. He couldn't imagine how difficult it would have been to deal with the loss of a sibling while adjusting to one's own paralysis. He felt extremely compassionate for her, but he was even more incensed over the fact that God would allow double fisted blows to strike this young woman. It was customary for the group to pray before making each delivery. Larry bowed his head out of respect for his friends, but internally his soul was shut off from God. The others sensed the tension, but said nothing. Each knew Larry would have to work this out on his own. It wasn't like he didn't know in his heart what he should do. He had consciously made a decision to handle things in ways that didn't include God. Every night, they each separately prayed for God's Holy Spirit to prepare his heart for continued healing.

SIX MONTHS AFTER RONNIE'S DEATH, Larry came to a place where he came face to face with himself. Seated on his couch, watching an exceptionally lewd movie, he felt a suicidal wave flow over his soul. Nothing had changed at work. He was still being acknowledged for his brilliance and hard work. When involved with his friends in the giving away of money, he felt pretty good during the activity. However, when he returned home the elation of the events subsided quickly. Larry attempted to be as kind as he could to everyone he encountered, in an attempt to be the person he wished to be. In an effort to feel better about himself, he discarded the pornographic movies he had purchased into a dumpster behind his apartment. Each act of kindness, and each attempt to be a better person, resulted in a short-lived sense of self-worth. However, there remained a nagging lack of peace within his soul. Larry knew what was wrong, but he just could not let go of his disappointment in God and his hatred for the man who ended his brother's life.

THE FOLLOWING WEEK, LARRY DROVE ALONE to Brandon Springs. He decided to talk with someone with whom he believed he could honestly and discreetly spill his guts before. He told no one he was going; not even Patsy. Though it would have been convenient to visit her in the neighboring town, he felt he had to handle this matter alone. That Saturday evening, he visited Alvin at the small church near the place where he was bitten by the snake. The older man didn't seem surprised to see him. It was as if he had expected to be contacted by this younger man. Larry went into details about his relationship with his brother, and of the events which led to his brother's death. He openly revealed his anger at God for not stepping into the situation. Alvin patently listened, as Larry emptied his soul. Alvin's supportive care reminded Larry of a time in his teen years when he returned home very drunk. Sickened by the excess of heavy liquor, he began to violently vomit the contents of his stomach. As he ranted about how sick he felt, his mother silently and lovingly cleaned up the vomit and tended to him. She didn't chastise him for his behavior; she patiently attended to his needs. Alvin did the same. He allowed the younger man to vomit the entire contents of his soul without preaching to him or chastising him for judging God. After the rant ended, the older man finally spoke.

"Maybe God did step into the situation," Alvin responded.

"My brother is dead!" Larry exclaimed, in frustration. "What is it about dead that you don't understand? He is gone!"

"We all are going to die, sooner or later," Alvin quietly stated. "Ronnie went before you, and it hurts when a loved one is taken away so violently and quickly. I really do understand. I lost my youngest son. He was chasing a ball and went into the road after it. This is a rural area, and cars pass by infrequently. What are the chances of one coming by exactly at the time he ran after the ball? For months I asked this question over and over. For months I ignored the living, as I grieved for the dead. For months I blamed God and felt nothing but anger towards Him. Then I began to think of the blessed times I had with my son while he was still with me on this planet. I remembered enjoying his baseball games, and how he hugged me when I came home from work. I remembered his baptism, and his sweet prayers before going to bed. It was at that moment I realized that he was in Heaven, and that he had only gotten there ahead of me. We all are going to die. We all are going to stand before God afterwards. In my spirit I knew he was alright. He's in a much better situation than he could have ever been in this world. It doesn't mean I don't still miss my little boy. You told me that Ronnie turned to God before he died. Eternity is forever, and it seems to me that God did step in. Ronnie had things settled with his Maker before he went to stand before Him. Because of that, you two felt a bond that you never experienced before. You will have it again one day. One day, you will go on to stand before God. And on that day, Ronnie will be standing right beside you telling the host in Heaven of how you helped him straighten out his life and how you helped him to prepare for the hereafter. That bond is eternal."

Those gentle words cut through the icy wall Larry had been building between his heart and God. He felt as if his head and chest were about to burst. He cleared his throat, and then turned to Alvin.

"I really miss him," he whispered. "I really miss him. The truth is, I wasn't there for him. I wasn't there to protect him. He was alone…the little guy was alone, facing a pair of monsters. Those guys were stinking monsters; they were a couple of tools of the devil himself. I should have been there.

I had planned to be there for him, but I didn't figure on those murdering pieces of garbage going to Ronnie's apartment. My brother was no match for those….killers."

During the conversation, Larry took care to check his words, for he had great respect for the man seated beside him. A great many other words came to mind, while speaking of Lee and Randy.

"You did everything you knew to do," Alvin confirmed. "You tried to warn him about his actions; you were a true brother to him. The Bible says there is a time for every man to die. Maybe it was just his time. There are a lot of things we won't understand until we leave this place and go to the next. One day you will understand, but it may never be in this world."

Months of anger poured from Larry. Though he felt exhausted, he sensed a peace sweep over him. Emotionally and physically, he felt very tired. However, his soul was rested as never before. Alvin reminded him of the Biblical story of the man Job. He told him that Job was a Godly man, who had been very fortunate most of his life. Then difficult times came his way, in which he lost the lives of his sons and almost all that he possessed. During those times his friends betrayed him, and they told him that God had turned against him as well. His wife believed he had done something to anger God, and she advised him to curse God. She also advised him to die and be done with his cursed life on earth. Job ignored the bad advice of his friends and his wife and remained as faithful to God during times of crisis and disaster as he had been during the years of blessings. In the end, God blessed him more than ever.

"I have no trouble believing that God exists," Larry began. "I just don't understand Him. God allowed me to walk out into that alley before Keith hurt Ronnie, but He left my brother on his own on another occasion. Why would He do that when Ronnie was trying so hard?"

"I can't explain everything that God does or doesn't

do," Alvin responded. "You know your brother pretty well. Do you think there was a chance that Ronnie would have eventually gone back into drugs and crime? Do you think maybe God knew this was the time to take him away, before he ended up hurting himself and other people?"

"Maybe," Larry replied. "He was really shook up, but I don't know what he would have done over time. He had a tendency to swing to extremes."

Alvin explained that life doesn't always seem fair, and that God sometimes allows things in our lives which seem to be unfair.

"It wouldn't seem fair for God to allow His only perfect Son to be brutally killed for our sake," Alvin said. "God gave his Son over to those who misunderstood Him, in order for Him to pay the price of the sins of people who seem so undeserving. Most of us pay little attention to our Creator. In fact, many of us purposefully choose to doubt the existence of the Designer of all that we see around us. You know, it takes a lot of effort to believe that the universe just accidentally came together on its own, with no Designer behind it."

Larry nodded in agreement.

"We all have faith," Alvin continued. "We just sometimes misplace it. Faith is a part of who we are. We are created to believe. To be honest, it takes a great deal of faith to believe that order accidentally comes from chaos, or that the structure and complexity of the universe just accidentally happened into existence. What are the chances of that? Do we have any evidence of this happening today? How often do we witness even the smallest example of this happening? Put the matter of the universe aside and consider just the human body. How small a part of the world around us we are, and just look at the detail. Many of us go out of our way to disbelieve, because we can't stand the thought of needing to answer to anyone but ourselves. Even forgetting our attitude toward God, look at what we do to each other.

Would you have given your son over to be killed for the likes of the people in this world? I don't think I could have; I know I could not have done it. We often concentrate on what we gained through the sacrifice of Jesus, because we are such a self-interested bunch. We think God is unfair when things don't go as we wish them to be, because we are so self-centered and small minded. God sees a much bigger picture."

As Alvin spoke, Larry's head lowered. His eyes began to water, and he felt it hard to swallow. He remembered the encounter with the snake, and the prayers of this plain spoken and plainly dressed older man. He remembered sensing the presence of God stronger than any time in his life, and he remembered the wonder of the miracle that happened that day. The doctors didn't call it a miracle, but Larry knew something very special happened. There was no proof, but Larry knew in his heart that God had reached out to him. He remembered the warm sensation his heart felt that day, and the peace that settled upon him in the bed of that pickup truck. As Alvin finished speaking in his slow southern dialect, Larry silently dropped to his knees in front of the pew where they had been seated. His fists covering his eyes, he lowered his head down toward the seat of the pew.

"Do you want me to pray with you?" Alvin quietly asked.

Still saying nothing, Larry nodded in the affirmative. The prayer of the older man wasn't eloquent, by any standard. No philosophical words of enlightenment were spoken, and no new spiritual truths were revealed. He simply asked God to show Larry the Love that He had for him, and to grant him peace in his heart. It probably wouldn't have mattered what words were spoken, for God's Spirit flowed over the younger man's soul like the warm radiant heat from a fireplace on a cold night. Larry let go of his anger. His anger toward God and his hatred for the murderers of his brother slid away and was replaced by a peace that defies understanding. Larry began to forgive himself for killing Keith, and for not being present the night his brother was killed. He immersed himself in the cleansing power of that peace, and his heart was at rest. He didn't know if there was some sanctified presence of God in that small church, or whether this humble man was a spiritual giant. He didn't care to understand, he just allowed himself to soak in the mercy of God.

Larry rested on his knees for almost a half an hour, as he was in no hurry to end the experience. Eventually, he turned and sat on the floor where his knees had knelt. He and Alvin talked for another half hour before he rose to his feet. Before leaving the small church, he gave Alvin a powerful hug that seemed to squeeze most of his physical strength from the older man. Alvin never complained about the fact that Larry almost crushed his ribs in the process of demonstrating his appreciation for him.

This time, he did choose to visit Patsy. He paid her a surprise visit after he left Alvin and told her of his visit with the older man. To her, Larry seemed to be almost radiant in his appearance. She carefully listened to each word. Afterwards, they prayed together for the first time in several months. The time flew by for each of them, and midnight arrived much sooner than they expected. He was exhausted, and she agreed to let him stay with her that night. They pulled out the sofa bed in her great room and slept mostly clothed. They were afraid to sleep in her bed, because they both knew that it might very well lead to the removal of the remainder of the clothing. She considered having him sleep alone on the sofa bed, but she didn't want to end their time together. Larry curled up behind her and held her in his muscular arms. Within just a few minutes he was fast asleep. Patsy rested as she felt the rising and falling of his chest against her back. Her small hand cupped under his larger hand, she relaxed and drifted off into the world of dreams. Patsy had seriously dated several men before, but this was different. As a nurse, she had gone to bed extremely tired after an exhausting night shift, but she had never slept as peacefully as she did that night. In his arms, she felt at home.

The next morning, both apologized for morning breath. While she showered, Larry made them blue berry pancakes, and the two laughed and talked throughout the breakfast. Larry showered while she cleaned up the kitchen. Before leaving Patsy's apartment for church that Sunday morning, Larry held her and kissed her. He had never felt so at peace in his life.

"Would you marry me?" he asked.

Only a couple of seconds passed before she answered.

"Yes, I would love to marry you," she replied.

Before leaving for the church, they stood together for several minutes in Patsy's apartment soaking in the realization of their new relationship and commitment. As they drove to the church, they discussed the situation of living in separate cities. It was obvious that this long-distance relationship would soon need to end. It would have been more difficult for Larry to find a job related to finance in Patsy's small town, and there would be ample opportunity for her to find a nursing job in Charlotte. It was settled. She would begin making plans to find a job in Larry's city.

Larry had only recently renewed his relationship with God, and he looked forward to hearing the first sermon attended in several months. Throughout the message he looked for God's guidance and he hoped to receive some type of spiritual touch. Though he thought the sermon had many good points, it didn't seem to speak to his soul. Somewhat inwardly disappointed, he left the church with Patsy to eat lunch. He thoroughly enjoyed her company, and the two planned to meet again the following weekend.

During the week, Larry informed Ryan of the new commitment between himself and Patsy. He let him know that he and Patsy planned to meet again on the following weekend. Larry told him about praying with Alvin. He suggested that he, Patsy, Layla and Ryan attend Layla's church on their next visit to Brandon Springs. Ryan reluctantly agreed, for he found himself feeling uncomfortable during services in that church. He was secretly hoping Layla would leave it for Patsy's church. In fact, Layla's church was the only uncomfortable thing he found about his relationship with her.

THE FOLLOWING WEEKEND, Larry and Ryan drove to Brandon Springs and met Layla and Patsy at Ryan's house. Patsy and Layla slept in the bedroom Ryan had prepared for his now deceased aunt. Ryan stayed in his own bedroom, and Larry took the couch. It rained most of that Saturday, so almost the entire day was spent playing cards and eating. The girls cooked breakfast, Ryan cooked burgers for lunch on a grill he had placed on the front porch, and Larry and Layla prepared supper. Most of the conversation focused on Larry's and Patsy's engagement. They stayed up until after midnight playing cards and board games, and conversing. Afterwards, they moved to their appointed sleeping quarters. Layla fell into a deep sleep minutes after her head hit the pillow.

Around 2:00 AM, Patsy slipped on a pair of shorts under her long night shirt and made her way to where Larry was sleeping on the couch. Kissing him on the forehead to wake him, she then kissed him on the lips. She crawled over Larry and slid between him and the back of the couch, so that she was lying behind him. She snuggled up to his back and kissed him on his bare muscular shoulders. Patsy covered both of them with the blanket lying at their feet, and then drifted off into sweet sleep. Feeling her light breath on his back, Larry was reminded of the early days of his previous marriage. He remembered how nice things were in the beginning, but things went wrong. Momentary doubts about Patsy crept into his tired mind.

"Will Patsy cheat on me in the end, as well?" he thought.

He reminded himself that there was a bond between himself and Patsy that he had never experienced. Within minutes, the doubts subsided, and he sipped into a heavy sleep.

He awaked the next morning with her head on his chest and his left arm over her shoulder. It was at that time that he realized she was not wearing a bra. Her soft body, under only her night shirt, pressing against his side caused him to experience a sudden erotic rush of emotions. As he became fully awake, he decided it best to slip out from under her to begin breakfast. For a couple of seconds, a sexual battle waged within his mind and body. His first marriage had failed, and Larry was uncertain as to why it ended with his first wife's infidelity. He desperately wanted to do it right this time and knew full well that he might become weak if he entertained the heated thoughts and feelings much longer. Larry didn't want to push Patsy into doing something that would be against her conscience.

He prepared pancake batter, and within minutes bacon began to sizzle in a skillet. He coated a second skillet with vegetable oil and began cooking the pancakes. Just as he flipped the first one, he felt the presence of Patsy leaning against his back. Turning, he found her standing behind him wrapped in the blanket from the couch. Her hair was a mess, and her eyes were still somewhat puffy. Larry allowed the pancake to take care if itself for a couple of seconds and wrapped his arms around the blanket clad woman.

"I have a pancake on the stove, young lady, don't make me burn it," he stated as he released her.

"I have to take a shower anyway," she said in a teasing manner. Patsy's glance spoke volumes. Her eyes intended to drive a mental picture of herself showering into Larry's mind. She easily succeeded, for he picked up the message immediately. Through the first six pancakes, he couldn't shake the mental picture. Since asking her to marry him, sensuous feelings for her almost constantly rumbled to the surface of his conscious mind. It was as if someone had turned on an emotional faucet, and his senses were on edge. Actually, the same was happening with Patsy. The commitment they made to be married, spoke loudly of things to come. She would often find herself fantasizing of Larry making love to her. In an effort to focus on something else, sometimes she would attempt to study her Bible. Most of the time, it didn't work. Though they had not yet been fully intimate, they each could sense the erotic pressure building within. The limits they had placed on their physical activity acted like a cork on a shaken soft drink bottle, as it sensually heightened the awareness of the other person. Neither had made mention of finalizing a date, but both secretly knew that it couldn't wait a great deal longer without fully giving in to desires.

Hearing the shower, Layla wakened. She slipped on a robe and exited the bedroom. She walked through the kitchen, and asked "Is Ryan up yet?"

"Not yet; or at least, I haven't seen him yet," Larry replied, as he poured batter for another pancake.

She proceeded through the kitchen, on to Ryan's bedroom door. She softly knocked and listened for an answer.

"I'm awake," he stammered. It was apparent that the knock on the door had wakened him.

"OK for me to come in?" Layla quizzed.

"Sure, enter at your own risk," he replied. She gave Larry a questioning glance, as if to ask what the risk might be. Then she heard Ryan issue an explanation.

"It's been hours since any of my teeth have been near a toothbrush."

"Me too," she said, as she opened the door. The bed was in shambles, with the comforter on the floor. Ryan rubbed the morning from his eyes, as she entered the room. It was as if the sensuous air between Larry and Patsy had permeated every square foot of the house like incense. Seeing Ryan lying on the bed, partially covered by the remaining sheet, she felt a pounding in her breast and a sudden flush. She slowly made her way over to the bed and sat on the side nearest the door.

Reaching out, he took her by the hand. Her thumb gently rubbed against his. Suddenly, he grabbed her and swung her small frame across his body and onto the other side of the bed. She let out a sudden and short scream. There he buried his head on her chest.

"I think I like this pillow," he whispered.

"I'm not just a pillow," she informed him, with a slight smile.

"You can say that again," he replied, lifting his head.

She immediately pinched him on the arm, and he pulled it back quickly releasing it from her grasp.

"Wow, you're pretty mean when you wake up," he accused.

"You're the one who tossed me across your bed," she replied, in a teasing tone. At that moment, Ryan could think of several things he would like to do to her.

A heavy voice sounded from the kitchen.

"Hey, do I need to close that bedroom door?" Larry jokingly called out.

"You better not, Larry!" Layla warned.

Reaching under the sheet, Layla pinched Ryan's leg and quickly leapt from the bed. She was as fast as a squirrel in danger. Ryan started to pursue, but he remembered that he was wearing very little. Grabbing his jeans from the end of the bed, he attempted to quickly slip them on and continue the chase. However, his feet were not quite as quick as his mind. His right foot made it through to the floor, but his left leg got hung up as the toes on his left foot were not pointed downward. His left foot became squarely lodged in the leg of the jeans, and Ryan fell squarely on his face. Hearing the loud crash, Layla quickly returned to the room. For a cautious second, she remained quiet, to ascertain whether he was hurt. Ryan was sprawled face down on the bedroom floor. His jeans were only halfway up his legs; revealing his underwear. Lifting his head, she saw what looked to be the infant stage of a rug burn on his nose. She burst into laughter. By that time, Larry had temporarily abandoned the pancakes and was viewing the spectacle from a vantage point directly behind the much shorter Layla. Quickly, the redness of the rug burn disappeared as it became indistinguishable from the increasing reddening of the remainder of Ryan's face. Larry let out a loud blast of laughter, as his friend was busily trying to free his stuck foot.

"It can't be that funny," Ryan stated, while turning his back to the small audience at the door. Once the foot was freed, he quickly slid the jeans up and fastened them.

"Oh, yes, it is," Layla blurted out from between gasps of air and laughter.

"OK, the show's over," Ryan said, as a slight smile began to invade his blushing face.

"Man, you almost made me burn my pancakes," Larry shouted, as he turned to rush back into the kitchen. As Ryan moved toward the door, he could hear his friend comment.

"It would have been worth a burnt pancake. That was great, Ryan!"

Still chuckling, Layla made her way to Ryan and slipped both arms around his waist.

"You skinned your nose. Boy, that's going to look goofy when it scabs over," she said, with a wink.

Ryan started to pull away, but her hold was firm.

"I love a goofy man, and I have one right here," she whispered.

Their eyes met, and it was obvious that she adored him, skinned nose and all.

"It might take a little while to get used to this new look on you, but I think it might grow on me," she whispered.

"Pancakes are up!" a bellowing shout sounded from the kitchen.

Ryan turned Layla around by the shoulders. As she took her first step towards the kitchen, he swatted her on the rear.

"That's for laughing at me, in my hour of need," he said.

She quickly reached back, without even looking at him, and pinched the skin covering his exposed abdomen. She then scampered off to the kitchen, with Ryan following close behind. As the two entered, they found a huge platter of pancakes and bacon placed on the table before a smiling Larry. A wet haired Patsy, fresh out of the shower, was leaning back against his chest.

"That wet hair of yours is cold, girl," Larry complained.

She turned around and gave him a kiss. She then turned to the other couple and said, "Let's eat!"

The food was good, and the conversation was even better. They talked about what they might do after church, during the couple of hours they would have after the service and before parting ways. The sky was cloudy, and rain was forecasted for the afternoon. It would be a great time to play a card game Ryan had brought along.

As the four filed into Layla's church, Larry was ripe with anticipation for a touch from God. Only he and Layla felt comfortable there, for both Patsy and Ryan believed the congregation to be made up of uneducated zealots. Besides the discomfort with the congregation, they felt the pastor was more like a cheer leader. In their view, he played on the lack of intelligence and the vulnerable emotions of the members of the church. The two believed him to be a master manipulator, who used his abilities to whip people into a slight emotional frenzy. Patsy and Ryan believed that an emotional expression was no sign of a deep and mature relationship with God, but instead was only the result of a type of "pep rally" being conducted in the presence of easily excitable individuals.

On the other hand, Layla and Larry saw a service with

little emotion as being shallow spiritually. The two felt deeply that a true inward relationship with God flowed outwardly. It was expected that a valid spiritual experience would be obvious to those around them during worship. They had some doubt as to whether true faith existed in someone who always retained a calm and quiet demeanor in their religious expression. These perspectives were never voiced to one another but were silently held within each. Regardless of the different views, the four were almost inseparable. It was a matter of trust, which went beyond theological perspectives.

As usual, the service began with an elderly woman playing a piano. The white-haired lady used no sheet music but played everything by ear. At first the music was played slowly and beautifully, with embellished runs of improvised notes flowing throughout the hymns. The fingers of this little woman danced across the keys of the piano, as if she had the dexterity of an eighteen-year-old. Her head, topped with a pure white bun of ancient hair, nodded to and fro to the rhythm which seemed to flow magically from her soul. Her eyes would close for several seconds, but when they opened her gaze seemed to be as if she were in another realm. Eventually, the soft flowing music evolved into a heart pounding ecstasy of power and excitement. She was amazing, for the transition was not even noticed until after she ceased to play.

When the pastor stood to approach the pulpit, the pianist began again with graceful slow and soft melodies. Even as he opened with prayer, she softly continued. Her playing seemed effortless. It was not until he began to preach, that she ceased to play for extended periods of time.

During the sermon, Larry began to feel a tingling move from his chest and into his head. Something seemed to flow out from the top of his head, somewhat like a movement of slight static electricity. It seemed to come in waves. He closed his eyes and felt as though he was standing in the actual presence of God. His thinking drifted way from the sermon, and onto the greatness of the Creator of the universe. His heart was filled with awe, for a God so great, yet so caring for each small person within His creation. As Larry's attention focused back on the sermon, he heard the following words.

"If God almighty calls a man unto himself for service, that man will know it," the pastor spoke. "He may try to run from it, and he may find himself fighting against his Creator at times. But, deep within, that man will know God's calling. Just as Jonah was called by God, and then fought against that calling; he was still compelled to do God's will. He cannot escape it."

At that moment, Larry felt the tingling sensation rush into almost an explosion within him. It felt as if the Hands of God were on his chest, as the paddles of a defibrillator. The sermon ended. As the closing hymn was being sung, Larry found himself moving up the aisle of the church and towards the altar. Once there, he dropped to his knees. The pastor took his place before him on the opposite side of the altar, and lightly placed his hands on Larry's shoulders. He quietly mumbled prayer, and then quickly placed his left hand on the top of the head of the kneeling man before him. At that point, Larry felt as if he were no longer in the sanctuary of that small wood frame church but had left that place for a more holy sanctuary. He soon became mindful again of the pastor. After the service was over, it seemed as if a weight had been lifted from him.

"What was going on, there?" Patsy questioned, as they descended the church steps.

"What do you mean?" Larry responded. "I just went up for prayer."

"You were kneeling there for over five minutes," she spoke, with obvious concern. "Are you OK?"

"I've never felt better," he replied. "Five minutes? You say that I was at the altar for five minutes?"

"At least," Patsy explained. "What was going on with you? "

"I don't know; I think God did something, but I am really unsure about it," Larry stated.

He could tell that she was concerned, and a little confused by his actions. He sought the words to offer an explanation.

"I'm not sure," he continued. "I just felt really close to God back there. I'm a little unsure about what, but I think maybe God is trying to speak to me."

"Speak to you?" she stated. "That odd little church seems really strange to me, and you are starting to sound a little creepy."

"What's creepy?" a voice spoke from behind them.

Ryan and Layla had finally caught up with them. The two had been delayed while Layla introduced Ryan to a couple of people in the church. Patsy said nothing. She just stared intently into Larry's eyes, trying to connect with what he was saying. She was truly concerned.

"I told Patsy that I thought maybe God was trying to speak to me," Larry explained. "I don't know. What's it supposed to be like when God talks to someone… or tries to talk to someone?"

"How should I know?" Ryan asked. "I've never seen a burning bush or anything. I guess God still talks to some people, but I don't know anything about it."

"What happened, Larry?" Layla asked. "Just tell us what made you think God was trying to speak to you."

"I probably should have just kept my mouth shut," he whispered. "Patsy asked me why I went to the altar, and what was going on." Turning to Patsy, he continued. "I don't want to hide anything from you. If you think I'm weird, then so be it."

"I just don't understand," she stated, as the four reached Ryan's parked car.

Leaning on the car, Larry tried again to explain.

"OK. I closed my eyes during the sermon, and I thought about how great God is. I mean, He created the entire universe, and He still is concerned about each one of us. I can't explain it. It just hit me. The Creator of a universe… it extends farther than any telescope can see… still personally loves each one of His creations. Isn't that amazing? He doesn't just keep track of us; that would be amazing enough. He actually knows what each of us thinks, and He cares about us. I started getting this tingling sensation in my back, or maybe it was my chest. It moved up into my head and felt like it was coming out the top of my head. It happened over and over. I had to go to the altar. I can't explain it very well, I just had to go. When that preacher prayed for me, it felt like I was in heaven or something. I don't know, it just felt like nothing else. Except for the time the snake bit me. It was a little like that, but only better. Do you remember, Ryan?"

"I still don't understand what happened that day," Ryan answered.

The four got into Ryan's car and headed back to the house in Brandon Springs. Along the way, they discussed the day of the snake bite and everything Larry said he experienced during this day's service. As they talked, Patsy became less afraid.

"I think it was the Holy Spirit," Layla stated, as they walked inside the house. "It had to be the Holy Spirit. I've heard some of the older people in the church say that when the Holy Spirit gets a hold on someone, it moves them. They say that people can try to fight it, but if God fills someone up with the Holy Spirit, they have to just do what God puts on their heart. At least, that's what I think."

"God doesn't treat us like zombies!" Patsy responded. "He gives us free will. He might put something on our heart, but He doesn't just take control of someone like that. He doesn't have them on remote control. It's not like He operates people with a joystick."

"What makes any of us an expert on what God can or cannot do?" Layla asked. "Not a one of us is a preacher."

"Maybe He wants me to be a preacher," Larry quietly said.

"Preachers usually go to seminary or to Bible College," Ryan replied. "You have a gift for finance, and that is the field God has blessed you with."

"Exactly!" Patsy responded.

"Moses spent a long time as a shepherd before God called him to be a man of God," Layla chimed in.

"I'm no Moses," Larry chuckled.

"You're not even Charlton Heston," Ryan replied.

The tension died away, and the mood of the afternoon became lighter. Conversation turned to less spiritual topics, and the couples began to be more aware that the time together was passing quickly. Larry and Patsy made sandwiches and chips for lunch, while Layla and Ryan packed for the return trip home. Layla packed for the girls, and Ryan for the guys. The realization set in that the following day would be a workday. After lunch, they said their goodbyes and departed as they had come.

Chapter 15

THE WORKWEEK WAS A NORMAL ONE for Ryan, but Larry continued to struggle with questions over what had occurred during the service at Layla's church. Eventually, he placed a call to the pastor who had prayed for him at the altar. He told him about what he experienced, and asked if it was a sign that God was calling him into the ministry. The conversation ended with these words of advice from the pastor.

"If God has truly called you into the ministry, you will not be content unless you are doing that work for God. I advise you to not become a pastor unless you believe you can not sense fulfillment in any other way. If you can be happy doing anything else, don't go into the ministry."

Those words sounded familiar to him, but he couldn't remember where he had heard them before. Later in the week, he placed a call to the pastor of the church in Charlotte where he and Ryan often attended. The minister advised Larry to take a couple of seminary classes to see if the ministry seemed to be the right direction. Larry called Patsy, and then Ryan, to tell them each that he planned to attend a class or two at a local seminary. After assuring Patsy that he was only doing this to see if God was indeed leading him in that direction, she seemed accepting of the idea.

However, this decision caused Ryan concern. He knew Larry better than almost anyone else, even better than his friend's future wife. Ever since the death of his brother, Larry's emotions seemed to not be in check. For weeks after Ronnie's death, Larry had little to do with his friends. For months, he seemed to be spiritually adrift. Now, he was seriously considering a career as a preacher. His behavior seemed to be erratic, and it caused Ryan to consider the possibility that Larry had suffered an emotional breakdown. The more he thought about it, the more concerned he became for his closest friend.

The following weekend, Ryan traveled alone to his house in Brandon Springs. He told no one, not even Layla. He really wanted to see her, but he wanted nothing to do with her church. Instead, he considered attending the church of his late Aunt Sally. During the week he contacted the pastor of the church, to let him know that he wanted to spend a couple of hours in personal counsel with him that Sunday afternoon. The old man invited him to the parsonage for Sunday lunch after the church service. Ryan accepted the invitation, but he became conscious of the possibility that someone at the church would leak word to Layla that he was in the area. Ryan was so determined to maintain privacy in the matter, that he didn't attend any service on that Sunday morning in Brandon Springs. The parsonage was located conveniently next door to the old church. He arrived at the pastor's home at 12:45 PM and was graciously invited inside. The first few minutes were spent with Ryan thanking the man for his ministry to his late aunt, but the conversation was politely redirected by the older man.

"I know you didn't make an appointment with me, and drive this distance, to talk about my acquaintance with your aunt," he began. "What concerns you?"

Ryan began by giving the pastor a few general facts about Larry. He told him of his intellect in financial matters and of his humble family history. Ryan then explained the tragedy of Ronnie's murder, and of the impact it had on his friend. He went into detail about Larry's volatile behavior afterwards, and of his recent experience in the neighboring church.

"That is an interesting congregation," the pastor began. "I have never attended, but I've heard stories. Actually, I make a point to periodically have lunch with as many of the community pastors as will meet with me. At first, I tried to start a monthly community luncheon with all attending at once. However, this idea proved to be unsuccessful. Now, I just individually invite a local minister to have lunch from time to time. I have never been turned down by the pastor of that particular church; so, I probably have lunch with him at least twice a year. He seems to be very serious about his profession."

"Since his last experience at that church, Larry is now considering becoming a minister," Ryan explained.

"Is that so bad?" the pastor asked, smiling.

"Maybe not for you, but I can't see Larry leading a congregation" Ryan said, in a tone of desperation. "I know him, and I think maybe he has suffered a nervous breakdown or something. I mean, he went from having nothing to do with God to wanting to be a preacher within a matter of weeks. Doesn't that sound erratic to you?"

"I'm sure the death of his brother had a real impact on his behavior," the old man responded. "Sally told me that you didn't pay her a visit for several years after your parents were murdered. I'm sure she was just as concerned about you, and you seem to have turned out just fine. What is your friend doing right now?"

"He says he plans to sign up for a couple of seminary classes," Ryan answered.

"Sounds like pretty risky behavior," the pastor said, with a twinkle in his eye.

"You don't seem to be listening," Ryan replied. "I know it doesn't sound like much, but you don't know Larry."

"I am listening," the old man replied.

The fact of the matter was that the ancient pastor was listening much more intently than Ryan suspected. He was not just listening to his visitor's words, but he was carefully searching out matters which lay beneath the surface. Years of counseling souls, in the gravest conditions, had given him keen insight into the internal rivers of trouble which ran beneath the words uttered. He listened to the breathing of those in his counsel; he watched eye and hand movements; he played particular attention to the inflection of the words spoken. He had learned to watch beneath the words and listen for the voice of a person's soul.

"Placing Larry's thoughts of ministry aside, what concerns you the most about your own life?" the pastor firmly asked.

"I really came to see you about Larry," Ryan stated.

"My advice on the matter is to let him take his classes and just see what happens," the old man consoled. "Just be patient and wait. Just try to relax and be his friend. Now, what about you? I've reserved two hours this afternoon, and we have only taken one. I would like to talk about your happiness. What concerns you the most about where you are in your life?"

Ryan sat in silence; his eyes fixed into those of the older man.

"Well, I don't know what to say," he replied.

"When was the happiest time of your adult life?" the pastor pressed.

Looking down in thought, Ryan quietly searched his mind and heart, and then tried to answer the question.

"It would have to be those days I spent with Aunt Sally here, while I was recuperating from that accident."

"What was so enjoyable?" the old man continued.

"Maybe the sense of having family, family that knows you thoroughly and still loves you," Ryan began. "I had lost my parents years before, and it was so nice to have family again. The absence of family was pretty much my fault. Sally had been there. I had actually neglected her, and for several years I had left her alone. She didn't hold a grudge, she just seemed to be glad I was visiting again. She was the most God-like person I have ever met. Since the time when I was a small child, I had never felt so at home. Her life was so simple; and for a time, it simplified my life. I can't begin to try to describe the peace I felt."

"Your life is not so simple now?" he questioned.

"Good grief, no!" Ryan exclaimed. "My last family member is gone, my best friend's brother murdered, Larry is going to get married, and I am dating a girl who attends a weird church. I'm telling you - each time I attend that church, I am just waiting for the snakes to be brought out! That's not even close to the most complicated issues that I experience on a continual basis. There are aspects of my life that I can share with almost no one. Not that I don't trust you, but I wouldn't want to put very many people in the position of hearing some of the things which are going on in my life. It's anything, but simple! My job is stable, but the rest of my life is nuts!"

"You can never go back to Brandon Springs," the old man stated.

"What!" Ryan snapped. "I own a house here, and my girlfriend lives here… what do you mean can't come back here?"

"No, I mean, you can never have that time again in Brandon Springs," he replied. "You can't go back. That time has gone. You desperately needed those days with your aunt. Your heart was thirsty for family and for God, and He provided what you needed. Your soul continues to long for that experience, but that time has come and gone. It is a lot like caring for a small child. There comes a time when the baby is no longer carried about the house. There comes a time when the child has to learn to walk. God is bringing you into a more mature relationship with Himself and with others. It doesn't mean that the peace of God goes away. It means you can't just sit around and only soak it in anymore. God wants you to stand up and take care of those around you. You can't stay in the same place. It doesn't work like that. There are people who need you. There are people who need peace and need to have that wonderful family experience passed on to them. If you could, who would you pass that on to?"

Ryan was silent, as he had politely and gently been nailed to the wall. He was looking for Larry to be his stable friend, his family. He also wanted to revisit his Brandon Springs experience. Larry could not be all of those things. During those days with his aunt in Brandon Springs, Ryan had felt as though he had entered another world. Family loved him unconditionally, and the presence of God seemed so real and close that he felt he could have reached out his hand and taken his Creator's. Life had become complicated since those days, and deep down he longed for the simple life he had shared with Aunt Sally. He had so enjoyed the sharing of breakfast in the morning, and the conversations at night.

"You can't go back, but you can take all of that with you in life," the old man explained. "You take it with you as you share it with others. That is the only way to experience anything like it again. Give that experience to someone else. Who deserves it the most? With whom would you most want to share it?"

"Layla," he whispered.

It was at that moment that he really understood how much she meant to him. He had been so careful. Ryan had not allowed her beyond certain areas in his heart. Those areas he retained for only himself. His inward safe places, he kept. If he was rejected by someone, if a situation didn't work out, or if he failed; those people and those experiences never got into those places. They were kept intact, safe. He knew that he would need to now open those areas to the risk of being abused. The pastor had not specifically told him this. Deep within, he knew that he had to sacrifice those areas for a chance to be where he needed to be. If it resulted in pain, he would have to rely on God to heal wounds.

"No one deserves that kind of peace of mind and heart, and that sense of family, more than Layla," he stated.

"Only you would know," the old man said. "I will tell you this, and I would say the same words to Larry. If you seriously become involved with the lives of those around you, if you seriously commit yourself to others, if you seriously place yourself in God's hands, and ask Him to take you where He wants you to be…you had better hold on tight. You may be in for a ride."

Something began to well up from within Ryan, as he looked up at the old man. His throat began to close, so that it was difficult to swallow. Whatever it was began to cause his vision to blur. Within a minute he felt it difficult to breathe. The walls which had sealed off private areas within him began to develop cracks, and all the loneliness he experienced since the death of his Aunt Sally began to flow away with the single tear that seeped from his left eye. Quickly wiping it away, he began to relax. He sat silently for a moment, and slowly shook his head from side to side. His throat began to loosen, and he took a deep breathe. He closed his eyes and emptied himself before God and the old man.

"You're right," Ryan admitted to the pastor. "You really are. I miss my aunt, my parents, and the simplicity of those days here in the little town. I think I'm not any less wacky than Larry. Maybe that's why we get along so well; we're two nuts from the same tree."

"You both have lost family, and you both went out on your own searching for something," the pastor explained. "You may not look much like each other, but you have a great deal in common. Not just in experience, but you have the same way of dealing with loss. You lost your parents, and Larry lost his first wife. You both ran away to Boston. Think of the odds. It's very possible that God knew you both needed each other. But now that's changing somewhat. Larry has found a woman, and soon he will need to make her more of his focus. Nothing stays the same forever, and it shouldn't."

Ryan nodded.

"I want to visit Sally's grave before I go," he said, as he gave the old man a firm handshake.

"You'll find it well cared for," the pastor said, with a sly smile.

"If the church has been maintaining the gravesite, I want to reimburse the church," Ryan began. "How much is it? Do I just make a donation, or is there a set fee?"

"Oh, the church cuts the cemetery grass in the summer, but that's not what I meant," the pastor replied. "How long has it been since you've been to the gravesite?"

"It's probably been at least ten months" Ryan stated. "I really shouldn't have neglected it. However, I know she is not really there in the ground. If anyone is in heaven, I know it would be Sally. But I should have taken better care just out of respect for her. I stay pretty busy, but that's no excuse. I'm in town fairly often."

"Regarding the church that gives you so much concern, a member of that congregation takes care of Sally's grave," the old man said. "A young woman from that church places artificial flowers on the grave every couple of months. Sometimes I see her there, and other times I just notice the new flowers. I'm not sure how well she knew your aunt, but I think she knows you pretty well."

"Layla?" Ryan asked.

"She must really care for you, son," he answered. "Either that, or she knew Sally a lot better than I guessed."

"She must care more than I realized," Ryan replied. "I had no idea. I don't think she knew my aunt very well. Before meeting me, she knew Sally was my aunt. I mean, in this small town it's hard not to know who everyone is. She's asked me questions about my aunt. In fact, once she asked me what kind of flowers Sally liked. To be honest, I didn't even know the answer to that question. I never noticed those things about Sally, and she never made an issue over the things she might have liked or wanted. She was always concerned with doing something for someone else. I guess I wasn't really listening to Layla, and I never picked up on what she might be doing. Do you know if she has relatives buried in your church cemetery?"

"Not to my knowledge," he replied. "But if her family has been here for a long time, it's very possible."

Ryan rose from where the two were seated and told the minister that he would be spending a few minutes in the cemetery behind the church. Leaving the parsonage, he walked across the side yard to the rear of the church. He passed grave after grave, as he made his way to Sally's. At the sight of her small marker, he thought how ironic it was to have such an insignificant reminder of such a wonderful person. However, Sally would have wanted it that way. She was not one to bring attention to herself. Gone was the vase and artificial flowers that he had stationed between Sally's and her husband's markers a few years prior. He suspected that they might have fallen victim to winds from any one of a number of powerful thunderstorms that often occur in the southeastern United States. Placed neatly before the headstone, was a plain white ceramic bowl with a short white ceramic vase within. In that vase, someone had taken great care to arrange artificial lilacs, which were mixed with an assortment of artificial wildflowers of various colors. The arrangement was plain, but simple and elegant. They seemed to be the perfect fit for a woman of such pure love and varied experiences. Sally seemed, on the surface, to be as common as flowers growing in the wild. However, on deeper review, one would have found an assortment of richly colored qualities in Sally's life. Her modestly kept wisdom was surprisingly impressive to anyone who took the time to listen for it. She was a gentlewoman, and she never forced herself on anyone. In many ways she was a true representative of God. It's been said that God is a Gentleman, who never forces Himself on anyone. He is just there; just as the truth is just there, for anyone to openly accept.

Ryan had planned his visit to be in secret, but he found he could not leave without first seeing Layla. Though the afternoon was passing quickly, he decided to drive to her trailer. He noticed her car parked near the road, and he pulled his vehicle in behind hers. Walls of a trailer aren't very thick. If the environment inside the mobile home is quiet, distinctive sounds from the outdoors may be easily heard on an otherwise quiet day. As he approached the trailer, the front door opened slightly. Ryan was able to catch a partial view of Layla's face in the opening. It was obvious that she was watching him as he approached, yet the door didn't open more than two inches. Suddenly, a flush of dread flowed through him. He had never paid her a surprise visit before.

Maybe she has another man in the trailer. After all, promises had never been spoken by either of us.

He glanced around in a pretended casual manner, in an attempt to spot an unfamiliar vehicle in the vicinity. He saw none.

At last, he was at the door, and was within a couple of feet of the woman peering from inside the trailer. He saw question in her eyes.

"Hey," she spoke, through the opening. "You didn't tell me you were coming."

"Maybe, I should have," he answered. "Can I come in?"

"Hold on," she replied, as she shut the door. Quickly, it opened again, but this time a little wider. "I had to take the chain off," she explained.

The door opened about ten inches, and he could see that she was only wearing a towel wrapped around her body. As he placed his hand on the doorknob, she continued. "I didn't expect anyone, so I took an early bath."

With eyes still narrowed, as if they were asking an obvious question, she stepped aside and allowed him in.

"I should have told you I was coming, but I've recently had a lot on my mind," he began. "I needed to talk with Sally's pastor, and I wasn't sure whether I would be coming by here."

"Can I put a robe on?" she interrupted.

"Oh... sure," he replied.

She turned quickly and left the room. Within a couple of minutes, she returned wearing a lavender robe, while passing a brush through her wet hair.

"OK" she said, looking down. "What's been on your mind?"

"You know, things sometimes change regarding someone you care about," he continued. "There have been some unexpected changes, and I wasn't sure what to make of them. I needed to talk to someone who I felt would give me sound advice, and I wasn't sure how long the discussion would last. I didn't want to promise to come by, and then end up not having the time to do so."

"So, did you get your answers?" she asked, still nervously brushing her hair.

"Yeah, he sort of told me that I was the one with the problem," he said. "He told me to just let it go, and he was right."

"Let it go?" she questioned.

"Yeah, he told me to quit worrying so much about changes in my life, and just trust God," Ryan explained.

"Trusting God is good" Layla agreed. "So, you drove all the way over here to hear him tell you that?"

"Well, it was a little more complicated than that," he continued. "I thought the problem was with someone else, but he showed me that it was really my problem. I've missed some things, and I've been trying to hold on to others in an attempt to make up for it. I have to just quit, and let it go."

She took a seat on the couch. The brush became still, as she held it with both hands in her lap. Her head still facing downward, she spoke.

"It's OK. I understand. I expected too much, and I've probably made things difficult for you. You don't have to come over anymore. If it makes it easier on you, I don't have to be involved with giving away that money to people, either. I won't tell anyone about it."

"What are you talking about?" Ryan stammered.

"Well, I guess you figured out that you really don't need me," she answered. "I don't blame you."

"You are the best thing that's ever happened to me!" he blurted. "Well, next to God."

Ryan reached and took a nervous hand from her lap.

"There is no way that I would want to stop coming to see you."

"What do you want?" she asked, as she lifted watery eyes to meet his.

"I want you," he said. "Did you think I was trying to say that I didn't need to hold on to you?"

"Well…well," she attempted to speak, but she couldn't find the words.

Ryan pulled her close and kissed her. He felt her cold wet hair brush his face, as she buried her head against his chest. She was trembling, and he realized that she had begun to cry. Finally, she whispered, "I love you so much".

"I love you too, Layla," he replied.

"Then what were you talking about all this time?" she asked.

"Larry," he replied. "Larry has been acting so weird lately, and I was afraid he was losing it".

"Larry?!?" she exclaimed. "You're talking about Larry?"

"Yeah, and the pastor told me that I've been thinking mainly about myself," he answered.

She began beating his chest and shoulders violently with both fists.

"You had me so upset over Larry?" she yelled.

Ryan took hold of both of her wrists, in order to stop the beating. He pulled them both apart and then brought them back behind his neck, so that her face was brought close to his. Her lips dropped on his, and she kissed him fervently. He leaned back onto the couch and brought her against himself. Both felt passion flush throughout their bodies, as the kiss became more fervent. Suddenly, the front door opened, and her daughter burst into the room.

"Mommy, we have flowers!" the little girl blurted. "See. Aren't they pretty?"

As the attention of the couple quickly shifted away from each other, and onto her daughter, they caught the sassy eyes of Layla's mother.

"Do we need to go find more flowers?" she asked with a grin.

Chapter 16

A TIRED, BUT THANKFUL, LARRY returned home. He had another difficult, but rewarding, day. As he opened the front door his cell phone began to ring.

"Is it done?" he asked, closing the door behind him.

"Not yet, but the drop will be made," Ryan replied.

He began to explain his difficulties in delivering the recent envelope of money to the selected recipient. Ryan had made his way to the home of Amy Mitchell. He circled the block a couple of times, and then parked his car in front of a home just down the street. He studied Amy's house for several minutes. Seeing no signs of movement outside or within the house, he proceeded. Amy was two months from graduating from college, and she was three months from giving birth to her first child. Unmarried, and looking at a steep student loan, she had struggled to maintain a high-grade point average in the field of bio-medical engineering. She had been advised to abort the pregnancy, but she found that she couldn't bring herself to do so. Amy had made a mistake, but she felt she that taking the life of her innocent unborn child would be a greater mistake. She had been engaged to be married, but four months after she found that she was pregnant her fiancé was killed in an accident.

The evening had been a cool, quiet, and cloudless night. The full moon illuminated everything around Ryan.

He approached her car in the driveway. As soon as he reached to open the driver's side door, he heard the sound of the front door of the small house shut. As he turned, a young woman standing on the front porch shouted in his direction.

"What are you doing?"

"Should I quickly toss the envelope into the car and run back in the direction of my parked car?" he thought, hesitating for a moment.

"I'm calling the police!" Amy shouted at him, as she began to dial 911 on her cell phone.

Ryan immediately made a run for his car. Once inside, he tossed the envelope into the passenger seat and started the vehicle. Quickly, he dropped the car into reverse and began speeding in reverse down the street away from her house. With his headlights still off, his body was partially turned as he looked through the rear windshield for objects faintly illuminated by the moonlight. Still moving in reverse, he glanced back to see Amy making her way down her driveway and into the street. Careful not to allow her the opportunity to read his license plate, he continued to travel backwards down the street. Once he was more than a block away, he temporarily stopped before immediately slamming it into drive and turning down a side street. He waited until he crossed the next intersection before turning his head lights on. For about a mile, he wondered if she had captured the numbers from his car tag. Ryan had a very bad feeling about his current situation.

He quickly made his way back to the freeway. Once there, a new fear flooded his mind. He couldn't remember whether he had actually touched Amy's car door with his bare hands. Ryan had been sloppy. He had been so preoccupied by the thoughts of this recipient; he had forgotten to put on the latex gloves. This meant he also had spread his fingerprints on the envelope itself. He would have to destroy the envelope and use another one for the delivery. As he traveled down the highway, he clearly remembered that he had not yet touched the door of her car.

If she didn't get the tag number, I should be fairly safe.

He could only hope that her view of him and his car wasn't good enough to give the police an accurate description. Ryan realized that it would be nearly impossible that night to make a second attempt to deliver the package to Amy Mitchell. His hands tightly clenching the steering wheel, he made sure that he didn't exceed the speed limit. He couldn't afford to give a policeman cause to pull him over. As he left the city limits, he breathed a sigh of relief. Passing the county marker on the highway, he breathed another. Ryan had made this attempted delivery alone. He had made many deliveries, and this time he felt no need to take the time of involving anyone else. Ryan volunteered to handle this one alone. Now, all he could think about was how stupid he had been to drive without his headlights.

What if I had hit someone? The donation effort would have involved tragedy.

It was as if the car was on autopilot, as he steadily traveled in the direction of Charlotte. It was almost 2:00 AM when he parked his car directly across the street from Larry's small house. He witnessed no burning lights inside and saw no signs of activity within the home. Ryan turned off the engine and breathed a nervous sigh of relief. He rolled down the driver side window of his car and felt the cool night air gently pass over the left side of his face. He sat motionless, listening to the crickets and the distant muffled sounds of the city. As the adrenaline rush of the event subsided, he began to calm down. Ryan closed his eyes for a moment and asked God to help him to not be in trouble. Thoughts of the pregnant young woman began to replace the thoughts of his personal situation. He prayed for her peace of mind and spirit. Feelings of guilt, for causing her additional stress, caused him to earnestly ask God to help Amy Mitchell not be afraid. It was the first time, since making his escape, he had considered her welfare.

Glancing over at the envelope in the passenger seat of his car, Ryan reconsidered the remote possibilities of delivering the money to her in other ways. Having serious doubts about ever risking another attempt, he decided to not to go near her home again. After all, he was sure she would not be leaving her car unlocked in the future. Then, as if inspired, he had an idea. He started the engine of his car, put it in gear, and allowed the vehicle to idle slowly down the street. As Ryan passed home after home, the thought became more strongly ingrained in his mind and soul. Before long, it became clear that this was the right course of action. A smile crept across his face as the idea continued to take hold. After years of making donations to worthy individuals, this seemed to be the most logical choice of any.

The next morning, Larry stepped out of his bedroom to face a long day of work. As he began to close the door behind him, he felt a smooth soft hand on his. Turning, he looked into eyes peering from the bedroom. Those eyes struggled to handle the light from the hallway.

"Are you leaving without saying goodbye?" Patsy softly spoke.

He pushed the bedroom door open again, and he took her into his arms. She slid her hands under his shirt and began kissing his neck. "Can I convince you to stay?" she whispered.

"If you don't stop, I'll be late," he replied. "This is a big day, and I would have a hard time explaining what kept me."

"OK," she answered, as she began tucking his shirt tail back in.

"Do you regret getting involved with me?" he asked.

"Not for a minute," she replied.

"Do you ever wish you had married a guy who would have provided you an easier life?" he asked. "I mean, about the money and all. I was making good money, and I was well on my way to being financially really well off."

"I am exactly where I should be," she said. "Wherever you go, I should be with you. You're stuck with me. How about you? Do you have any regrets?"

"Sometimes I think about how easier life would be for you, if I hadn't given it all up," Larry quietly spoke.

"I have everything I need, and almost everything I really want," she assured. "You know what I want most, but all in good time."

He kissed her on the forehead and turned to leave the bedroom again. This time, he successfully made it out of the room.

As he walked down the hallway of the small house, he thought about some of the financial struggles they had shared over the two years of marriage. Larry thought about how close they came to calling off the wedding, after he told her he had made a decision to become a minister. That announcement had shaken up her plans for them both. She had pictured a large home, and new cars. None of that was to be. He thought about his mother, and her life. He imagined that earlier in her life she may have had greater expectations than to share a small house with violent man. Since the death of his father, Larry sent his mother round trip air tickets twice a year, to enable her to visit. Twice yearly, he visited her in Alabama. Larry thought about the furniture he had purchased for his mother during those early years of financial success. He considered the home repairs he had been able to do for her. Due to his own current financial situation, he could no longer do any of this.

He slipped behind the steering wheel of his aging car and considered regrets in his own life. The first, and foremost, he regretted the night Ronnie died. Larry had forgiven himself, but he still missed his brother terribly. He placed the car in gear and headed down the street. It was a new day, and things would be different. Soon, he was to give a presentation to the leadership of a church that included exceptionally wealthy members in its congregation. A year earlier, Larry had become the director of a mission for the homeless in Charlotte, and today he would attempt to win support from that church. The mission needed financial help, and he wasn't too proud to beg for it. He took only a meager salary from the mission, to support Patsy and himself. She was still a nurse, but they were seriously considering having a child. He had used his entire savings to purchase the very small home where they both lived. It would be big enough for one child, but the neighborhood was not the best. He looked at this watch and took note that he had half an hour to make the 7:00 AM meeting. The meeting was to take place before Mission Committee members of the church had to be at their places of work.

As he drove down a mostly empty street, his cell phone rang. Not expecting a call this early, Larry fumbled the handling of his phone and it fell to the floorboard of the car. Making sure there were no cars immediately in his vicinity, he bent over to pick it up. He quickly straightened himself and answered.

"Hello?"

"The drop has been made," Ryan informed.

"Good," Larry replied. "Have you been up all night on this one?"

"Yep" his friend answered. "I screwed things up earlier, and it took some time to handle things."

"I bet you'll sleep well tonight." Larry responded. "Hey! I've got a big day today. Say a prayer for me this morning."

"Will do" the voice on the other end replied.

It took several minutes for Larry to drive to the large church complex, and it took at least five more minutes to find the meeting room within. His presentation was simple, honest, and straightforward. Several of the members of the committee remembered him from his days in finance. Though most didn't understand the thinking behind a gifted financial wizard's decision to leave a field for which he seemed to have been born, they were truly impressed with his dedication to help less fortunate individuals. His financial gifts were not entirely wasted, because he was extremely good at running a most efficient ministry. On the side, he still gave stock tips to individuals. He only asked that they share a little of their profits with the mission. When he arrived, he was given the directorship because the previous director considered it a failed cause. That person was leaving the mission to pastor a church. The mission had been in the red, and the city was about to shut it down because there was no money to bring the building up to code. Larry visited a few acquaintances. These people had made a great deal of money via his stock tips, and he was able to obtain enough temporary support to make the repairs. Years before, he viewed his ability in areas of financial investments as being a gift to himself from God. Now he simply saw it as a gift to pass on to others.

The presentation was given, and a promise was made that a decision regarding support would be given in the near future. He left the church confident that the matter was in God's hands. Larry drove through wealthy neighborhoods and arrived in the more destitute area of the mission. Larry parked his car and quietly entered the front door.

Evelyn was an elderly widow, whose husband had been a minister. She required very little salary, since her husband had left her a pastor's pension. The job of administrative assistant to the mission was perfect for her. Many years of accompanying her husband, as he ministered to others, caused her to feel quite at home at the mission.

As Larry made his way to his office, he was met by Evelyn. She took him by the coat sleeve and led him hurriedly into the office.

"You need to see this," the elderly woman spoke in almost a whisper.

She was holding something behind her back; and once he was seated in his chair, she dropped it on the desk before him. At once he recognized the familiar large envelope.

"This envelope is full of money!" she proclaimed. "Whoever gave this package shoved it through the donation drawer. It's a good thing that you replaced that old mail slot with a drawer that would accommodate clothes and other items. This fat envelope would have never gone through a mail slot."

Larry said nothing, but simply opened the package and peered into it. There was no question in his mind regarding the source of the money. Larry had only asked his friend Ryan if the package of money had been given away. He never thought to ask if it had been given to Amy Mitchell, as planned. Reaching into the envelope, he brought out a large bundle of bills. The feel of the money in his hand, immediately brought memories of occasions when he and Ryan loaded the bills into envelopes for other recipients. He looked down at the hands that once beat a man to death. Larry marveled at the fact that, in his mission to others, these hands were now placed on needy individuals who came to him for prayer and help. As he considered God's remarkable grace and irony, a lump began to form in his throat and his grateful heart began to beat faster. Larry thought about the money he and Ryan had given to his brother, and regret began to take hold of his heart.

"If I had not been so careless as to let Ronnie know about the money and the charitable effort, would my brother still be alive?" he painfully asked himself.

His hands shook as he placed the bills back inside the envelope. A glance from him told Evelyn that his emotions were on the verge of bursting. She was old enough to have witnessed a lot of people in many situations. His countenance was not difficult to read.

"Do you want to be alone for a few minutes?" she politely asked.

Larry nodded, and Evelyn closed the door behind her as she stepped outside. He could hear her whispering to the staff, of the tears she saw welling up in his eyes. One member of the staff offered the explanation that Larry must be so moved by the amount of money in the donation, that it had brought him to tears.

Evelyn suspected the cause to be more than the amount of money contained in the envelope. She had become very astute at reading mannerisms and facial expressions of individuals. For years she accompanied her husband as he counseled females. This was done as a precaution against placing a man of God alone with a troubled woman. This was to ensure he would not be tempted to take advantage of a vulnerable female. Also, a woman would have no grounds to accuse him of behaving inappropriately with her. He did the counseling, but Evelyn had listened and observed people for many years.

Alone in the office, Larry immediately dropped to his knees in prayer. He considered the fact that the dangerous situation, resulting from Ronnie's unwise spending activity, may have had a sobering effect on his younger brother.

"It could have been the factor that caused my brother to straighten out his life and turn to God," Larry considered.

Larry began to thank God for His hand in Ronnie's life and in his own. He was tired, and his volatile emotions jerked his thoughts in different directions. He was thankful that God had touched Ronnie, but negative thoughts plagued his view of himself. Though he had finished his seminary studies, he didn't see himself equal with other ministers.

"How many other men of the cloth have inflicted physical violence on another human being to the point of killing someone?" he thought.

He felt so inadequate, and so undeserving of God's Mercy. As he prayed, Larry felt an internal spiritual warming. He sensed the presence of God's Spirit as strongly as he did the day Layla's pastor prayed for him in that old white wooden church. A tingling sensation moved from his head down into his chest. He closed his eyes and pictured the janitor of Layla's church standing in Heaven with his brother Ronnie. In this mental picture, it was almost as if the two were communicating without speaking. He knew the janitor, Alvin, to be a man of serious prayer.

"Maybe Alvin had prayed for Ronnie at some point," he thought. *"Maybe God is letting me know that Alvin had a role in my brother's life, and that I never knew it."*

Larry wasn't sure why he had thought about the older man, as he sensed Gods presence to be so real. It didn't matter. It was as if his Creator was speaking directly to his heart, without words. He felt as if his brain was being bypassed, for God needed no verbiage in meeting his need. No scripture was being read and understood for the first time. He sensed God's acceptance, and his soul rested in it.

The root cause of his feelings of inadequacy ran much deeper. As a child, his father had wounded his spirit with brutal words and often brutal actions of physical violence wounded his body. In his office, Larry dropped to his knees in prayer. Words would not have convinced him of his father's love. There are unspoken messages of love communicated, which go beyond words. During this time of communion with his Creator, he felt God was speaking directly to his soul.

Opening his eyes to the familiar sights of his small office, his troubled soul was at rest. He felt refreshed. Larry looked at his watch and took note that it was 9:45 AM. He had been alone in the office for about a half hour. He rose from his knees and made his way to Evelyn. She was seated at her desk typing a newsletter to the churches in the community. As he handed her the envelope, Larry gave her direction concerning the cash.

"Please place this in the safe," he requested. "I'll deposit it in the mission's account this afternoon."

Larry began his rounds at the mission. He greeted each staff member and client, and then proceeded to provide counseling for a newcomer. After helping serve meals at lunch, he sat with the new man to eat his own meal. He wanted to get a feel for the person, and he understood that a conversation over food provided a more relaxed atmosphere than speaking with him from behind a desk. After Larry taught a class on personal hygiene, he retreated to his office to give Ryan a call.

"I thought we had decided on who was to receive the donation," Larry stated. "I see you took a little creative license with this recent delivery of money."

Ryan explained how difficult it would have been to make another attempt at giving the money to Amy Mitchell. Larry agreed with the remote chance of success, but questioned Ryan's gift to the mission. They laughed, as Ryan went into the harrowing details of almost getting caught during the delivery of the recent donation.

"After all these years, it would have been ridiculous to get caught making a delivery!" Ryan exclaimed. "I was careless. I even forgot to bring a pair of gloves."

Though they had not grown up in the same household, Larry had come to know and trust Ryan as no other. He grieved at the loss of his physical brother, Ronnie, and continued to miss him. However, in one sense, he felt as though he still had another brother. The spiritual bond between himself and Ryan made them brothers of the soul. Ryan and Larry sometimes met for lunch at the mission. Larry's work at the mission called for long hours, and he now had less time to give to the charitable effort. However, both men vowed not to neglect spending at least one weekend a month visiting the other. The weekend always included Patsy and Layla.

Unlike the previous professional financial work in an office, the needs of the mission work rarely ended on Friday afternoon. Larry imagined the mission work to be as demanding as that of a medical doctor on call. Incidents and situations occurred almost every day requiring his attention, and occurrences could happen at any time of day or night.

Although he had a fairly able staff on rotation, his responsibilities ran twenty-four hours daily and usually seven days a week. During that one weekend each month with Ryan, he allowed the staff to provide hours of coverage so that he was not required to be physically present. The overall responsibility of the mission was entirely on the shoulders of Larry and his God.

That afternoon, Larry called the committee chair at the church he had visited earlier in the morning. He confessed to receiving the large quantity of cash from an anonymous donor, and he felt this information would probably cause the committee to believe the needs of the mission were no longer as critical. In truth, only the immediate needs would be met by the donation. What the mission needed was a regular flow of donations, as to ensure continuous operations.

The following day, he was visited by the main pastor and the Missions Committee Chair of the wealthy church. When word got out about the large donation, it was assumed that a wealthy member of the church had made it. The pastor decided that this particular mission must be at the heart of at least one heavy giver to the church, and he felt he should make sure the ministry was supported.

"I want to propose something, if you will give me your attention for a few minutes," the pastor began.

"Sure," Larry responded, as he brought an extra chair into his office.

As Larry took his seat behind the small desk, the pastor continued.

"The Missions Committee members and I have discussed the need at this mission, and we have come to an agreement."

"Yes?" Larry said, anticipating a meager commitment to the mission.

"We want you to allow the church to adopt the mission as a direct ministry of our local church, and I want you to be on our church staff as the Minister of Missions to the

Community," the pastor offered.

"I didn't know you had a Minister of Missions to the Community," Larry stated in astonishment.

"We do now, if you will take the position," the pastor said with a smile. "Your work here has been impressive, and we believe you would be a great asset to our church. There is no question that you are a great asset to the community. Would you be interested in that arrangement?"

"Yes, I will gladly accept," answered Larry.

"We haven't even discussed your salary for the position," the pastor noted. "That aspect will have to be placed before a separate committee, which decides the church financial matters regarding employed ministers. This committee will meet at 7:00 tonight."

"I trust you," Larry responded. "I know that you will be more than fair. My concern is that the people here remain to be served and cared for."

It was almost 9:00 that evening when Larry entered the front door of his small house. A familiar voice from the kitchen called out.

"It's about time," said Patsy. "When I heard you drive up, I put your dinner in the microwave. It should be ready in a minute."

"We need to talk," he replied.

"Is everything OK?" Patsy questioned, as she walked into the small living room.

"Looks like I may have a new job," he said, playfully trying to add a little suspense to the conversation.

"What will happen to the mission?" she asked.

Larry couldn't stand waiting any longer. He filled her in on the events of the day and the offer from the pastor. Each week, he would attend two committee meetings and a roundtable meeting for ministers at that church. During the rest of the week, he would spend his time conducting his ministry work at the mission. Larry explained to her the phone call he received from the church committee shortly after 8:00 PM. He would receive no parsonage or housing allowance from the church. Instead, he would retain his normal salary from the mission and be paid an additional $20,000 annually by the church. As a minister of the church, he would also take part in pensions and insurance plans. The church would also contribute at least another $30,000 annually to the mission, as part of its budget. The mission would still be allowed to accept direct charitable gifts from businesses and individuals. At last, Larry and Patsy would be financially in a position to have a child.

Larry and Patsy celebrated the blessings which had come their way. After the excitement somewhat settled, they knelt before the couch in the living room and prayed for God's continued direction. After supper, Larry sat on the front steps of the small home in the still moonlight. Glancing down at his hands, he again thought of the life those hands had taken and of the gracious work they were now doing on a daily basis. He felt at peace. The guilt was finally gone.

His thoughts were interrupted by his wife.

"Ryan's on the phone," she announced.

He excitedly told his friend of the news. Ryan congratulated him, and then soberly informed his friend of the purpose of the call.

"Layla called," Ryan began. "Do you remember the janitor of the church who prayed for you when the snake bit you?"

"Alvin," Larry responded.

"He died this morning, around 9:30 AM," Ryan replied.

Larry was silent for a few seconds, remembering the wisdom and deep spirituality of this seemingly common man.

"How did he die?" Larry asked.

"Apparently, he suffered a massive aneurysm in the brain," Ryan explained. "He was gone almost immediately."

The remainder of the call was spent with Larry giving his friend details of the opportunity presented by the church.

After Larry ended the call, he told Patsy about Alvin passing away around 9:30 that morning. He thought about his time in prayer earlier that morning and having the mental picture of his brother and Alvin standing together in Heaven. Larry had felt so close to God. It was at that point that he realized the unusual coincidence. He remembered looking at his watch that morning, and the fact that the watch read, "9:45 AM".

Chapter 17

RYAN AWAKENED TO A SENSE of complete peace. The red glow of the morning sunrise began to spill across the partially nude form lying beside him. He reached for the sheet to cover the sleeping woman, but he had second thoughts. Ryan hesitated for a few seconds, as he genuinely enjoyed what he saw. He continued the placement of the sheet over Layla and also covered her with the spread. Ryan moved close behind her and placed an arm over her swollen pregnant belly. He left it there just long enough to feel a slight push of a tiny arm or foot poking its way from inside, and then gave a small prayer of thanksgiving to God. Glancing around the familiar bedroom, he lay there for a couple of minutes. He remembered the broken springs and the lumpy mattress of his Uncle Andrews bed, and of how he replaced it with the one on which he now lay.

Remembering what Saturday mornings usually brought, he quietly rose from the bed. He was careful not to wake her. Ryan slipped on a pair of jeans and made his way across the bedroom and slowly opened the door. In the hallway, just outside the door, a small voice whispered.

"Can I come in?" Layla's daughter asked.

"OK," he responded. "But, you know, she is sleeping pretty well right now."

The little face grinned, and then turned its attention to

the person still sleeping.

"I'll be real quiet," Kaylee promised.

The little girl tip-toed across the room, and slowly climbed upon the bed. She positioned herself beside her mother and began to gingerly stroke the sleeping woman's hair. She glanced back at Ryan, as if to say, "See, I'm being really quiet."

He gave her a quick smile and left the bedroom to begin the Saturday morning ritual. This ritual only came into play on Saturday mornings at the house in Brandon Springs. Once in the kitchen, he started the coffee. Assured that this first task was successfully underway, he began frying bacon and scrambling the eggs. Larry made a small amount of pancake batter. He opened a small box containing some of his Aunt Sally's recipes and selected the one for buttermilk drop biscuits. Voices of laughter from the past ran through his mind, and they brought him back to those special days he spent with his aunt. In his imagination, the kitchen still echoed with loving conversation and moments of enjoyable teasing.

Those thoughts were interrupted by the ringing of the phone. He quickly answered, hoping to not wake the woman asleep in his bed. The ancient voice of the woman on the other end, was asking if the month's delivery of charitable funds had been made. Ryan assured her that it had been given to a very worthy recipient. He heard a deep and restful sigh, and then in a distinctive clear voice.

"You know, my husband and Sam chose you a long time ago," Mrs. Thompson stated.

"What?" he politely asked.

"Bill knew you were the one, as soon as he heard you share Layla's story with the Sunday school class," she explained.

Mrs. Thompson told him how the older men realized that their time on this earth was limited and that their activities with the donations were quickly coming to an end.

Each believed a worthy younger man should be found to finish their work.

"You've proved him right," she said. "You and your friends have done such a wonderful job in continuing the charitable cause they began. I don't know if those in heaven are mindful of things still going on in this world after they die, but I can tell you that Bill would be so very proud of you."

As he hung up the phone, he heard a sweet feminine voice from behind him.

"Who was on the phone, so early?" Layla asked.

"OK, it was another woman," he stated, trying not to crack a smile.

"Well, it had better have been your Aunt Sally calling from her grave, if you know what's good for you!" Layla exclaimed.

She pinched a portion of his skin covering his bare abdomen between her thumb and finger.

"Aghh!" he let out a cry. "You are really a violent person, you know that? Maybe I should call the police; you continually abuse me."

"Not so fast," she replied. "Would you want me to spill the beans on your illegal financial dealings? I know for a fact, that a lot of ill-gotten gain has passed through your hands."

Just then, the phone rang again. This time Layla quickly picked it up.

"Hello," she politely answered.

She listened for a couple of seconds, and then replied.

"Oh, I'm feeling fine. How are you doing?" She was silent for a few seconds, and then answered. "OK, I'll tell him. Bye."

"Well?" Ryan asked, placing his hands over his tender abdomen in an effort to protect it from another violent attack.

"Mrs. Thompson said that she forgot to tell you that she sent a package to you, and that it should be delivered sometime today," she replied.

"That's interesting," he responded.

"So, when were you going to tell your wife that you were receiving phone calls from another woman?" she asked, holding back a smile.

"Well, I don't know what to say," he replied, while shrugging his shoulders.

She walked up closer and opened her robe.

"Maybe I can take your mind off that other woman," she whispered.

His hands moved away from protecting his recently abused abdomen, and he placed one hand on her swollen belly. She moved closer and placed the exposed upper portion of her body against his bare chest. He pulled her form against his and caressed her neck. He silently thanked God for his life.

"I am so glad I married you, Layla," he whispered.

"This baby is so lucky," she replied. "You're a natural at being a father. You're so good with my daughter Kaylee. I was drawn to you the first day I met you, that day in Elva's Café. I felt like I had always known you. I can't explain it."

Raised on her toes, she pressed her face against his neck. She lowered herself and kissed his bare chest. Raising herself again on her toes, she whispered in his ear.

"You're a good man, and I am so in love with you."

She heard a small voice call out from the other bedroom.

"OK – I'm dressed and I'm ready for the day!" Kaylee shouted.

At the sound of the young footsteps speeding into the kitchen, Layla quickly closed her robe and gave Ryan a kiss.

"I guess that's all you get for now," she told him, in a teasing manner.

"Hey, nobody else is ready for the day!" Kaylee scolded. "I'm the only one who is dressed and ready."

"Well, I've been cooking breakfast," Ryan said in his defense. "See, I made you a mouse pancake."

He showed her a plate with a round pancake with two smaller round protruding areas coming off it, resembling a mouse face with two ears. He spread a little butter on it and handed her the plate.

"I love mouse pancakes," she said, with a grin.

She took the plate to her place at the table, hopped up in her chair, and began to pour maple syrup on it. She then held out both hands and looked up at Ryan.

"You look like you're ready to eat," Layla stated.

"Can I?" Kaylee asked Ryan.

At that point Ryan and Layla each took one of the little girl's hands and bowed their heads.

"Do you want to say it, Kaylee?" Ryan asked.

She nodded her little head and began.

"God, thank you so much for my mouse pancake, and bless it to make me healthy and strong. Please bless my daddy and my mommy, and bless their food, too. Thank you for this day in Brandon Springs. Amen."

They released hands, and she began to eat. Layla announced that she would shower and get dressed while Ryan finished cooking the biscuits. He watched her walk back to the bedroom, and then he glanced over to the little girl just in time to witness a fork full of mouse pancake being consumed. Ryan thought about the day that he legally adopted Kaylee as his own daughter, and he thought about how he had grown to love her. He tried to imagine the birth of his own flesh and blood child, who was due in two months. Ryan couldn't see how he could love this child any differently than the little girl sitting at the table. He hoped that he would never show favoritism between the two, but he realized that only time would tell.

Just as Ryan placed the breakfast on the table, Layla arrived from her shower. She was dressed, but her hair was still wet. She walked up behind him and tossed her wet hair against his bare back.

"Good grief!" he shouted. "Now look, I made you

breakfast, and you repay me by slinging your cold wet hair on me. You had better watch yourself because you may be due for a spanking."

"I expect you to wear a shirt in the presence of my daughter," she teased. "That's what you get."

The whole situation made Kaylee giggle. She hoped down from her seat, took them both by a hand and led them over to the kitchen table.

"Now, behave or you may have to be sent to your room," she said, smiling.

Breakfast was enjoyed by all, and afterwards Ryan excused himself to cut the grass outside. This was supposed to have been the main reason for spending that warm sunny weekend at the house in Brandon Springs, but he found it easy to come up with an excuse for leaving Charlotte for a weekend at the house. While he was working outside, Layla swept the house and cleaned the bathroom. Kaylee, now six years old, pulled a chair up to the kitchen sink and did her best to wash dishes.

Ryan showered after mowing. Later, they sat down to a lunch of sandwiches and iced tea. In an effort not to dirty Kaylee's freshly washed dishes, they used paper plates and disposable cups. Ryan had installed a satellite dish for a small TV, but it was rarely turned on. The family usually just enjoyed the quiet country sounds of birds singing and the distant barking of dogs, while working on a puzzle that would be placed on a card table in the living room. He remembered wishing for a TV as a child, while visiting his aunt and uncle at the home. He was often bored during those years, but things were different now. Ryan now welcomed the slow pace and simple living there, as an escape from the busy and demanding life in Charlotte. By now, he had been given greater responsibilities at his job. Ryan had accepted the life that went with marrying a woman with a small child, and he looked forward to another child on the way. He kept tabs on many of the individuals who had been given packages through the charitable work. Some would move, and he would lose track of them. However, he was very interested in seeing the results of those gifts in the lives of those people. His life was more complicated than ever, yet life never felt so worthwhile.

That afternoon the package arrived from Mrs. Thompson, and both Ryan and Layla were curious as to what it contained. There were two envelopes and a book. Inscribed on one envelope were the words, *Open First*. It was a letter from Mrs. Thompson explaining that the other envelope held pictures, and that the book contained the memoirs of her late husband, Bill. She expressed her trust and confidence in Ryan and asked that the memoirs be kept in a safe place. Bill Thompson's widow requested that only those persons involved in the charitable effort be allowed to read the memoirs. The information within could prove troublesome for her family, should it be read by others. She promised that he would find the accounts captured by her husband to make for a very interesting read.

The envelope was found to have an early picture of Bill Thompson and his wife. Ryan and Layla agreed to have it framed and kept at the Brandon Springs house. Other pictures were of seven different men. Some of them wore Army uniforms. There was one picture of an oriental woman holding a baby. The words, *Min Yon and little Max,* were written on the back of the old photo. Ryan studied the face of the woman. He placed his finger over the slightly smiling mouth, to focus on her eyes. Though he was not accustomed to reading the expressions on the faces of oriental people, her eyes seemed sad to him.

The writing on the back of another photo of a man in uniform read, *Henry Pope*. The name written on the back of another photo of a man in uniform read, *Louis Simpson*. There was a portrait photo of a very handsome man wearing a suit. It was professionally done in Los Angeles, with the name of the studio and address printed on the back of the photo. His face seemed to exude confidence and intelligence. The handwriting on the back of the photo read, *Tom Richards*.

"These men must have been important to the Thompson's, and I would guess they had early involvement with the charity work," declared Ryan.

The next faces in the photos were familiar to him, even though the pictures had been taken many years earlier. They were of Bill Thompson, Charles Moore, and Sam Wells. He turned each picture over to confirm with the penned writing on the back of the photos. Bill and Charles were the easiest to recognize, but he was fairly surprised at the younger face of Sam Wells. His hair was thicker, his powerful jaw line was much leaner, and his eyes were somewhat softer than the man he knew. Although he didn't entirely have the handsome features of a movie star, his presence was striking.

It was the face in the next photo that took him by surprise. Most of the other pictures were in black and white, but this more recently taken color photo was of his Uncle Andrew. He and Layla looked at each other in astonishment.

"OK, I want us to read these memoirs together," he said to Layla. "I'm a little creeped out by that last photo."

"You read first, and then I'll read to you," she suggested. She snuggled up to her husband and pulled a blanket over her legs and feet.

The entrees by Bill Thompson began in 1956, where he made a full confession of how the gold was found in Korea. He listed each of the men involved in the arrangement and wrote a short paragraph about each of them. Bill wrote in detail of how Sam Wells introduced Max Cunningham to Mr. Park and Min Yon. He described the marriage between Max and Min Yon, and how she was left with their baby boy in South Korea. Ryan found the murder of the Korean businessman to be particularly interesting.

"I wonder who else in South Korea knew about that money," he said to Layla. "I wonder if the guy was killed over that gold, or because of involvement in some other illegitimate business."

As Layla was about to take her turn at reading, Kaylee entered the room.

"I'm tired of playing in my bedroom, can I go outside and play on the porch?" she asked. A coloring book was neatly tucked under one arm, and she held a box of crayons in her hand.

"Sure, Honey," Layla replied. "Just don't leave the porch, unless you tell us."

"OK," she answered, before opening the front door.

Kaylee enjoyed fishing in the pond behind the house, and Layla was concerned that she might wander back to it. Ryan and Layla had made a point to give her swimming lessons, and Kaylee had become a very good swimmer. However, they often found snakes in the vicinity of the pond. The little girl's mother was familiar with the story about Larry being bitten by the copperhead a few years earlier, and these snakes were known to frequent the pond.

Layla began reading at the point where Bill Thompson sadly wrote of the death of his friend Henry Pope. He was puzzled as to who could have cut the brake lines of the truck, but he suspected the death had something to do with the Korean money. For several months after Henry's death, he watched to see if the family appeared to be living more affluently. Instead, the wife and two daughters struggled to make ends meet. Mr. Pope's life insurance policy was small, and his widow eventually found a job in a textile factory. There was no sign that he had left them with any of his share of the money. Bill wondered if that money had been abandoned in a train station locker, or if Henry left it somewhere else. However, he couldn't escape the possibility that someone had learned of the cash and had killed him for it. He felt it was a shame for the family to struggle, when so much money had been at Henry's disposal.

Bill Thompson was even more shocked at the execution

style murder of Tom Richards and Louis Simpson in Chicago. Their murder caused him to feel sure that someone with knowledge of the money was picking off the members of the group. Tom was a bachelor, so he doubted that money was left to anyone in his family. Like Henry Pope's family, the widow of Louis appeared to struggle financially after her husband's death. It was apparent to him that the killer was taking the money from each victim. Only Max, Sam, Charles and Bill now remained. Bill didn't know whom to trust. He wrote of the care he took in communicating with the others, and how he felt that Charles would be the least likely to commit murder.

Still, he was not about to leave either his wife or himself in a vulnerable position. It was at this point that he decided to reveal some of his secrets to his wife. He let her know that he and the other men had brought a large quantity of money back from Korea, and that United States government knew nothing of it. No taxes had ever been paid, and they both could be in big trouble should this come to the attention of the IRS. He didn't tell her about the death of the Korean businessman, but he let her know that he suspected the deaths of Henry, Louis, and Tom to be linked to someone who knew about the money. Within the handwritten pages of the memoirs, he left a detailed account of how shocked she was to find out about the money.

Bill told her of his plan to attempt to hide the funds. If he was murdered, he wanted to make sure the money would be available to her. Mr. Thompson decided to deposit the money in several lockers at train and bus stations. He put some in a safe deposit box at his bank. He gave his wife a list of the places and the amounts and put a spare key to each in separately marked envelopes. The envelopes were placed in different places of the house. A note, detailing the presence of each key and each location of hidden funds, was kept in the safe deposit box. If the murderer broke into his home, Bill wanted it to be difficult for every key to be found.

The entire situation caused Mary to be very nervous and afraid. She was uneasy that her husband had hidden money from the government, and she was surprised that Bill would risk his career over not declaring the money to be taxed. However, she knew that her father had financial dealings which were not always above board. Other than this vice, her father had always been a kind man. In her heart she trusted Bill, for she knew that he had told her about the money because he was concerned for her welfare. It was now apparent to them that both their lives could be in danger. Fearing for her safety, Bill bought a small 38 caliber revolver for her. She had always been a lady whose expertise was in the kitchen. However, this quickly changed. He took her to shooting classes and taught her how to clean the gun after each shooting. The gun stayed loaded in her nightstand. Their plans of having children were put on hold, as both could not bear the thoughts of endangering a child by the presence of a loaded gun.

One day, Bill received a call from Sam Wells. He wanted Bill and Charles to meet him at his home in Atlanta on the following weekend. He asked Sam why Max had not been invited, but no answer was given. Bill came to the conclusion that Sam and Max may have teamed up to get rid of the other partners. He had suspected the murderer to be one of their own, because it was doubtful to him that an outsider would have known about money held by so many men. Bill strongly considered the possibility that more than one person could be involved. Scenarios vividly played through his imagination.

"What if the invitation by Sam to have me in Atlanta, involved a plan to have Max come to my home and search for my share of the money," he thought. *"Sam could easily kill me, and Mary would be left to the mercy of Max."*

Frightened, Bill sent his wife out of the house before leaving for the meeting. She went to stay with her sister for a couple of days.

Charles was the first of the two to arrive at Sam's house. Shortly afterwards, Bill rang the doorbell and was invited into the home. Bill and Charles greeted each other with suspicion. Each assured the other that they knew nothing regarding the subject of the meeting, and each questioned why Max was not invited. Sam insisted that they each take a seat. He told them that he had been investigating the deaths of the Army acquaintances. Bill insisted that he knew nothing regarding who could have committed such terrible acts. Sam raided his hand to call for silence.

"I had to kill Max," Sam bluntly stated. "Max killed the three men and took their shares of the money."

Seeing doubt in their eyes, he excused himself for a moment and stepped over to his gun safe. In the memoirs, Bill expressed the fear he experienced as he considered the possibility that his host might be going for a gun. It took several seconds of silence before Sam open the door of the gun safe. During that time, the two men seated on the couch periodically glanced at one another in attempts to determine whether either had knowledge of what was about to happen. Bill told how relieved he was when Sam reached inside and produced four bags.

Sam struggled as he gave them the details of killing Max and finding the key to the locker. The policeman gave Sam and Charles each a bag of money, and he retained two bags for himself. They appointed Sam as the handler of the money sent to South Korea, and they decided they should do something for the families of Henry and Louis. Charles said that he would handle helping Henry's family, if Bill would do the same for the family of Louis. They would give the families $10, 000 apiece from the funds in the bags given to them by Sam. Each of the two retained the rest of the money in the bags.

Sam told them of the envelope containing the information noting how Max was sending money to Min Yon and his son in South Korea. He informed them that he planned to continue sending the money to Max's widow and son.

As soon as Charles and Bill departed in separate directions from Sam's house, Bill called his wife to let her know they would now be safe. He told her he would give her the details when he returned home. After she heard of that Sam had risked his life to remove them all from the path of a killer, she found a sincere reverence and respect for the man. Previously, she had not thought much of him. Out of all of Bill's army buddies, she viewed Sam to be rather frightening. From that day forward, she saw him in an entirely different perspective. She knew that he would long carry the sting of guilt for taking Max's life. Her family was now safe, and she would be forever indebted to him.

"I FOUND ANDREW," Ryan announced, as he stepped outside and onto the front porch. He observed Layla examining several of her daughter's completed selections from the coloring book, and he listened as Kaylee busily gave her mother descriptive details of the handiwork. Seeing Ryan standing near the door, Layla responded.

"OK, I'll come back inside in a few minutes."

She again turned her attention to her daughter.

"This one is really good" she said to Kaylee.

Ryan wanted very much to read more, but he realized the period of time the little girl had been entertaining herself. After all, the trips to the house in Brandon Springs usually meant that Kaylee would get to have plenty of quality time with her family. He decided the memoirs could wait. He dropped down cross legged beside the little girl and began to comment on the quality of the coloring effort.

"You stay inside the lines much better than I did when I was your age," he told her.

"That's because you were a boy," she explained. "It's not your fault. You were just born that way."

The reading of the memoirs of risk and murder had been so captivating, that a certain amount of tension had risen within Ryan. Kaylee's comment was so much to the point, and funny, that Ryan couldn't help himself. He burst out laughing and gave her a tight hug.

"Yeah, I know," he replied. "I was just born that way."

They visited with her for a few more minutes before returning to the couch for more reading. Ryan read how Sam and his Uncle Andrew had met at an American Legion center in Atlanta. Andrew had purposely selected an out-of-town center to frequent, because no one there knew of the incident that caused him to leave home and join the military. No one knew that he had neglected to use his parking brake, leaving his car on a slight hill overlooking a lake while fishing. No one knew that his car rolled down the hill and pinned a boy under it in the lake. No one there knew that his careless mistake had led to the death of a child. At an Atlanta American Legion center, he was just another American who enlisted to protect his country. He enjoyed the camaraderie of the people there.

One night, when he and Sam had had too much to drink, Andrew attempted to confess to his new friend.

"You don't really know me," he said to Sam. "There's a person who died because of me."

Sam held out his hand, objecting to where the conversation was might head. He then placed his finger over his mouth to signify to his new friend that nothing more should be said.

"Let's not go there," he quietly stated. "Neither of us are young men. Things happen, if you live long enough. Let it rest."

These words were true, and he was thankful for them. Sam was his comrade, regardless of failings. Andrew thought about the fact that he could have ruined the friendship by saying too much. He had too much to drink, and he knew words have a tendency to slip through drunken lips.

"Words, normally held tight, can become loosened through alcohol," Andrew thought. *"He's right, I need to leave it alone."*

Sam sometimes drank to push out thoughts of the night he killed Max, and he had no intention of allowing himself to become involved in a confessional match with this new friend. In the beginning the two met only at the American Legion, but they became good friends over time. Sam became intrigued when Andrew repeatedly brought up the subject of his nephew, Ryan. Andrew was very proud of the success of this young man, who lost both parents at the hands of a criminal. Eventually, Sam invited Andrew to his home in Atlanta for supper. Andrew talked about the accomplishments of his nephew, and let it be known that he and his sister Sally were Ryan's only remaining relatives.

As Sam Wells, Charles Moore, and Bill Thompson continued the practice of giving away the large sums of money, the topic of longevity came up. Each believed they would die before giving all of it away. They discussed the option of giving out larger quantities, but they were fearful that the larger amounts might lead the recipients to change their personal behavior for the worse. They considered passing the charitable activity to their children, but none of them wished to place the burden of forcing their flesh and blood into a situation that would cause them to hide their lives from the law. The only agreed upon action was to find someone outside the family to continue the practice. This person had to be significantly younger, someone who could be trusted, and someone who had little chance of bringing risk to their own family members. Sam told them of the conversations he had with Andrew about Ryan Walker. Although, he had never met the young man, he had come to gain respect for Andrew. He generally believed in the saying, *"the apple does not fall far from the tree"*.

Sam began to invite Andrew more often to his home on

weekends, and eventually he invited other guests to join them. The guests usually consisted of his old army buddies Charles and Bill. In time, these buddies would sometimes be accompanied by their wives. Over time, Ryan's uncle was brought into the circle of friends, but not into the knowledge of the charitable effort. They all liked and enjoyed the company of Andrew, but they also had the ulterior motive of hearing more about Ryan. Sam began to travel more often to Boston for visits with Bill, and he also used the visits as opportunities to tail the young man in question. Sam would give a report of Ryan's activities to Bill. Bill had meticulously documented Sam's observations in the memoir.

Andrew died, and although Ryan did not attend the funeral, Sam Wells and Bill Thompson were in attendance. The fact that Ryan was absent from the burial, caused the older men some concern. Nevertheless, Sam continued to observe Andrew's nephew. The older men allowed Ryan to catch glimpses of particular activities, in order to capture his curiosity. They planned to slowly draw him closer to them. This provided each of the Korean War veterans time to make their own evaluations as to Ryan's fitness to play a part in their discrete plan.

It didn't take them long to decide that Ryan should be intimately involved in the operation. The deciding factor came during the time Ryan spent with his aunt, after he was almost killed in an auto accident. Because of the fact that Ryan was hospitalized, Sam drove to Brandon Springs and rented a motel room during the entire time the young man visited with his aunt. He followed Ryan and Sally to the visitation at the funeral home for the family of the woman killed in the accident with Ryan. There, Sam witnessed the compassion Andrew's nephew showed to the children of the woman who had been killed in the other car. The three older men determined they would attempt to fully draw him into the charitable cause.

Even from a distance, Sam could see the love and respect Ryan had for his Aunt Sally. From outside the little café where Layla had been a waitress, Sam watched the facial expression of Ryan while he treated his aunt to lunch there. He also took note of the waitress who served the two. It seemed that Ryan hardly noticed the young woman, but it was obvious to the retired policeman that Layla was interested in him. As she served other customers, her attention often shifted in the direction of the young man seated with his aunt. On another occasion at the restaurant, following Sally's death, Ryan and Layla shared a long conversation. Though Ryan may not have realized it at the time, there was a genuine chemistry between the two. On one evening, Sam followed Layla as she drove to her mobile home after getting off work. Careful not to be noticed, he listened just outside the window of the trailer to a conversation between Layla and her mother. During the evening, Layla seemed almost obsessed by her interest in Ryan. She talked at length with her mother, regarding him.

"Why shouldn't I be able to find a man like him?" he heard her ask her mother.

Sam observed Ryan when he visited Brandon Springs, and it became Bill Thompson's responsibility to watch him in Boston. Ryan had been selected to be brought into the circle, and the three older men were in discussion as to how they should go about pulling him in.

"It would be easier if Andrew was still alive," Bill told Sam. "We could easily become part of his life through the uncle."

Observing Ryan in Boston, Bill once considered Larry to be a candidate to receive a package. He believed it might be the means of drawing Ryan into the charitable work. Eventually, he abandoned the idea for another plan. He told the other two men he would make an attempt to bring Ryan into his church. Bill waited for Andrew's nephew to leave work for his lunch break. He then went inside the office and left a church bulletin on the corner of his desk. The older man hoped Ryan would visit his church, and he did. However, he didn't expect Ryan to attend his Sunday school class and request prayer for Layla. It was if the answer had fallen into Bill's lap, and he viewed it as a confirmation that Ryan was the correct selection to carry on the work. This was the avenue the older men had been waiting for, and they decided to act immediately. The plan was now clear to them. Layla was to be the next recipient for a donation. These men had practiced in the shadows for many years, and they had become quite proficient.

The package of money was delivered to Layla's car, and the older men correctly believed she would think it came from the man who occupied so much of her thoughts. Sam was a policeman, and he knew how to conduct an investigation without being noticed. However, this was not his intent. He purposely left hints of his presence and made a point to stir up concern in Layla. Sam made sure she saw his car outside her trailer, and then at her school. For him, it was as easy as leaving breadcrumbs along the pathway to a trap. The effort was planned to the letter by the older men. Bill expected a return visit by Ryan to his Sunday school class. Because of the scholarship, Charles expected a visit, as well. They wove a web to capture Ryan's attention with the combination of the package of money, the scholarship, and the intentional sightings of Sam. They would have him nibble at hook, and then they would set it and reel him in.

As soon as Ryan made an appointment with Charles Moore, the attorney contacted Bill Thompson and had his friend schedule an appointment to meet with him at the hour just prior to Ryan's visit. The two older men purposefully allowed their meeting to run a little late, as to ensure Ryan's recognition of Bill Thompson. The two intended for Ryan to see them together, and they were successful in creating an air of suspicion. The older men were placing before the younger man a mystery, which they knew would be difficult for him to ignore. Ryan thought he was conducting an investigation of them, but the more experienced men were actually pulling him inside their circle.

As Ryan and Layla continued their reading, they became more and more fascinated at the brilliance of the old men. He had always pictured himself as being a rather smart person, but Ryan now realized that he was not in the same league as these seasoned veterans. He was a very capable student in school. In the workplace he displayed savvy business sense. These men had spent a lifetime in study of human nature and the complexities of relationships. These veterans were survivors. They had not only survived war, but had escaped the brutal intent of a murderer. They had given themselves to careful study of people for decades, and they had become very successful in their effort to find worthy candidates. Honed skills in stealth, enabled them to anonymously deliver the donations.

It soon became apparent to Ryan and Layla that they had brushed shoulders with very special people. The men had made serious mistakes in their youth in obtaining the Korean money, but they grew in wisdom through their experiences over time. These were not men who were recognized as being significant by the world around them. In fact, in attempts to prevent anyone from stopping their charitable efforts, they had become accomplished at blending into the sea of humanity. In secret, they meticulously researched candidates, and gave away millions of dollars to those needy persons found to be worthy. While lesser men fervently called attention to themselves, they quietly lived greatness.

A STOPPING PLACE in the memoirs was marked, and they were laid aside by the couple. As Layla began preparation for supper, her thoughts were consumed by the words she and Ryan had been reading.

"I can't imagine the terror Mrs. Thompson felt when Bill Thompson told her about the murders of his associates," she thought.

Ryan remembered the prayer given by Kaylee at breakfast time that morning, where she gave thanks for their time in Brandon Springs. He thought about the impact of that small community on his life, as he walked out the front door and onto the front porch to check on this little girl. The crayons and coloring book had been abandoned. He found Kaylee petting a kitten. Her attention was totally fixed on this small warm gray furry creature. Ryan saw the mama cat at the end of the porch. She was busily nursing the other members of the liter, and seemed unconcerned that one of hers was in the hands of a small child.

"Oh, can I have this kitten?" Kaylee asked, smiling up at him.

"We'll see," he replied, as he sat down next to her. Reaching over, he began to pet the kitten. He thought about loved ones who had passed over to the next world, and he considered those still in his life.

"She's so soft," the little voice whispered. "Please?"

"Keeping an animal is a big responsibility," he replied. "You would have to feed it and give it water every day. You would have to clean out its litter box."

"What's a litter box?" she asked.

"It's sort of a box with tiny pebbles in it," he explained. "It's where a cat goes to pee-pee and pooh-pooh. It smells really bad, and it wouldn't be much fun to clean that out."

"I can do it, if you teach me," she promised. "I can do work."

"Yes, I seen you work," he agreed. "You washed dishes for us today, and I know you are a hard worker."

"So, can I?" she pressed.

Ryan paused for a few seconds, and then he answered.

"OK, you can have it," he said.

Kaylee stretched her right arm around his waist, while

still holding the small animal in her left arm. With the kitten pressed firmly between them, she gave him a tight hug.

"Don't squish the kitten," he advised.

"I made a kitten sandwich," she teased. "But I was careful not to squish her."

Layla came out onto the porch to announce that supper was ready. As soon as she spotted the kitten, Kaylee proclaimed the news that Ryan decided to let her keep it.

"I know we didn't talk about it," he began. "I guess I'm a sucker for a pretty little girl and a kitten."

Layla bent over and gave Ryan a hug and a kiss. She then sat down on the other side of Kaylee and petted the kitten. Ryan considered the risk he took in getting involved with Layla. Most career minded men of his age would have run from that situation. She was an unmarried woman with a small daughter. He thought about the closeness he had shared with his Aunt Sally, and the family he was now blessed to have.

Ryan felt truly blessed by God. He had lost his mother, father, and all other living relatives. But he had made a decision to allow the love he received from them to continue, by passing it on to the woman seated on the porch. He would also give it to the children they would share.

Kaylee had thanked God for this day in Brandon Springs, but Ryan understood that it wasn't entirely the peaceful setting that was so special. It was the spiritual and loving aspects he had found in Brandon Springs, which he now shared with the little girl and her mother.

I can never go back to the time shared with my parents, or to the days with Aunt Sally. However, the richness of those days continues in lives now shared.

Ryan could have retreated back to his former lifestyle, that of living for himself. However, he made a conscious choice not to do so. He took the risk. Ryan had stepped out into the unknown, by continuing the secret charitable work and by sharing intimately in the lives of others. Ryan found that, by his own choosing, the experience he found in Brandon Springs went wherever he went. He carried it with him.

About the Author:

Rob Williams, currently residing in Nacogdoches Texas, has served in multiple roles supporting the Christian community. Included in this long list of mentorships was his service as youth director of an inner-city church in Atlanta and working with children in some of the toughest housing projects in that city. Rob worked at a rehabilitation center for five years, where he became acquainted with the homeless. The center helped those on work release from jail and those who were physically and mentally handicapped. He has taught adult Sunday school classes for more than thirty years and led youth in Boy Scouts and Cub Scouts for twenty years. Retired from the high-tech industry in Huntsville Alabama, he writes Christian fiction and science fiction in his free time. Rob is a husband, the father of four, and a grandfather. He is the author of the three novel Brandon Springs Christian fiction series, the dystopian science fiction novel *Sins of Variance*, the Christian fictional crime novel *Gathering of Six*, and Christian mystery *Cabin by the Stream*.